FROZEN MINDS

A murder mystery set deep in Wales

CHERYL REES-PRICE

THE
BOOK
FOLKS

Published by The Book Folks

London, 2020

This book is a work of fiction. Names, characters, businesses, organizations, places and events are either the product of the author's imagination or are used fictitiously. Any resemblance to actual persons, living or dead, events or locales is entirely coincidental.

ISBN 978-1-913516-56-7

www.thebookfolks.com

FROZEN MINDS is the second standalone title in a series of murder mysteries set in the heart of Wales.

Chapter One

The jangle of the phone alarm woke Leah from her dream. She snatched the phone from the bedside table, hitting snooze before bringing her arm back under the warm duvet. Curling up, she closed her eyes and willed the dream to come back.

It was no use, she was awake and could already feel anxiety snaking its way around her body, knotting her stomach and crushing her chest. A feeling of impending doom was with her every morning now. Work served as a distraction but the feeling was always present, heavy in her stomach.

She flung back the duvet and felt the cold air raise goosebumps on her arms. She shrugged on a robe before walking into the bathroom. Avoiding the mirror, she washed, brushed her teeth, then swilled down her medication with a glass of water. Back in the sleep-in room she hurriedly dressed in jeans and a jumper before pulling back the curtains. Outside, frost crystallised the grass on the lawn, heralding another chilly November day.

It was quiet in the corridor, most of the residents were still asleep. At the first bedroom on the right, she knocked before entering.

'Leah!' A young man with white-blond hair and small, narrow eyes set in a boyish face grinned at her.

'Morning, Liam,' she said and immediately felt her spirits rise.

'Look, I already dressed myself,' he announced, standing proudly before her.

Leah looked at the inside-out T-shirt hanging over his jeans and the sandals on the wrong feet.

'Wow, you must have woken up really early this morning.'

'I've been waiting hours, days, and months for you to come,' he said, with a mischievous grin.

'More like a few minutes, I think.' Leah couldn't help smiling too. 'You might want to put a jumper on this morning. Look outside.'

Liam shuffled to the window. 'The sun is out.'

'Yes, but look at the frost, it's going to be cold.' Leah went over to the wardrobe and took out two jumpers. 'Which one?'

Liam screwed up his face in concentration. 'Um... the blue one.'

'Excellent choice, now how about some socks and trainers.'

Leah helped Liam on with his trainers and they left the room.

'Better hurry up or Kevin will eat all the cereal,' she teased as they walked down the corridor.

Liam giggled as he trundled along beside her. They entered the kitchen where one of the other residents, Kevin, sat at a large pine table stuffing spoonfuls of cereal into his mouth. Two other staff members, Cillian and Gemma, stood at the kitchen counter. Cillian turned as soon as Leah entered the room.

'How did you sleep?' He smiled warmly.

She felt her heart flutter at the sight of him.

'Good. It was a quiet night.'

'Not for me,' Gemma said as she took a sip of tea. 'Kev was up twice, and Eddy had a seizure.'

'You should have buzzed me,' Leah scolded. She took a bowl from the cupboard and placed it in front of Liam.

'It wasn't a bad seizure, besides, you looked so tired yesterday I thought you could do with a night of unbroken sleep.'

'Thanks, Gemma,' Leah said as she handed a box of cereal to Liam who carefully measured it into his bowl with a spoon. 'But if you want to catch a few hours' sleep I'll be alright with Kev and Liam for the moment.'

'I'm good, I want to stay up or I won't sleep tonight. Your turn for night shift tonight, Cillian.'

'Don't remind me.' He grinned then winked at Leah. 'I'd better make a start getting the others up.'

Leah watched him leave then turned her attention back to Gemma.

'Well, if you're flagging this afternoon the offer still stands.'

'Thanks, Leah, but we've got a busy day planned today, haven't we, Kev?' Kevin looked up from his bowl but continued to fill his mouth. 'Hey Kev, what day is it today?'

'Ice cream day!' he cried out, bits of cereal flying from his mouth.

Liam gave Kevin a shove. 'Pig!'

'No, it's pantomime day, but it is ice cream day as well. Better check we have enough.' She pulled open the top drawer of the freezer and let out a sigh. 'Oh great, looks like someone had a feast.'

Leah moved closer to the freezer and peered into the drawer. A hole had been dug out of the large tub of ice cream, the lid discarded to the side.

'Who's been eating the ice cream?' Leah looked at Kevin who sniggered and kept his head down.

Liam looked alarmed. 'It wasn't me. I didn't do it.'

'I know you didn't,' Leah said as she ruffled his hair fondly. 'Come on, you can help me get another tub. We don't want Kevin to miss his ice cream tonight.'

They left the kitchen and Leah grabbed the keys from the office then opened the cellar door.

'Hold the rail when you go down,' she advised. She watched Liam take his first two heavy steps then followed. The chill penetrated her jumper and she rubbed her arms. 'Bloody freezing down here.'

'Bloody freezing,' Liam repeated and giggled.

They reached the bottom of the stairs and Leah walked towards the large chest freezer. Using two hands she pulled up the lid and peered inside. Two glassy eyes stared back. The air caught in her throat, and every muscle in her body tensed leaving her grounded. She wanted to look away, but she was transfixed.

Ice glimmered on the dead man's lashes, his mouth gaped open, and his skin had a purplish hue. She tried to draw in a breath while beside her Liam leaned forward and began poking the body.

'Bloody freezing,' he said, laughing. 'He's bloody freezing.'

Chapter Two

Detective Inspector Winter Meadows sat at his desk staring at the computer screen. Around him was the usual office chatter, which he had perfected fading out until it became a low hum in the background. His thoughts were not on work this morning, but on the upcoming sentencing taking place at Swansea Crown Court following his last case.

'Morning.' A mug of coffee was set on the desk, snapping Meadows from his thoughts. He looked up and smiled at Detective Constable Edris.

'Thanks.'

Edris took a seat, laying a file on the desk, and turned to Meadows.

'Are you alright?'

'I'm fine.' He picked up his coffee and took a sip, grimacing as it burned his tongue.

'Is it the sentencing today?' Edris asked.

'No, it's tomorrow…'

'Are you going to go?'

'I don't think it's a good idea. It's up to the judge now.' He indicated the file on the desk. 'What have you got?'

'Missing person. Alan Whitby, fifty-five years old, married. Reported missing by his wife yesterday morning. According to her he went out Monday evening saying that he would be back in a couple of hours. He never came home and didn't show for work the next day.'

'So, about thirty-six hours.'

'Yes, something like that. Uniform have done all the usual checks. No accidents reported and no sign of his car. They want to know if you'll look into it.'

'Why not? Nothing much happening at the moment.'

Meadows was getting used to the ways of the small police department. Having transferred from London eighteen months earlier, he'd found it a little too quiet at first. Now he was used to taking cases usually dealt with by uniform, and when his department needed assistance, he was never short of help. There was no "them and us" in the valleys.

Meadows read through the file while he finished the rest of his coffee. There didn't appear to be any obvious reason for Alan Whitby's disappearance. No depression, financial troubles or arguments according to his wife.

'Not high risk, but we'll go and see Mrs Whitby.'

At least I can get out of here for a while.

Meadows logged off the computer and grabbed his coat. They were heading down the stairs when they met Sergeant Dyfan Folland.

'Just coming up to see you,' he said, wheezing.

'I think you need to spend some time in the gym, fit up,' Edris said.

'I could still put you down, boy. Got a few pounds on you.' Sergeant Folland patted his paunch. 'Anyway, it's not like you set foot in the gym, from what I hear the only exercise you get is in the bedroom.'

'You shouldn't listen to gossip,' Edris retorted, his face reddening.

'What have you got for us, then?' Meadows asked, keen to put an end to the banter.

'Suspicious death in Ynys Melyn, Bethesda House. Do you know it?'

'Yes,' Meadows replied.

'No,' Edris said at the same time.

'Residential home,' Folland explained. 'Doc and SOCO are already there. Uniform called it in.'

'Well it looks like our missing man will have to wait a bit longer.' Meadows started down the stairs. 'Have you informed the DCI?'

'Yep.'

'Good, I'll keep you updated.'

Folland headed for the front desk, and Edris and Meadows for the exit. A blast of cold air hit them as the doors opened.

'Nice crisp morning,' Meadows noted, pulling up the collar on his coat.

* * *

In the car Edris turned up the heater as Meadows drove through the centre of Bryn Mawr. He stopped at the traffic lights and watched the shoppers scurrying across the road.

'They have some good plays on in there,' Edris said.

Meadows turned his head to look at the old miner's welfare hall.

'Go there often, do you?'

'Yeah, it's a cheap night out. Watch a play, have a few drinks. If you go into Swansea it costs a fortune to get a taxi home.'

'It used to be full of old men when I was young,' Meadows said.

'Yeah, I guess this place has changed a lot since then.'

'Not really. Same old building, just different shops. Not even a decent restaurant.'

'You've spent too much time in London.'

The lights changed to green and Meadows pulled away.

'Well this shouldn't take too long, some old biddy probably croaked it in the night and they are being over-cautious.' Edris adjusted the seat and leaned back.

'Bethesda is a residential home for adults with learning difficulties.'

'What's that then, like a psychiatric hospital? There was one when I was a kid. Hillside. My parents used to threaten to send me there when I was naughty.'

'Sometimes I worry about you.' Meadows laughed. 'You were obviously a very naughty boy. Hillside is a young offender institution. Bethesda is assisted living.'

A half hour later they turned off the main road and crossed the bridge that led to Ynys Melyn.

'It's like the twilight zone here.' Edris glanced out of the window. 'One road in and out – that's if you ever get out. All the undesirables live here.'

'It's not that bad, I've been in far worse places.'

Meadows glanced to the side where a group of ponies huddled together in a field; beyond, the scars of the open-cast mining in the area were still visible.

They drove a few miles on a straight road, passing the old National Coal Board offices which had been turned into a community centre. A sign announced that they had entered the village, which was dominated by a large council estate. Side streets led off the main road, lined with terraced houses which had once housed the miners.

'It's like a ghost town,' Edris said. 'Wednesday morning and no sign of life.'

'Maybe they're all in work.'

'In bed more likely.'

Meadows swung the car around a sharp bend and proceeded up a steep hill until they came to a converted church with a large extension to the side. He pulled up in the adjacent car park and they left the warmth of the car. As they walked, he surveyed the building. It was a tall grey stone structure with the original bell tower. The name *Bethesda* was carved into the stone above the door. To the left of the building a large oak tree stood, its branches stretching over the roof.

'Strange place,' Edris said. 'Don't think I'd like to live in an old church.'

'Afraid of ghosts, are you?'

Meadows looked at the front entrance where he could see PC Reena Valentine moving from foot to foot and rubbing her hands together.

'Poor girl looks frozen.'

'I wouldn't mind warming her up.' Edris grinned.

Meadows clicked his tongue and shook his head. What had happened to the quiet constable who had followed him around six months ago, desperate for approval?

'Morning, Valentine.' Edris smiled as he approached.

She returned Edris' smile before addressing Meadows. 'Morning, sir.'

Meadows returned the greeting as he appraised the young woman. Shoulder-length ebony hair was pulled back in a loose ponytail and glistened in the sun. She was tall and slender with soft brown eyes framed by long dark lashes. 'What have you got for us, Val?'

'Body discovered at approximately 8 a.m. in the storage freezer in the cellar by a staff member, Leah Parry, and one of the residents, Liam Casey. The body is believed to be that of the supervisor, Mr Alan Whitby. The manager, Jane Pritchard, and another member of staff, Cillian Treharne, went down the cellar when they heard shouts from Leah.'

'Looks like we've found our missing man,' Edris said. 'In the freezer?' He raised his eyebrows.

'Yes. I've taken down the names of all the staff and residents present this morning.' Valentine rubbed her hands together nervously.

Meadows guessed there was more she wanted to say, but it was obviously causing her embarrassment. 'Anything else?' he prompted.

'Leah and Liam left about fifteen minutes ago to get some ice cream.'

'Ice cream?' Meadows felt a flicker of annoyance.

She should have known better.

'Yes… Apparently that's why they were down the cellar, to pick up some more ice cream. The manager was insistent. She said it would calm Liam down after his ordeal. I'm sorry.'

No point humiliating her in front of Edris.

'OK. Let me know when they return. In the meantime, make sure no one else leaves. If you have any problems with the manager give me a shout and I will deal with it.'

'Thanks, sir.' Valentine gave him a weak smile.

Meadows nodded. 'Right, let's take a look.'

'The manager has requested that you use the back entrance to the cellar. She doesn't want the residents disrupted any more than they have been.'

'I'll look forward to meeting her later.'

'See you,' Edris said with a wink.

'Have you and Valentine got something going on?' Meadows asked as they walked around the back of the building.

'I'm working on it!'

'Well, just make sure you keep your mind on the job.'

They met with PC Matt Hanes, who stood at the entrance to the cellar.

'Alright, Hanes?' Edris said.

'Freezing my arse off,' Hanes complained. 'SOCO are in there, so you'd better suit up.'

Meadows pulled on a protective suit and stepped into the cellar. The first thing he noticed was a smell of bleach lingering in the air. *Someone has tried to clear away any evidence.* His gaze roamed around the room. It had a low ceiling with fluorescent strip lights, giving Meadows the urge to bend his head. Along the wall were shelves holding various household cleaners and a large toolbox. Cardboard boxes were stacked in a corner. Along the opposite wall was the chest freezer, about five feet in length. Meadows recognised the police doctor stood next to the freezer scribbling notes. He turned as Meadows approached.

'I've pronounced him dead, it's the best I can do. Impossible to make an examination.' He frowned at Meadows as if he was somehow to blame for the situation. 'Don't even think about asking for a time of death.'

Meadows stepped forward and peered into the freezer. Alan Whitby's body lay hunched, his knees bent and arms laying twisted on his chest. There were no obvious marks on his face. *Poor bugger, now what did you do to deserve this end?*

'Frozen to death?' Edris stood next to Meadows.

'You'll have to wait for the post-mortem. And don't expect it to be quick. They've got to thaw him first. Glad it's not my problem. If that's all, I'll be on my way.'

'Yes. Thank you,' Meadows replied without taking his eyes from Alan Whitby.

'Cheerful sod,' Edris commented once the doctor had left the cellar.

'From what I can gather he's rarely friendly, but he's efficient nonetheless.'

'Yeah, he was a great help. So, what do you think?'

'Well he certainly fits the description of Alan Whitby. He's not a small man.' Meadows sized up the body. 'I'd say at least fourteen stone. It would take considerable strength to lift him.'

'Maybe he was pushed in and the lid shut on him.'

'I would guess not. Do you think you could wrestle me into this freezer?' Meadows turned to Edris and raised his eyebrows.

'Maybe not, but we could give it a try if you like?' Edris said with a grin.

Meadows turned his attention back to the body. 'I would imagine he was either already dead or unconscious.'

'Not a very good place to hide him, but I guess someone with learning difficulties wouldn't have the capacity to come up with a way to dispose of the body.' Edris glanced around the cellar.

'That's assuming it was one of the residents.'

'You don't think so?'

'No,' Meadows rubbed his hand over his chin. 'If it was one of the residents it would have been a spur of the moment attack and they would have just left the body, or even called another member of staff. This is a more calculated act. I think you are right about it not being a good place to hide a body, especially if the freezer is in daily use. I expect they panicked and put him in here to buy some time and move him later.'

'They?' Edris raised his eyebrows.

'There has to be more than one person involved. No way could you lift him in alone. Even with two it would be a struggle. I don't see much food in there. So it was either nearly empty or the food has been removed and dumped somewhere.' Meadows turned away from the freezer to survey the room. A forensic officer stood nearby. 'Any signs of forced entry, Mike?'

'No, both doors are intact. The door to the main house is locked. There are very few prints, you would expect there to be a lot more if this room is in constant use. I think someone did a good clean up job.'

'With bleach by the smell of it,' Meadows said.

'Yes, but there is always the possibility something was left behind. We'll search for blood. I don't see why anyone would thoroughly clean with bleach unless they were trying to cover something up. I don't see any sign of injury on the victim though.'

'There could be, just have to wait until he is moved.'

'Good luck with that.'

'Probably have to cut him out.' Mike grimaced.

As Meadows turned to leave, his eyes fell on a hoist in the corner of the room. He pointed it out to Edris.

'That would work. Drag the body on the hoist, crank it up and tip him in.'

'So it could be down to one person then?' Edris said.

'I still reckon more than one, or a very strong man. Mike, can you make sure that thing's checked, please.'

Mike looked over at the hoist. 'I'm on it.'

'Thanks. Come on, Edris, let's go and see Jane Pritchard.'

They walked outside and Meadows scanned the car park.

'I think we can assume from the description and the fact that three staff members identified him, that it is Alan Whitby in there. But if that's the case, I don't see his car. The missing person report stated that he left the house driving a silver Jaguar XF.'

'Nice car. Do you think they killed him and nicked the car?' Edris looked at the building. 'Are these people able to drive?'

'No, which is another reason why the killer is unlikely to be one of the residents. The killer or killers are likely to have parked the car up somewhere or dumped it. Get Traffic to keep an eye out.'

Edris took out his phone as Meadows surveyed the back of the building.

They could have just dumped the body in the boot and got rid of the car. They must have been afraid they would be seen.

He looked up to the top floor and saw a man, who he assumed to be a resident, in the window. He was rocking back and forth, his face expressionless as he kept a watchful eye over the scene.

Chapter Three

Jane Pritchard stood at her office window. By angling herself at the far left she could watch the police officers come and go. An ambulance was parked near to the door of the cellar but so far there had been no sign of the body having been removed.

A cold shiver ran through her body despite the protection her office gave her from the outside elements. She moved away from the window and sat at the desk where she shuffled through some papers. She couldn't concentrate, the words bounced off the pages. Anxiety constricted her ribs, and her heart rate increased until she felt the heat rise and prickle her skin. She tugged at her collar trying to stay cool, but she could feel the perspiration gathering on her neck.

The office door flew open, making her start. Miles stepped through the door and shut it behind him.

'Well there's a stroke of luck, Alan dead in the freezer,' he said with a smirk.

'What do you think you're doing, coming in here?' Jane hissed. 'We shouldn't be seen alone together.'

'What are you talking about, you daft cow, we have to act normal. I'm always in here. The last thing we want to do is draw attention to ourselves.'

'Act normal!' Jane shrieked. 'Are you out of your mind? There's a fucking body in the freezer!'

Miles flew across the office and leaned in close until his face was inches from hers. 'Pull yourself together. I'm not going down for you, you stupid bitch.'

Jane leapt from her seat. 'Are you threatening me?'

'That's bloody rich coming from you.'

'What's that supposed to mean?'

Miles ignored her and moved to the window. 'Looks like there's some movement.'

Jane walked to his side where she could see two men leaving the cellar. They stopped and surveyed the car park, then the younger one took out his phone while the other stared up at the window.

'What are they doing?' Jane could hear her voice quaver and struggled to keep the panic at bay.

'Coming in to see you, I expect. You better sort yourself out and use your head. The residents all have the capability of violence. They're unlikely to look elsewhere if you point them in the right direction.' He walked to the door. 'Use your charm, flirt with them. You're good at that.'

He left, pulling the door closed.

Chapter Four

Meadows followed Valentine into the entrance hall, with Edris close behind. To his left was a large sitting room where noise billowed out from the residents. He could see a hive of activity and it was evident from the squeals and shouts that the police presence at Bethesda was causing a disturbance. He noticed Edris move away from view. He was obviously uncomfortable around the residents. Meadows felt a smile play on his lips.

There was a homely feel about the place. Coats were piled on to a rack with an assortment of boots and shoes underneath. Meadows let his gaze travel the hallway until it rested on a wide staircase. At the top stood the man he had seen in the upstairs window. He was slim, dressed in black trousers and a mauve shirt with a bow tie. In his hand he clutched a black book. Meadows smiled but got no response. The man started to descend the staircase, his shoulders held straight and chest puffed out.

'Hello,' Meadows said when the man reached the bottom of the stairs.

The man continued to walk as if the group were invisible; he entered the sitting room without a backwards glance.

'Jane Pritchard's office is through that door and first on the left.' Valentine pointed out a door on the opposite side of the hall.

'That's good, I thought for a minute we would have to go through there.' Edris indicated the sitting room with a tilt of his head.

'You could go and have a chat with the residents if you like,' Meadows said.

'No thanks, I'm sticking with you.'

Meadows turned to Valentine. 'You can stay here and warm up – that's if you're not uncomfortable like Edris.'

'Not at all, my feet are like ice!' Valentine smiled.

Meadows proceeded through the door with Edris following silently behind. They reached the office and he gave a sharp knock with his knuckles then opened the door before waiting for a reply.

A woman sat poised behind a desk, she had cropped bleached hair and hard grey eyes. She greeted them with a false smile. Her eyes roamed over Meadows before she turned her attention to Edris.

'I'm Detective Inspector Meadows and this is Detective Constable Edris.' He showed his identification and Edris followed suit.

The woman stood up and held out her hand. 'Jane Pritchard. How can I help you?'

Meadows pulled up a chair in front of the desk and Edris took a seat next to him, notebook out and pen poised.

'I would like you to talk us through what happened this morning.'

Meadows noticed her shoulders relax and she leaned back in her chair.

'I arrived just after eight this morning. Gemma, one of our support workers, was in the kitchen with Kevin, a resident. I said good morning and was making my way to the office when Leah came up the stairs from the cellar with Liam. Leah is Liam's support worker. She was calling for Cillian and was clearly distressed.'

'Cillian is a member of staff?'

'Yes, he is also Leah's boyfriend. Liam was elevated and shouting that Alan was hiding in the freezer.'

'Elevated?' Edris looked up from his notebook.

'Yes, it's a term we use to describe a resident's exaggerated state of mind, or behaviour. Liam was overly anxious and excited, and needed to be talked down to prevent him from becoming aggressive.'

'Right.' Edris scribbled down a few notes.

'Did you go down into the cellar?' Meadows asked.

'Yes, I went down with Cillian. We saw Alan in the freezer and I asked Cillian to quickly check on the rest of the residents. I locked the door then called you lot.'

'Why did you ask Cillian to check on residents?'

'To make sure they were all here, of course. This isn't a lock-up. The front door is easily accessible and if one of them had… well, if one of them was afraid they may have run off.'

'I see.'

She doesn't look very shaken considering she hasn't long seen the dead body of a colleague.

Meadows sat forward in his chair.

'When was the last time you saw Alan?'

Jane sat forward, folded her hands together and placed them on the desk. 'Let me see. It was about six o'clock on Monday evening.'

'So you didn't see or speak to him after that?'

A slight hesitation. 'No.'

Meadows noticed she kept still as she answered the questions.

I don't think you are telling us the truth.

He didn't break eye contact with her.

'Is the door to the cellar usually kept locked?'

'Yes, the key is kept here in the office.'

'Who has access to the key?'

'All the members of staff.'

'Do the residents go down to the cellar?'

'Not alone, although they all know the location of the key.'

'How many residents?'

'Six. I'm afraid all of them have displayed outbursts of violence in the past.'

Meadows raised his eyebrows. 'So, you think one of the residents is responsible for what happened to Alan?'

Jane squirmed in her seat. 'I wouldn't like to say, but all the staff know the risks they take working here.'

'How many staff members are employed here?' Edris asked.

'Besides myself and Alan, twelve. Six work during the week, they take it in turns to cover the night shift and sleep in. Relief staff come in Friday afternoon until Monday morning.'

'So there is always someone on duty?'

'Yes, each resident has a key worker. The staff organise their own shifts. Each member of staff can be assigned two residents, but not more. After 9 p.m. there are two staff members, one as a sleep-in, who is on call during the night if there are any problems; the other stays awake all night.'

'What time did you leave on Monday evening?' Meadows asked.

'Half six.'

'And you were expecting Alan for work on Tuesday morning?'

'Yes. I phoned his mobile when he didn't turn up. It went straight to voicemail so I left a message. His wife rang me shortly after to ask if he had been into work.'

'Had he missed work before without contacting you?'

'No.'

'Did he have any problems in work with the staff or residents?'

'None at all. We're a happy family here.' Jane smiled.

'So, you got on well with him?'

Another hesitation and Jane's shoulders tensed. 'Yes, I can't think of any major disagreements.'

'So, what do you think happened?'

Meadows saw the colour rise in her face, she shifted in her chair and ran her hand through her hair.

'I wouldn't like to guess. Like I said before, all the residents in the past have shown violent behaviour. I suppose one of them could have pushed him in the freezer and shut the lid without realising the consequences.'

'I see, but that doesn't explain the car.'

'The car?'

'Yes. Alan's car is missing.'

'I see, well I wouldn't know anything about that.'

'According to Alan's wife he left the house about nine o'clock Monday evening. Can you think of any reason he would come back to work?'

'No, maybe he forgot something.'

'Does he keep a laptop here?'

'No, all administration work is done on the work computer in here.'

'Who was on duty Monday night?'

'Gemma, and I think Leah was the sleep-in.'

'Then one of them would have seen him if he came into the house,' Edris said as he looked up from his notepad.

'Unless he used the back door to the cellar.'

Meadows let the comment hang in the air. He could tell from Jane's demeanour she regretted her words.

Could she have got him into the freezer? That's doubtful, even with a hoist. Unless she had help…

'Would Alan have had keys to the back door?'

'Um, no. The door is kept locked unless we have a delivery. The keys to both doors are kept together.'

'So if he came in the back door someone would have let him in.'

Jane shrugged her shoulders.

'We'll need to interview all the staff and residents as well as take fingerprints for elimination purposes.'

'You do realise that a majority of the residents don't have the mental capacity to answer questions. They get confused easily and it's likely that your presence here will upset them.' Jane's eyes narrowed and she folded her arms across her chest.

'I can assure you any questioning will be handled with sensitivity and I will ensure that an appropriate adult is present during the interviews.'

'I would prefer you to use the staff members as appropriate adults. It will be less stressful than having a stranger. It would also be better if you dressed in casual attire. The residents associate suits with professionals such as doctors.'

'I'm sure we can manage that.' Meadows gave her a tight smile.

'I would also be grateful if you would leave the questioning until tomorrow. The residents have a planned day out and it is crucial to their wellbeing that their schedules are not disrupted. I think there has been enough upset for one day.'

'For the residents' sake I will agree to leave the questioning until tomorrow, but this is a murder investigation and I would appreciate your full cooperation with my officers. I will need a list of all members of staff, names and addresses and length of employment. Also a list of residents and their medical conditions.'

'That's confidential information.'

'I can get a warrant if you prefer?'

Jane seemed to be weighing up her options. 'Fine,' she snapped.

Meadows stood and Edris put his notebook back into his pocket. Relief was evident on Jane's face.

'We need to take a look around the house before we leave,' Meadows said.

'I'll show you.' Jane stood.

'I would prefer you get the information ready for when we leave. I'm sure another member of staff can show us around.'

'I'll ask Miles, he'll be able to answer any questions about the running of the house.'

Meadows saw a sly smile play on her lips before she walked towards the door.

As they stepped into the corridor, they met a young woman and man walking towards them. Meadows' eyes travelled the height of the man who dwarfed his own six-foot-one frame.

Bloody hell, I wouldn't like to face him in a boxing ring.

Chapter Five

Thick legs supported a hefty body, while meaty hands like shovels swung back and forth at his sides. His face was round, with dimpled cheeks and a mop of unruly sandy hair topped his head. The girl by comparison was extremely petite, with long brown hair. Dark circles were visible beneath tired hazel eyes.

'This is Kevin and Gemma,' Jane said.

'Hello, Kevin. I'm DI Winter Meadows.' Meadows stepped forward.

'Winter?' Kevin's eyes grew wide.

'Yes, Winter.'

'Winter, Winter!' Kevin cried as a broad grin lifted his face. 'Make it snow, make it snow, Winter Man!' He leaped up and down, his hands flapping widely.

'Shit,' Edris hissed and moved behind Meadows.

'Interesting name,' Jane commented.

Gemma put a calming hand on Kevin. 'Snow in fourteen days, remember.'

'Fourteen days,' Kevin repeated. 'You make it snow in fourteen days.' He eyed the inspector.

'Well, I…' Meadows saw Gemma nod at the side of Kevin. 'Yes, fourteen days.'

Kevin gave a booming laugh which shook his body. 'The Winter Man makes it snow. Do you want to build a snowman?' Kevin sang.

'Kevin's favourite film is *Frozen*,' Gemma explained. 'We're going to Lapland in two weeks.'

'*Frozen*! That's appropriate, don't you think?' Edris whispered.

Meadows ignored his constable. 'Kevin, would you like to show me and Edris around the house?'

Kevin stopped singing and looked at Edris. 'Show you?'

Edris looked relieved that his name hadn't sparked another outburst. 'Yes.'

'I think it might be better if Miles—' Jane began but Meadows cut her off.

'You can show us around your home,' Meadows coaxed. 'You can be the boss.'

Kevin grinned. 'Like boss lady.' He looked at Jane. 'Yes.'

'OK'

Meadows turned to Jane. 'I think we'll manage fine with Kevin and Gemma. If you could put together the paperwork, I'll collect it when I've finished my tour.'

'Very well,' Jane snapped and she turned back into her office, firmly shutting the door.

'Come on then, Kevin, where shall we start?' Meadows said with a smile.

'Boss lady's room,' Kevin pointed to the office door.

'Do you go into this room?' Meadows asked.

'No.' Kevin frowned.

'Can't say I blame you,' Edris said.

Kevin ambled to the next door, humming and swinging his arms. Edris kept close to Meadows as they followed.

'You were on duty Monday night?' Meadows said, addressing Gemma.

'Yes, why? Is that when Alan was…?' Gemma's eyes widened.

'We aren't certain, but as Alan was last seen on Monday evening…' Edris said.

'Who was the sleep-in?'

Meadows watched her movements closely. She seemed frightened. Was it because she had been alone that night with a killer roaming the building? Or is it something else?

'Leah.'

'Did you see Alan on Monday evening?'

'He came into the sitting room about six o'clock to say he was leaving.' Gemma folded her hands across her chest as she spoke.

'And after that?'

'No.'

'Other than Leah, did you see anyone else on Monday evening?'

'No, well, just the residents.'

Kevin was hopping from foot to foot by the next door. Meadows sensed he was eager to get on with the tour. 'So what door is this, Kevin?'

'Food store.' Kevin's eyes danced. 'Lots of ice cream.'

'Do you like ice cream?'

'Yes.' Kevin nodded and a grin spread across his face.

'Do you go to the cellar, I mean food store, to eat the ice cream?'

'No, not allowed. The door's locked. Boss lady has the key. I eat the ice cream in the kitchen when they are all asleep.' Kevin gave a booming laugh which shook his body.

'So it was you that ate all the ice cream!' Gemma said and shook her head playfully.

'What night did you eat the ice cream?'

Kevin looked blankly at Meadows.

'He doesn't really understand the concept of time. I'm afraid days of the week are meaningless,' Gemma explained.

'Do the residents get up during the night?'

'Sometimes?'

'And Monday night?'

'No,' Gemma looked at Kevin. 'We had a quiet night on Monday.'

Meadows noticed the colour rise in her cheeks but didn't comment. 'OK. Next door, Kevin.'

'Yes, Winter Man.' Kevin shuffled to the adjacent door. 'Sleepy room.' He knocked loudly on the door. 'No one home.'

'Can we have a look?'

Kevin turned to Gemma, who nodded. He opened the door and stepped inside. It was a small room, sparsely furnished with a single bed and bedside table. A door led to an en suite.

'The room is fitted with an alarm to alert the sleep-in when assistance is needed,' Gemma explained.

They left the room and proceeded to the next door.

'Liam's room.' Kevin knocked. 'No one home.'

'The rooms are close to the cellar,' Edris said.

'Close enough to hear an argument,' Meadows agreed.

'Come on, Winter Man,' Kevin said.

They stopped at the last door on that side of the corridor.

'My room.' Kevin beamed. He tapped his fingers on the door. 'No one in.'

Meadows laughed. 'Can we see your room?'

'OK.' Kevin led them inside.

It was not what Meadows expected. They stood in a sitting room with comfy seating in the centre and a large television mounted on the wall. A table was set against the wall with two chairs. The room was decorated in various shades of blue, with winter landscapes in frames. A shelf held rows of DVDs and underneath it stood a large plush snowman.

'You have a very nice room.' Meadows smiled at Kevin.

'All the residents' rooms are similar, with sitting room, bedroom and en suite. Some have a small kitchen to make a drink and snack,' Gemma explained. 'We've just redecorated this room, haven't we, Kevin?'

'I picked the colour,' Kevin said proudly. He moved across the room and picked up the plush toy. 'Do you want to build a snowman?' he sang.

Meadows laughed. 'I'll have to learn that song.'

They left Kevin's room and moved to the room opposite.

'Nicole's room,' Kevin said.

Meadows knocked the door and waited. 'Nobody home.'

Kevin giggled then led them back to the hall where Valentine was standing guard at the main door.

'There are another three rooms upstairs and a separate bathroom and massage room,' Gemma said.

'I don't think we need to go up,' Meadows said. 'What about this door, Kevin?' He pointed to a door near the entrance.

'It's the place that no one has been,' Kevin said.

'Stairs to the bell tower and roof,' Gemma explained. 'The door is kept locked.'

The front door opened and they all turned to see a young man and woman enter.

'Leah and Liam,' Valentine said.

They stopped at the sight of the strangers. Both were the same height and the first thing Meadows noticed was Leah's pale complexion. Despite being out in the cold, her skin was ivory, with dark shadows under pale blue eyes. Her skeletal figure was evident beneath her coat. In her hand she clutched a plastic shopping bag.

Liam moved behind Leah, glaring. His narrow lips were set into a round face. His hair was white blond and showed the pink of his scalp beneath.

'Hello, Liam, the Winter Man is here,' Kevin said.

'We've got the ice cream.' Leah lifted the bag up.

'Yeah, ice cream!' Kevin danced happily.

'For later. We'd better take it to the kitchen before it melts. Come on, Liam.' She smiled weakly at Meadows before entering the sitting room with Liam shuffling close behind.

Meadows turned to Edris, who was eying the sitting room with unease. 'Why don't you go and see if Jane has the paperwork ready while I see the sitting room and kitchen with Kevin.'

Relief flooded Edris' face. 'I'll see you back here.'

'Come on then, Kevin, show me the sitting room.'

They entered to a hubbub of noise. The sitting room was spacious with several sofas and chairs, where the residents sat doing various activities. Meadows looked around, then up at the high ceiling with the original church beams still visible.

'Everyone is here,' Kevin said.

The residents took no notice of Meadows and continued with their activities. All except the man Meadows had seen on the stairs earlier. He stood staring, the black book still clutched in his hand, his face expressionless. Meadows tried smiling but got no response. The man took a pen from his pocket, opened the book and started scribbling.

'That's Eddy, I think your presence is unsettling him,' Gemma said. She turned to Kevin. 'Do you want to show us the kitchen?'

Kevin nodded and led the way.

Meadows took one more look around the sitting room then followed Kevin into the kitchen area, where Liam was sitting at a large pine dining table. Leah acknowledged them with a smile as she made tea.

'Get out!' Liam shouted, his eyes challenging the detective.

'Hi, Liam. Kevin is just showing me the kitchen,' Meadows explained, trying to keep his voice friendly and smiled.

Liam leapt out of his seat. 'Get out, I don't want you here.'

'It's OK, Liam,' Leah said as she put a reassuring hand on his shoulder.

Kevin shuffled in front of Meadows. 'Don't shout at the Winter Man, Liam.'

'Fuck off, Kevin,' Liam bellowed.

'That's enough, Liam. Now say sorry to Kevin. You know you shouldn't say bad words.'

'Alan says the F-word,' Kevin said.

Meadows noticed the look exchanged between Gemma and Leah. Maybe Alan hadn't had much patience with the residents. Liam's fists were clenched and he appeared to be struggling to hold his temper.

'It's OK, Liam, I'm going now. Thank you for showing me around, Kevin. I'll come and see you again.'

As Meadows left the kitchen, he heard Kevin shout at Liam. 'You made the Winter Man go away.'

He couldn't help smiling.

In the hallway he met with Edris who was clutching a stack of files.

'The residents' personal files. Jane Pritchard says she wants them back ASAP.' Edris grinned.

'She'll get them back when I've finished with them,' Meadows said and then turned to Valentine. 'They shouldn't be much longer in the cellar. At least you look a little warmer now.'

'I am, thanks,' Valentine said with a smile.

'Come on, Edris, we'd better break the news to Alan Whitby's wife.'

'See you later.' Edris winked at Valentine before leaving the building.

Chapter Six

'Are you OK?' Meadows glanced sideways at Edris who was looking out of the car window.

'Yeah, I'm good now we are away from that place.'

'You surprise me. I wouldn't have thought you would be prejudiced against those with mental health conditions.'

'I'm not.' Edris bristled. 'It's just… They make me feel uncomfortable.'

Meadows sensed there was more to it.

'You were really good with Kevin. I was impressed,' Edris said.

'Thanks. There was a guy called Billy in the commune when I was growing up. He was a bit like Kevin. He was about forty with a mental age of ten. He used to like to play with us kids. We just accepted him as one of us. It was the reason his family came to live in the commune. Little understanding of mental health in those days. He never harmed any of us, even when he threw a tantrum, and boy did he have a wicked temper when he didn't get his own way.' Meadows smiled at the memory.

'I wouldn't like to see Kevin throw a tantrum. Did you see the size of his hands? I reckon he could easily have put Alan Whitby in the freezer,' Edris said.

'You're kidding? Why would he want to do that?'

'Well, all that talk about snowmen and *Frozen*. Maybe he couldn't wait to make a snowman.'

Meadows chuckled. 'He has a mental age of about six. If he did shove Alan Whitby into the freezer, I doubt he would have kept quiet about it.'

'I suppose not, but what if someone helped him cover it up? He would've wanted to show Gemma his handiwork and she could've told him not to say anything, then moved Alan's car.'

'But why would she do that?'

'I don't know. Maybe she's fond of Kevin and didn't want him taken away.' Edris turned in his seat to face Meadows. 'Maybe they don't want the home to get a bad reputation or be shut down. That Jane was a bit shifty.'

'Yeah, she was. She certainly knows more than she's letting on. I think you're right, we have to treat this like any other investigation and keep an open mind. Gemma did look a bit worried when I asked her about Monday night. Then again, it would be worrying to know someone was murdered so close by. If Leah was asleep that would have left Gemma alone and vulnerable. What if the killer thought she saw or heard something?'

'What if Gemma knows who the killer is and is too frightened to come forward?' Edris added.

'I think it would be wise to keep a round-the-clock presence at the home.'

'As long as you're not suggesting that I take that job.'

'Well if you're offering…'

Bryn Coed village was a mixture of terraced houses, a newly built estate, and old stone semis. The river Amman ran through the centre. Over a bridge and down a narrow road, houses were set amongst the trees. It was here that the Whitbys lived. Meadows stepped out of the car and surveyed the well-kept semi-detached house. Large clay pots flanked the door and a caravan stood on the gravel driveway.

'He seems to have done well for himself,' Edris commented. 'The caravan looks new, and the missing Jag is less than a year old. They don't come cheap.'

'No, I don't suppose he earned that much as a supervisor. He could have had a windfall or maybe he just saved. Worth checking into his finances.'

They got out of the car and Meadows saw the curtains twitch. He hated this part of the job.

As they approached the house the front door was flung open and a woman in her early fifties stepped out. She had short brown hair speckled with grey. It stuck out at an angle where she had obviously been running her hand through it.

'Mrs Whitby?' Meadows asked.

'Yes.' She twisted her hands together, looking frantically between the detectives.

'Detective Inspector Meadows and this is Detective Constable Edris.'

'Have you found him?' Her voice was high-pitched, anxious.

'Perhaps it would be better if we went inside.' Meadows smiled kindly.

'Oh, God!' Her hands flew to her mouth. 'It's bad news isn't it?'

'Please, Mrs Whitby – Melanie. It would be better if we came in,' Meadows coaxed.

She led them into the sitting room and turned expectantly to Meadows. 'Please just tell me.'

'I'm very sorry–' Meadows began. 'The body of a man answering the description of your husband was found this morning.'

The colour drained from her face and she let out a wounded howl. Meadows took her arm and gently led her to the sofa where she sank down, her arms wrapped around her body.

'Edris, go and make Melanie a cup of tea, please, plenty of sugar.'

Edris left the room and Meadows took a seat in the chair opposite Melanie Whitby. The shock of the news made her body tremble and she rocked slightly as she sat. There were no tears, but Meadows knew they would come when the news sank in. He waited for the inevitable questions. In the background he could hear Edris tinkering in the kitchen.

'Are you sure it's Alan?'

'We are fairly certain, yes. There will need to be a formal identification from a family member,' Meadows said.

'Was it a car accident?' she asked, her voice barely a whisper.

'No, I'm afraid it wasn't an accident. Is there someone we can call for you?'

She shook her head.

'It would be better to have someone with you.'

'My daughter. Claire. She's at work.'

Edris came back into the room and placed a mug of steaming tea into Melanie Whitby's hands.

'Oh God, how am I going to tell her?' Sobs wracked her body and the tea spilled over her hands. Edris moved quickly, taking the mug and placing it on a nearby table.

'We'll contact her for you, can you give us her number?' Edris asked.

'My mobile's on the kitchen table. Claire's work and mobile numbers are in the contact list. But you can't tell her on the phone…'

She hiccoughed.

'Don't worry, we'll tell her when she gets here.' Meadows nodded at Edris who left to search for the phone.

'What happened?' She wiped the tears with the back of her hand.

Meadows picked his words carefully. 'Your husband was found at Bethesda House early this morning. I'm afraid we are treating his death as suspicious.'

Melanie looked blankly at Meadows, then confusion gave way to anger. 'You mean one of those loonies killed Alan?'

It saddened Meadows that blame would be laid on those who couldn't defend themselves.

'I don't think–'

'I told him it wasn't safe to work there, but he wouldn't listen,' Melanie ranted.

'Please, Melanie, at this stage we don't know the circumstances surrounding Alan's death. I can however tell you that we don't believe any of the residents of Bethesda are responsible for what happened.'

'What are you saying?' she asked, her forehead creased with confusion. 'Was there a break-in?'

'We don't know at this stage, but I promise you we're doing everything we can to find out what happened to your husband.'

'Oh God.' Melanie put her hands over her face. 'I can't believe this is happening.'

'Claire is on her way and I've requested a family liaison officer,' Edris said when he walked back into the room. He had a box of tissues in his hand and placed them on the table next to Melanie.

'What did you tell her?' Melanie grabbed a handful of tissues and blew her nose.

'I told her there had been an incident involving her father and asked her to meet me here. I'll explain when she arrives,' Edris said.

Melanie nodded mutely then turned her attention back to Meadows. 'How did he die?' The words trembled on her lips.

Meadows could see the pain on her face and knew from the way she bent forward with her arms around her body that it gnawed at her stomach.

'I'm afraid there will have to be a post-mortem. We will know more then. I'm very sorry, Melanie, but I'm going to have to ask you some difficult questions. It's better to do this now. I understand how difficult this is but it is necessary.'

Melanie nodded and took another wad of tissues and dabbed her eyes.

'The last time you saw Alan was Monday night, is that right?'

'Yes.'

'How did he seem to you? Was he happy?'

'Just his usual self. He came home from work, showered, then relaxed with a glass of wine before we ate.'

'Had he been worried about anything recently, problems at work?'

Melanie's eyes narrowed. 'You're not suggesting that he—'

'No, nothing like that,' Meadows cut in quickly. 'I just want to find out if he was troubled.'

'No, if anything he was really happy these past few months.'

'So, no money worries?'

'No, it's been a really good year financially.'

'Alan recently purchased a new car?'

'Yes, it was his dream car.' Melanie's voice trembled.

'Did he buy it outright or take out a loan?'

'He bought it outright. What's the car got to do with what happened? Did someone take the car, is that it?'

'The car is still missing. At the moment we need to have as much information as possible. I'm sorry if some of the questions seem intrusive.' Meadows paused for a moment. 'So, had you come into money recently?'

'Alan received some large bonuses from work over the last few months, I expect it was to show their appreciation for all his hard work and extra hours. He wasn't paid overtime.'

'Did Alan plan to go out on Monday evening?' Meadows asked, leaning forward, his hands placed on his lap.

'No, after we ate, we planned to watch a film together but that bloody woman phoned.'

'What woman?'

'Jane Pritchard. She said he needed to come back into work.'

Interesting that she didn't mention that when we spoke to her.

'Did he often get called back into work in the evening?'

'No. Well, it seemed to be happening more and more recently. He said he wouldn't be long and that was the last I saw of him.'

Fresh tears ran down her face and her hand trembled as she wiped them away.

Meadows waited for her to compose herself. He noticed that Edris stood by the window watching out for Melanie's daughter.

'Did Alan give a reason why he kept getting called in? Was there any particular problem at work?' he asked.

'No, I expect Jane couldn't cope with something or other. Alan should have been the manager... He's been there longer than she has.'

'I'm sorry, Melanie, but I have just a few more questions. Did Jane Pritchard call on the house phone or Alan's mobile on Monday evening?'

'The mobile. She wouldn't call on the house phone.'

'And he took his mobile with him?'

'Yes, he always kept his phone on him. I knew something was wrong when I couldn't get hold of him. It kept going straight to voicemail.'

Meadows made a mental note to ask SOCO if they had found Alan's phone. The number and provider were listed on the missing person's file.

'How was your relationship with your husband? Any recent arguments?' he asked.

'No... what are you implying?' Melanie frowned.

'I'm not implying anything. I'm sorry we need to ask these things.'

'We were happy, we had the odd argument like any couple that's been together for a long time but nothing serious. There certainly weren't any affairs on either side if that's what you're getting at.'

Meadows saw Edris move away from the window, as with a nod of his head he indicated the arrival of Melanie's daughter.

'Can you think of anyone who would want to harm your husband? Any recent fallings out, a grudge maybe?'

Melanie was distracted by the sound of the front door opening. 'No.' She looked away as she answered.

Hushed voices could be heard in the hallway followed by howls of distress. Claire Whitby came charging through the door and flung herself into her mother's arms, sobbing.

'Family liaison officer is here,' Edris said.

Meadows stood as the officer entered.

'Melanie, I'm going to leave you with PC Williams. She will answer any questions you might have and keep you up to date with the investigation. We may need to come back to ask some more questions.'

Melanie nodded.

'There will also have to be a formal identification,' he reminded her.

'I'll do it.' Claire looked up at Meadows through her tears.

'No, love.' Melanie looked horrified at the idea. 'I'll do it. When can I see him?'

'As soon as we have heard from the hospital. PC Williams will make the arrangements.' He nodded at the PC who stepped forward.

Meadows felt relieved to step outside. The Whitbys' house was heavy with grief.

'So, what do you think?' Edris asked as they climbed in the car. 'Do you reckon Alan was banging Jane Pritchard?'

'I suppose it would give him a reason to go back into work for the evening. It'll be interesting to see what Jane has to say about the phone call. Let's get hold of the phone records first. See if she was the one to make the call. Someone lured him back.'

'Yeah, and I can imagine Jane Pritchard shutting the lid on the freezer,' Edris said with a grin.

Chapter Seven

I hate being on the bus. I feel sick, my tummy feels all squashy like someone is stirring it with a spoon.

'Are you OK, Liam?'

Leah is sitting next to me. She's looking at me now. She is smiling but she looks like she is going to be sick too.

'I don't feel well.'

'It won't be much longer.'

She puts her hand on my head. It's cool like a flannel, it feels good. Leah always makes me feel better.

Why don't you look out of the window? See how many red cars you can see.' Leah smiles.

There are lots of cars going past. It's loud, the bus is loud, and Kevin is singing. The noise scratches at my skin. A red car, that's one. I don't want to look for red cars. Red is angry, I hate red. I want to ask Leah about Alan. I'm glad he is frozen like ice cream. I bet he will be mad when he melts. Leah says we mustn't talk about it but I need to let the words out. There are too many words in my head, pushing and squashing. My head will break if the words don't come out.

'Leah.'

She's talking to Cillian. 'Leah!' *I pull on her sleeve.*

'What's the matter? Are you going to be sick?'

'No. Is Alan going to come back?'

'No, sweetie. Alan is never coming back.'

'Are you sure?'

'Yes.'

'Is it my fault?'

'No, Liam.' Leah touches my arm. 'You were asleep when Alan got hurt, weren't you?'

Leah looks worried. I nod and look out of the window. I don't remember things. Sometimes I get angry, the red comes and fills my head like fire. My head and hands hurt. I want to punch, kick, and bite to make the fire go away. Then everyone hates me, except Leah. Alan makes me angry, makes the fire come; but not anymore, he's cold like Kevin's snowman. I can see pictures in my head. Hear people shouting. It makes bubbles in my stomach. Leah says I was asleep. Leah doesn't lie.

'You OK now, Liam?'

Leah's voice is yellow like the sun, it makes me feel warm.

'No, I want to go home.'

'We're going to the pantomime. You'll have fun.'

I smile for Leah but I don't want to go. Too much noise and people look funny at you. I want to go home. No, the policeman might be there. I know what they do, they will come and take me away, lock me up. I want to stay with Leah. I have to keep the words in my head. I didn't do it. I didn't do it.

Chapter Eight

Meadows' stomach emitted a low growl as he entered the police station. He had skipped breakfast that morning and there hadn't been time for lunch. Now he could feel hunger gnawing inside him.

Sergeant Folland was sat behind the reception desk talking on the phone. He acknowledged Meadows with a nod of the head as he walked by. Meadows stopped at the bottom of the stairs and turned to Edris who was following.

'Do me a favour, go to the canteen and see if they can rustle up a sandwich.'

'I thought you'd never ask.' Edris grinned. 'I'm bloody starving.'

'While you're at it see if Valentine is back and ask Folland if he can spare her for a few days. We're going to need some extra help. Oh and can you check in with SOCO, see if they found Alan's phone.' He took the pile of files from Edris' hands.

'Anything else while I'm at it?' Edris teased.

'No, that will do for now.' Meadows grinned before heading up the stairs.

The office was quiet when he walked in. The first thing he saw was DS Stefan Blackwell engrossed in a game on his computer, and he didn't appear to have noticed Meadows.

'Good to see you've got some time on your hands,' Meadows commented.

'Just taking a break,' Blackwell said.

'Make the most of it, we have a murder investigation which should keep us all busy.'

Blackwell scowled and shut down the game.

'Briefing in half an hour,' Meadows called to Rowena Paskin, a smartly dressed DS who was busy typing. She looked up and nodded before smoothing back her wispy brunette hair and returning her attention to the screen.

Meadows dumped the files on his desk then set up the incident board. Alan's name was positioned in the centre, on the left-hand side he listed the residents and staff members, on the right side the relief staff.

Edris returned and handed Meadows a sandwich and mug of tea. 'Valentine will be up shortly. She seemed really pleased to be joining us.'

'Good, try not to distract her.' Meadows bit into the sandwich.

'Wouldn't dream of it,' Edris said, putting on a look of mock innocence. 'I've got the phone from SOCO, they've already checked it for prints. It's dead after being in the freezer but we might have some luck when it has dried out.'

'Better put in a request for the phone records. It will be interesting to see if Jane Pritchard did call Alan on Monday evening, even better if we have the evidence to confront her with.' Meadows gobbled down the rest of the sandwich and swilled it down with tea before turning back to the board.

When Valentine entered the office, Meadows called for everyone's attention. Blackwell dragged his chair over and plonked himself down. Paskin and Valentine pulled up chairs and sat with notebooks and pens poised.

Meadows surveyed his small team before turning to the board.

'We were called to a suspicious death in Bethesda House residential home at 8 a.m. this morning. The victim, Mr Alan Whitby, was found in a large chest freezer in the cellar. He went missing Monday night. Until we have a confirmed time of death, we will work on the premise that he died sometime on Monday evening or the early hours of Tuesday morning.'

Meadows saw Blackwell's lips twitch. *He would find it funny.*

'Bethesda is a home for adults with learning difficulties ranging from autism to schizophrenia.'

'Are you sure it wasn't a knife in the shower?' Blackwell mimicked a stabbing knife as he screeched the legendary Hitchcock theme tune. 'My money's on the schizo.'

'That's *Psycho*, you fuckwit,' Edris snapped. 'Schizophrenics are not psychopaths.'

'Like you would know, you keep your brain in your trousers,' Blackwell growled.

'OK, that's enough.' Meadows looked at Edris whose ears were glowing red. 'We're supposed to be a team.'

'Yeah,' Blackwell said, glaring at Edris. 'You can start by showing a little bit of respect. I still outrank you even if you are the golden boy.'

Irritation crawled at Meadows' skin but he refused to rise to Blackwell's dig. He knew there was some good beneath Blackwell's negative attitude but had yet to uncover it.

'If you have a problem, Stefan, let's hear it.' Meadows kept his voice even. He deliberately used Blackwell's first name to dispel the use of rank and superiority among his team.

'No, I'm not the one with the problem, Detective Inspector.'

So he's still pissed that I got the job and he missed out on promotion.

'Good.' Meadows smiled. 'Then let's get on, shall we?' He turned back to the board. 'There are six residents in Bethesda: Kevin, Liam, Edward, Steven, Vanessa and Nicole. They are all potential witnesses. However, gaining information from them will be difficult.'

'So you're ruling them out as suspects?' Paskin asked.

'I think it's unlikely that one of them committed the crime but I think we need to keep an open mind. If one of the residents is responsible then they would have had assistance in covering it up. Alan Whitby's car is missing and the residents don't have the capability to dispose of a vehicle.'

'Are you sure about that?' Blackwell asked.

'Fairly certain. I think it would be a good idea to learn as much as we can about the medical condition of each of the residents before we start questioning. There are files on my desk. Perhaps you would like to do the research and brief the team in the morning.'

He might learn a thing or two.

'If you insist.'

'Good. Now there are six full-time staff, each a support worker, the manager Jane Pritchard and Alan Whitby who was the supervisor.' He pointed to the names listed on the right. 'Leah Parry is Liam's support worker. She discovered the body this morning. She was also the sleep-in on Monday night. Gemma Scott is Kevin's support worker, and she was on duty Monday night. I have yet to meet with the other members of staff. Relief staff come in on Friday evening and work through to Monday morning.'

'According to Alan's wife Melanie, Alan received a phone call from Jane Pritchard at 9 p.m. on Monday asking him to go into work to deal with a problem. We interviewed Jane this morning and she told us the last time she saw and spoke to Alan was at 6 p.m. Monday evening.

Either she's lying or someone else made the call to get Alan out of the house.'

'He was driving a silver Jaguar XF which is still missing. I've asked Traffic to keep an eye out for it, my guess is it's been dumped somewhere,' Edris said.

'We're waiting for the reports from SOCO but I don't hold much hope of finding fingerprints. The cellar had been cleaned down with bleach. Until we have the post-mortem report we don't know if he was dead or alive when he went into the freezer. I would guess Alan weighed about fourteen stone, so it's highly unlikely that someone could have wrestled him into the freezer on their own. It's my guess that we are looking at two people to move the body.' Meadows looked around the group. 'Any thoughts, questions?'

'There was no sign of a break in,' Valentine said. 'The cellar was obviously a prearranged meeting place. Can we assume that it's someone within the house as opposed to an outsider?'

'Or it could be the wife,' Edris offered. 'She would know her husband's workplace and the routines well enough. She could have followed him there, saw him having it away with the manager then shoved him in the freezer.'

'Thinking with your dick again.' Blackwell sniggered.

'Well, I suppose it's not an impossibility,' Meadows commented. 'But she would have needed help.'

'Maybe Jane was fed up of being the other woman and the two of them were in it together,' Edris suggested.

'And the motive?'

'Maybe to split the insurance policy.'

'It's worth checking out Melanie's alibi and seeing if Alan had an insurance policy. If only to satisfy Edris.' Meadows grinned. 'According to Melanie there were no problems in the marriage and certainly no money worries.'

'Alan seems to have been splashing the cash recently,' Edris said. 'New car and caravan. A large bonus from work apparently.'

'Drugs?' Paskin offered. 'Any of the residents on permanent medication? He could have been selling.'

'Good point,' Meadows said. 'I'm sure any medication will be listed in the files. Can you check that out, Blackwell?'

'Yep.'

'Paskin, I think you should pay Melanie Whitby a visit in the morning. See if Alan has a laptop, also get any bank statements and see if you can get an alibi. Valentine, can you make a start on interviewing and checking alibis for the relief staff please.'

'Does this mean I can ditch my uniform?' Valentine's eyes lit up.

'Yes, while you're with us,' Meadows said. 'Leah and Gemma were the only staff on duty Monday night. The sleep-in room is close to the cellar. I'm sure one of them or one of the residents on that floor must have heard or seen something. I have requested a constant presence at Bethesda House, and Matt Hanes is over there at the moment. Edris and I will go to the hospital tomorrow, see if there's anything to be learned from the post-mortem. We'll meet back here for Blackwell's briefing after.'

Meadows moved away from the board. There was a scuffing of chairs as the team moved back to their own desks. He sat at his computer and started adding the information to the database. He looked up every now and then to see Blackwell engrossed in the files, his forehead creased with concentration. Meadows smiled.

He might develop a bit of compassion yet.

Chapter Nine

Steam rose off the bonnet of Meadows' old Ford Mondeo as he sat outside Edris' house with the engine running. He could see the frost glittering on the pavement and parked cars. Inside his car, warm air blew from the vents and the speakers vibrated to the sound of AC/DC. Meadows sang along as he beat out a rhythm on the steering wheel.

The passenger door opened and Edris entered with a blast of cold air. 'Morning,' he shouted over the music.

'Morning.' Meadows shifted the car into gear and pulled off.

'What the hell are you listening to?' Edris reached out and turned down the volume.

'Wakes me up in the morning.' Meadows smiled.

'I wouldn't have thought old-school rock was your thing.'

'What did you expect? Classic FM?'

'No, folk music. The sort of stuff you listen to around the campfire.'

'Bloody hell, Edris, you haven't got much of an imagination.' Meadows laughed. 'Talk about stereotypes.'

'So you're telling me that AC/DC is hippy music' – Edris raised his eyebrows – 'and you rocked it out around the campfire.'

'You've got a fixation on campfires. It wasn't the boy scouts. I'll take you up to the commune one day and you can see for yourself.'

'Really? That's awesome.' Edris beamed. 'Do you visit often?'

'I've been up a few times since I've been back, mainly to take Mum. I left there when I was fifteen years old and they still welcome me.'

Meadows felt the nostalgia of childhood memories stir his emotions. It was a time he felt safe and happy, a time when his father was a man he could look up to. He shook away the memories and concentrated on the road.

'Let's hope we gain some insight from the post-mortem this morning. I hope for Alan Whitby's sake he was dead before going into the freezer.'

'Oh, I don't know, I can think of worse ways to die. Apparently you just fall asleep,' Edris said.

'Yes, but not until you're so cold you can't think. Then there's the panic of being locked in a confined space.'

'Yeah, you've got a point. You're going to enjoy meeting Daisy Moore this morning.' Edris grinned.

'Daisy?'

'The pathologist. I met her when I was training. I heard she's taken over from Glyn Thomas.'

Meadows conjured up an image of a sweet grey-haired lady leaning over the body as she pointed out injuries.

'She's awesome,' Edris continued.

Must be someone younger if Edris is impressed.

'Don't tell me you've dated the pathologist as well,' Meadows said with a groan.

'No, and what do you mean, "as well"? I'm not a complete slut!'

Meadows laughed as he drove into the car park. 'Come on then, let's meet this awesome pathologist of yours.' He pulled up his collar as he stepped out of the car and walked briskly towards the hospital with Edris at his side.

'You can lead the way, as you've been here before,' Meadows said.

They walked past the reception desk and to the lifts.

'I hate the smell of hospitals.' Edris wrinkled his nose as he pressed the call button.

'It smells a lot worse where we're going,' Meadows said as he stepped into the lift.

The lift took them down to the basement where a corridor led them to the morgue. As Meadows pushed open the first set of double doors the smell of formaldehyde tickled his nostrils. It always reminded him of the biology lab in school where frogs would sit in jars ready to be dissected.

They stood in a bright white room with filing cabinets lining one wall. A desk sat in the centre with trays filled with paper. A door led to a separate office where loud music thrummed.

Edris knocked on the office door and opened it.

A young woman who Meadows guessed to be in her late twenties sat at a desk. Raven hair was pulled back and secured with a band at the nape of her neck. A few wisps had escaped and coiled around her ears. She looked up at the visitors with sapphire eyes set behind long dark lashes. Meadows took a sharp intake of breath.

She leaned across the desk and turned off the music giving Meadows a few seconds to compose himself.

'Hello, Edris.' She smiled. 'Nice to see you again.'

Meadows expected Edris to go into flirt mode but to his surprise he didn't see any mischief in his eyes.

'Hi, Daisy, this is DI Winter Meadows. I don't think you two have had the opportunity to meet.'

'No, then again people generally don't go out of their way to meet me.' She laughed as she held out her hand.

Meadows took her hand, it felt soft and delicate in his own. 'It's a pleasure to meet you.'

It's a pleasure? Prat!

'I take it you are here to see Alan Whitby.' Daisy rose from her seat.

Meadows was impressed that she referred to Alan by name. Most of the pathologists he met used the term "victim"; it was as if they had to dehumanise the person to carry out their work.

Daisy slipped on an apron and snapped on latex gloves. 'Come on, I'll take you to see him.' She led them to an adjoining room, where Meadows could feel the drop in temperature. The room looked and smelled sterile. Two large stainless-steel sinks were positioned against the wall and various tools sat on a trolley. Against the far wall was a set of storage drawers.

'I haven't long finished the PM. I had to let him warm up a bit, poor fellow.' She approached a drawer, checked the label then slid out the gurney with ease. 'I've sent off blood samples to toxicology, I'm afraid it might take a while to come back, I've marked it urgent. His clothes have been bagged and sent to the lab.'

Meadows was transfixed by the movement of her lips as she spoke. They were an attractive deep wine colour, set against an ivory complexion. Her smile was warm and inviting. He noticed a small hole below the left side of her bottom lip. *A piercing? Probably takes it out for work.* He became aware that Daisy had stopped talking and was waiting for him to speak. *Say something, idiot!*

'So what have you got for us? Keep it nice and simple,' Edris said.

'OK. He's dead.' Daisy grinned.

Meadows saw a twinkle in her eyes.

'Maybe not that simple,' Edris added.

She reached out her hand and moved Alan's head gently. 'He was hit on the head at least three times and with considerable force, enough to break the skin. There would have been a lot of blood. Something blunt and heavy. If you look here' – she pointed to a slit in the skin –

'there is a groove. I also removed small fragments of plastic.'

'So is that what killed him?' Meadows asked. He had regained his composure and was now fully focused.

'No, my guess is he would have been knocked unconscious. He died of asphyxiation. I take it there wasn't much space in the freezer. He wouldn't have survived much longer in the cold.'

'Any defence wounds?'

'I was just getting to that.'

'There is a scratch under his chin.' She lifted his head. 'And one on his face. I would say fingernails.'

A scenario played in Meadows' mind. Perhaps Alan attacked someone, a woman, and she tried to fend him off. A man would more likely have punched him, not scratched his face. Sexual assault? Rape? Maybe someone came to the victim's aid – another woman? He's hit from behind…

'So a woman, probably two?'

'That's for you to work out, Detective.' Daisy smiled. 'But either a man or woman could have inflicted the head wounds with a heavy object.'

'Any signs of sexual activity before he died?' To his horror Meadows felt a flush spread up his neck.

'No obvious signs. I've sent swabs to the lab.'

'Good. Time of death?'

'It's difficult to tell with accuracy. My best guess would be sometime Monday night or early hours of Tuesday morning.' She pushed the gurney back into storage before she snapped off her gloves and walked to the sink where she scrubbed her hands. 'As soon as I have the results back from toxicology, I'll let you know. Meanwhile I'll finish the PM report and email it to you.'

'Thank you.'

'You're welcome.' She turned away from the sink and smiled.

Meadows wanted to say something but couldn't think of a parting comment.

'Catch you later.' Edris smiled and turned to leave.

'Bye,' Meadows said and followed Edris.

'So what do you think?' Edris asked as they entered the lift.

'She was very nice,' Meadows said.

'I meant about Alan Whitby.' Edris laughed.

'Oh, right.' Meadows squirmed.

'I think you've got a bit of a crush there!'

'Don't be daft,' Meadows snapped. 'She's more in your league, I think.'

'League?' Edris chuckled. 'Hey, not my type.' He held up his hands in surrender. 'You go ahead, I think she likes you.'

Meadows felt a warm tingle spread through his body.

'So, what do you think? Two women? Maybe Alan tried it on and it got out of hand. Someone came in to help and picked up the nearest object and hit him over the head.'

'So we are back to the case now?' Edris' eyes twinkled mischievously.

'Well, Gemma and Leah were in the house alone.'

'Not totally alone. One of the residents could have woken up. Then there's Jane Pritchard. She could have arranged to meet him in the cellar and things got out of hand.'

They left the building and walked towards the car. Meadows unlocked the door and climbed in.

'It doesn't make sense though. If Jane was having an affair with Alan why would he suddenly turn on her?'

'Maybe she changed her mind. Who knows what goes through women's minds.'

Meadows started the engine and pulled out of the car park. As he drove he reached out to switch on the stereo, and AC/DC vibrated through the car once more.

'So, would you like me to get you Daisy's number?' Edris shouted above the music.

'No, I don't have much luck with women.'

Chapter Ten

Jane Pritchard paced her office. Her eyes stung from lack of sleep and her stomach churned with worry. She pinched the bridge of her nose and tried to dispel the train of thought crashing through her mind.

Jane inhaled deeply, holding her breath as she counted to eight then blowing out. She repeated the process until she felt calmer. *OK, that's better.* She opened her handbag, took out a compact and dabbed some powder on her face before leaving the office.

The staff were already waiting in the sitting room where she had asked them to gather. Only three residents were present. Kevin sat next to Gemma carefully selecting jigsaw pieces, Eddy paced the room, emitting a repetitive droning noise, his black book clutched tightly in his hand, and Liam stood against the wall, fists clenched and eyes narrowed.

Jane looked around at the expectant faces and pulled back her shoulders.

'Firstly, I would like to thank you all for keeping the house running with the minimal amount of upset yesterday. I understand that this is a difficult time for you all, well for all of us. We have lost a valuable member of staff in very distressing circumstances.'

She paused and looked around the staff trying to gauge their reaction. No one looked particularly upset. She checked the faces again.

'Where's Leah?'

'She isn't feeling well today,' Cillian said.

'I see. Well, I suppose she had a bit of a shock yesterday.'

'A bit of a shock?' Cillian's eyes hardened. 'She should have been sent home straight away.'

'She seemed to be coping alright. We all had a shock, Cillian. Will she be coming in tomorrow?'

'We'll have to wait and see if she feels better.' Cillian's eyes challenged Jane.

She turned her gaze away from him. 'As you are all aware, the police will be coming in later to question the staff and residents. While we want to co-operate with the police, you must bear in mind that our first priority is to protect the residents and the reputation of this house.'

'Even if someone here shoved the poor bastard into the freezer,' Miles said from across the room.

'I don't think anyone here would have done that,' Gemma said and looked pointedly at the residents.

Jane snapped her head towards Gemma. 'Are you sure about that? Maybe there's something you know that we don't. Would you care to share with us?'

'I don't know anything about what happened. I'm just saying I don't think anyone here would do something like that.' Gemma's face reddened.

Jane's attention was caught by Liam rocking back and forth, his hand banging out a rhythm on the DVD shelf.

Jane felt irritation crawl at her skin. 'That's enough, Liam,' she said firmly.

'Want Leah,' Liam bellowed.

'Well, she's not coming in today. Now settle down or go to your room to relax.'

Liam swiped his hand across the shelf, sending the DVDs crashing to the ground.

Cillian jumped to his feet and put a hand on Liam's shoulder. 'Take it easy, buddy. Take a deep breath. Come on, you can give me a hand to put these back on the shelf.' Cillian crouched down and started collecting the scattered DVDs as Jane turned her attention back to Gemma.

'You were on duty Monday night. Who was awake during the night?'

'No one.' Gemma visibly squirmed in her chair. 'It was a quiet night.'

Jane tried to force a smile. She looked around at the rest of the staff, the meeting wasn't going the way she planned.

'What I'm trying to say is that there is little understanding of our home and the complex needs of the residents. People will be happy to jump to conclusions, especially the police. Like any other workplace, there is always gossip. I would appreciate it that if any of you have heard any rumours, or if the residents have said anything or acted out of the ordinary, then please let me know first before you say anything to the police. Bear in mind we will all lose our jobs if the house is closed.'

She let the statement hang in the air. So far Danielle and Harry had remained silent. It didn't surprise Jane, as they hadn't been on the premises Monday evening.

'We all know that the residents say the most outrageous things sometimes. I ask each of you to be vigilant during the interviews. If at any time you feel the police are badgering the residents or if any of the residents become distressed, you must stop the interview immediately and refer the police to me.' Jane looked at each of the staff in turn. 'Are there any questions?'

Kevin looked up from his jigsaw. 'Do you want to build a snowman?' he sang.

'No,' Jane snapped. 'You better behave yourself when the police are here, Kevin, or there will be no snow.'

'No snow!' Kevin leaped from the chair. 'I want snow.'

'Thirteen days,' Gemma said in a soothing voice.

'A word in private, Miles,' Jane said, then walked out of the sitting room.

'You really know how to keep your cool,' Miles snarled when he caught up with Jane.

'Gemma knows something, I'm sure of it. Find out,' Jane whispered.

Miles grabbed her arm and spun her around to face him. 'How am I supposed to do that?'

'Use your charm, you're good at that. Let me know when the police get here and keep your eyes and ears open.' Shrugging off his hand Jane walked into her office, slamming the door behind her.

Chapter Eleven

Meadows and Edris arrived in the office to a hive of activity. Paskin sat at her desk, her cheeks still flushed from the cold. Meadows guessed that she hadn't long arrived. She had a laptop open on her desk and was searching through files.

'I'll check to see if Alan's phone has dried out,' Edris said as he headed for his desk.

Meadows' eyes roamed around the office. Valentine's eyes were fixed to a computer screen, her fingers flying over the keyboard. Blackwell swung back and forth on his chair as he talked on the phone.

Meadows waited until Blackwell ended the call then called for the team's attention. They all dragged their chairs and gathered around the incident board, the two women sat with notebooks open, Blackwell slouched in his chair, legs apart and his hands resting on his thighs. Meadows briefed them on what they had learned from the trip to the morgue as Edris put the phone together.

'It's working,' Edris exclaimed, then started scrolling through the information.

'Good,' Meadows said.

'So, do you think we're looking for a woman?' Valentine asked.

'From the scratches on Alan's face I would say yes, however the wound inflicted on the back of his head could have come from anyone. Someone called Alan on Monday evening and got him to return to Bethesda. Alan's wife said it was Jane Pritchard, or at least that's what he told her.'

'It was Jane,' Edris said. 'According to the call history she phoned him at 9 p.m.'

'Interesting.' Meadows nodded. 'That would tie in with what Melanie Whitby told us. Run a check on the number to make sure that it is Jane Pritchard's and he wasn't using her as a cover name on his phone. We'll talk to Jane later. We need to find out why she was meeting him. Were they having an affair? And who else was with them?' He turned to Paskin. 'I see you have Alan Whitby's laptop. Did you get any useful information from Melanie Whitby this morning?'

'Not from Melanie, she's sticking to the story that her husband was a well-liked man. Good husband, good father. No recent arguments. I did get to speak with her daughter, Claire, alone. She told me that four years ago there were allegations of abuse at Bethesda House. Two members of staff involved, Alex Henson and Rhys Owens. Alan gave evidence at the tribunal.'

Meadows felt a spike of anger at the thought of someone in a position of trust abusing those too vulnerable to defend themselves.

'Did she elaborate on the nature of the abuse?'

'No, but she thinks the men were prosecuted. I'll look up the details of the case. If it went to court it should be on file.'

'Bastards,' Blackwell hissed.

So he does have a heart after all.

Meadows turned and added the names to the board. 'Both men would certainly have motive to kill Alan.'

'Why wait four years to get back at him?' Valentine asked.

'They could have just been released from prison,' Edris offered.

'I doubt it,' Meadows said. 'Sadly, very few cases of neglect and abuse get a custodial sentence. The longest I've heard of is two years and that was only because an undercover reporter recorded it.'

'I saw that documentary. It's fucking disgusting, they should have been locked up and had the same treatment.' Blackwell glowered.

Meadows didn't condone Blackwell's language or his eye-for-an-eye attitude, but the injustice of the case riled him too.

'I agree the sentences were lenient in that particular case. In most cases of this kind it's difficult to get sufficient evidence for a prosecution. The victim may not have the capacity to give evidence. It's the word of the whistle-blower against the accused. In this case it sounds like Alan may have been the one to report the abuse. Once Paskin has all the details, we will interview these two as priority.' Meadows underlined the names of the two men on the board.

'I'll go and interview them,' Blackwell said.

An image of Blackwell throttling the suspect flashed across Meadows' mind. He was about to decline the offer when Kevin came to his mind, the big man with his child-like eagerness who had touched his heart. Maybe they deserved to have Blackwell inflicted on them.

'OK, you can take Alex Henson; better take Paskin with you. Edris and I will interview Rhys Owens, see if their stories tally. Try and keep your temper in check.'

'I'll play it strictly by the book.' Blackwell smirked. 'I won't leave any marks.'

Edris sniggered and Meadows groaned inwardly, hoping that Blackwell was joking.

'OK, while we wait for the information on the abuse case, I would like to make a start interviewing the residents of Bethesda. Blackwell, would you like to fill us in on what you gleaned from the personal files? I think we will all benefit from some insight before we start the interviews.' Meadows smiled then took a seat allowing Blackwell to take the floor.

'The files were very enlightening,' Blackwell said. 'Of the six residents in Bethesda two are severely autistic – Edward, known as Eddy, and Nicole. Most of you are probably familiar with autism, especially if you've watched *Rain Man*.' He looked around the team and smiled.

Meadows gave a nod and leaned back in his chair, giving Blackwell his full attention.

'The condition varies according to where you are on the spectrum. Nicole for instance is non-verbal, she can communicate but you're going to have to rely on her support worker Danielle. Nicole responds better to women. It's doubtful you'll be able to get much information from this resident.'

'All the same, it will be interesting to see if we get a reaction when we mention Alan's name,' Meadows suggested.

'I agree,' Blackwell said.

Meadows smiled, surprised.

'It is important to remember that there will be a lack of understanding of social cues and the ability to read facial expressions. The sensory world can also be confusing, some don't like loud noises or bright lights. Nicole can be unresponsive to strangers. According to her file, both parents are still alive and she has two brothers. All visit regularly. She has been in Bethesda for five years.'

'How old is she?' Paskin asked.

'Twenty-eight.'

Meadows was impressed that Blackwell didn't have to consult any notes to answer the question.

'Eddy's life is dominated by routine,' Blackwell continued. 'Any deviation from that routine will evoke an outburst.'

'Violent?' Edris asked.

'On occasions he has had to be restrained, but mostly these outbursts involve head-banging, squealing, that sort of thing. His support worker is Harry, who it appears has a good connection with Eddy. Eddy always carries a book with him.'

'We saw him yesterday,' Edris said.

'He records anything out of the ordinary in his book – an outing or a visitor to the house. The book is used to alleviate his anxiety when there is a break in his routine and it appears to be working.'

'That's interesting.' Meadows leaned forward in his chair. 'There could be some information in the book. I saw him looking over the car park yesterday, he would've had a clear view of anyone entering the back door of the home.'

'He could have noted an argument between Alan and one of the staff or residents,' Edris said.

'What's important to Eddy may not be what we deem important, he may just have recorded a change in his breakfast cereal,' Blackwell said.

'It's certainly worth looking at the book, though. It may hold something interesting,' Meadows replied.

'Good luck with that. Eddy always keeps his book with him. The file does note that he has difficulty sleeping so he may have witnessed something on Monday night. For the record, Eddy has been a resident of Bethesda for six years and receives regular visits from his family.'

Meadows scribbled some notes and underlined *Eddy's book*. He looked around at the rest of the team, who were taking notes and appeared equally as interested in the residents of Bethesda.

'Vanessa is the oldest resident, at fifty years of age,' Blackwell continued. 'She has Down's syndrome, which I assume needs no explanation. She requires less care than the others, her support worker is Cillian but he also shares responsibility for some of the other residents. Both of Vanessa's parents are dead and she has no other siblings.'

'That leaves us with the other three residents whose conditions are a little more complex. Liam has a low IQ; according to his file he suffered from foetal alcohol syndrome. That is, his mother drank heavily during pregnancy. He has poor short-term memory, difficulty in interacting with groups and anger issues to name a few. His condition is quite complex.'

'Does that mean he's violent?' Paskin looked up from her writing pad.

'He is prone to violent outbursts, yes. There are several incidents recorded in the files, biting, punching and kicking. Two of the attacks were on Alan Whitby.'

'Do the files record what triggered the outburst?' Meadows asked.

'No, but it's worth noting that foetal alcohol syndrome can cause a variety of other problems – kidney failure, poor immune system, and physical weakness to name a few. Liam is five foot four and may not be very fit, so I can't see him lifting Alan into the freezer.'

'Family?' Meadows asked.

'No, Liam has been in care all his life. There are no records of any visitors.'

'That's sad,' said Valentine.

'Liam's support worker is Leah. They have a good relationship and sometimes she's the only one he will communicate with.'

'Just to remind you all, it was Leah and Liam who discovered Alan's body yesterday morning,' Meadows added.

'Kevin, like Liam, has a low IQ equivalent to that of a six-year-old. Complications at birth left his brain starved of oxygen. He is not known to be violent but can throw a tantrum. According to his file he's a big bugger, six foot five.'

'He certainly is,' Edris said. 'Frightened the life out of me yesterday.'

'It wouldn't take much,' Blackwell quipped. 'Kevin has the physical capability of lifting a body into a freezer, but I doubt he would have the ability to hide a body and keep it a secret.'

'Or drive away in Alan's car,' Meadows said.

'He could have been acting under instruction,' Edris commented.

'Yes,' agreed Blackwell, 'but it would be one hell of a risk. Gemma is Kevin's support worker. He has a brother who visits from time to time. That leaves us with Steven, who suffers from schizophrenia, a condition which I, like many others, misunderstood.'

'You made a mistake?' Paskin arched her eyebrows.

'Misunderstood,' Blackwell snapped. 'Steven's condition started in his late teens with hallucinations, seeing and hearing things that weren't there. This developed into delusions, thinking that people were spying on him and listening to his thoughts.'

'So he was perfectly normal before the hallucinations started?' Edris asked.

'Yes, he was studying for a degree in chemistry.'

'Does it say in the file what triggered the condition? Was there a family history of the illness?' Edris asked.

'No, why?'

'Just curious.' The constable leaned back in his chair.

Meadows glanced across at Edris. He thought he saw an expression of worry flit across his face before he cast his eyes downward to his notepad.

Maybe there's more to his discomfort than he's telling me.

He turned his attention back to Blackwell who was listing other symptoms of schizophrenia.

'Steven takes a mixture of antipsychotic drugs to suppress the symptoms but these cause side effects. Poor sod.'

'Violent?' Valentine asked.

'Not according to his file, he can be uncooperative and gets agitated easily. It seems he has difficulty organising his thoughts and his speech can be garbled. I have done further reading on the condition and would like to be the one to conduct the interview with Steven.'

'OK,' Meadows said. 'Edris and I will interview Eddy, Kevin and Liam. Valentine and Paskin, I think it best that you interview Vanessa and Nicole as they respond better to females.'

Blackwell took his seat so Meadows stood up and looked at the team. They were all dressed smartly.

'The manager has requested that we dress casually. We'll take it in turns to go over there, too many of us at once will upset the residents. Any questions?'

There was a general shaking of heads.

'Good, try to get as much information out of the support workers as you can. Get a feel for how they regarded Alan Whitby and if any of them know about the abuse allegations. Edris and I will go first. Paskin, can you get all the details on Rhys Owens and Alex Henson?'

'I'll get onto it straight away.'

'Valentine, how did you get on with the relief staff?'

'Most of them have alibis. I just have to check them out.'

'I'll give you a hand with that,' Blackwell offered.

'Good. Come on then, Edris, I'll take you home to get changed.' Meadows walked out of the office feeling like he was part of the team for the first time since he took the job.

Chapter Twelve

I want Leah. I'm going to stay in my room until she comes. She promised she wouldn't leave me so she has to come. I hate Jane, I bet she made Leah stay away. She is always making people go away, shouting at them, taking away treats.

'Liam, are you alright, mate?'

I'm not going to turn around. If I don't look at him, he will go away. He shouldn't keep coming in my room without knocking, it's the rules.

'Liam?'

'Go away, Cillian.'

He's closed the door but he is still here, I can hear him coming up behind me.

'Come on, Liam, you don't want to stay in here all day. We can go out for a walk if you like.'

He is standing behind me now.

'I don't want to go for a walk. I'm staying here until Leah comes.'

'She can't come in today. She isn't feeling well. You want Leah to get better, don't you?'

I have to turn around and look at him now or he'll think I don't care about Leah. He will tell her I don't care.

'Is she really ill or are you lying?'

'Of course she's ill, why would I lie?'

He wants Leah to himself, always touching her, smiling and laughing.

'Jane always lies and so does Alan. I'm glad he is in the freezer.'

'You don't want to go saying things like that. The police will be here soon and they will want to talk to you. It's OK, I'll be with you.'

He's smiling, he shouldn't be smiling. He knows.

'I don't want to talk to the policemen, they will take me away.'

There's something heavy in my chest. It's getting bigger, the red will come. I have to squeeze my hands tight. Cillian is stepping away, he's afraid. People are always afraid of me. Except Leah. I don't mean to hurt people. They get in the way.

'It's OK, mate, no one is going to take you away. Remember what Leah said?'

'Alan in the freezer, I didn't do it.'

'No you didn't, you just saw him when you went to get ice cream.'

'I don't like Alan. Alan is mean to Leah.'

'Yes I know, but you mustn't tell the police that.'

He's making my head hurt. I can't remember.

'Go away, Cillian.'

'OK, I'll come back and see you later.'

He's gone. Good. I don't want him to come back. I don't want to stay here. My arms and legs hurt, I have to keep moving them. Swing, stamp, jump, swing, stamp, jump. Leah told me a secret but I can't tell anyone. It wants to come out of my head, there is not enough room in my head for the secret. I mustn't tell.

Chapter Thirteen

Meadows drove down the farm track that led to his cottage. It had been his family home, now he lived there alone. He'd bought it from his mother to enable her to move to a ground floor flat. As he pulled up outside, he tried to imagine his home through Edris' eyes. A run-down place in the middle of nowhere with a farmhouse, the only neighbour, a mile further down the track.

'I won't be long,' Meadows said.

He left Edris in the car with the engine running to keep him warm as he dashed into the cottage. It was cold inside with a faint smell of damp. The walls were brightly coloured, his mother's choice, he hadn't yet found time to redecorate. He went straight to his bedroom where he changed out of his suit and into a pair of faded jeans and a grey and blue striped Baja hoodie. He checked his reflection in the mirror. *It will have to do.* He pulled on a pair of boots then walked onto the landing where he pulled down the hatch leading to the attic. The ladder slithered to the floor and he climbed with ease. Several large boxes stood against the wall filled with things his mother didn't have room for, but was reluctant to part with. He rummaged around in the boxes until he found what he was looking for, pocketed the object then climbed back down, closing the hatch.

'You took your time,' Edris said as Meadows slid behind the steering wheel.

'I couldn't decide on a jumper.' Meadows looked at Edris who was dressed in a pair of loose jeans with a plaid shirt open over a black T-shirt. 'I didn't want us to clash.'

Edris gave a half-smile but didn't comment.

'Are you OK?' He put the car into gear and pulled off. 'You haven't been yourself since we left the station and you seemed particularly interested in Blackwell's presentation on schizophrenia. Are you worried about the interviews? Because if it makes you uncomfortable—'

'It's not that,' Edris said. He sighed and looked out of the passenger window. He remained silent for a few moments then turned to look at Meadows. 'I have an uncle who is schizophrenic, my father's brother. He used to stay with us sometimes.'

He wriggled in his seat. Meadows could sense his discomfort but remained silent.

'When I was seven years old he came to stay for a week. He was OK at first, then one night he came into my bedroom when I was asleep. He put his hand over my mouth and dragged me out of bed. He took me into the kitchen and started opening the drawers until he found Mum's filleting knife. I just stood there too terrified to call for help.' Edris paused and rubbed his hand over his face.

Meadows kept his eyes on the road while Edris composed himself.

'He unlocked the back door then grabbed me again, he had the knife in his other hand. I thought he was going to kill me and chop me to bits. He dragged me down the garden, I remember my whole body was shaking and I couldn't stop my teeth from chattering. It was winter and I was dressed in pyjamas, no slippers, but I don't think it was the cold that made me shake.

'We went into the coal shed, he constantly mumbled strange words that didn't make any sense. He got me to help him pile the coal against the door. I was in that shed for hours. Eventually my parents came. I could hear Dad shouting for him to let them in. It only made my uncle more agitated, he shouted back waving the knife.'

Meadows could imagine a seven-year-old Edris covered in coal dust and huddled in the corner of the cold shed.

And I thought I had some bad childhood memories.

'How did you get out?'

'It was my mum who eventually persuaded him to come out, she told him he would be safer in the house – they could lock the doors. As soon as my uncle opened the door he was grabbed and taken away in an ambulance. He never came to stay again.'

Meadows pulled the car into Bethesda's car park, switched off the engine and turned to face Edris.

'That explains why this place makes you so uncomfortable. You should've said something sooner. I can manage the interviews here. You take the car and interview Rhys Owens. Don't worry, no one else has to know about this. You can pick me up later.'

'Thanks, but I'm fine doing the interviews here, honestly. They don't frighten me. Funnily enough my uncle thought he was protecting me. In his own little world he thought I was in great danger from some outside force. That's why he barricaded us in the coal shed. He thought it would be safer there. It was never his intention to harm me.' Edris sighed. 'I'm afraid of what I might become. When I see them in there' – he nodded towards the house – 'I see my future.'

'So you're afraid of something that probably won't happen?'

'You heard what Blackwell said about Steven. He was normal until the hallucinations started.'

'Does anyone else in your family suffer from mental health problems?'

'No, but that doesn't mean anything. It can run in families.'

'The chances of it happening to you are probably very slim. Worrying about it isn't going to help or stop it happening. You have to confront your fears. Go and see your GP for reassurance. In the meantime, you know the signs and symptoms and so do your parents. I'll soon let you know if I think you're losing the plot.' Meadows grinned.

Edris visibly relaxed. 'I guess you're right. Thanks.'

'Come on then, we'd better make a start.'

Meadows climbed out of the car. As he walked towards the building he looked up and saw Eddy watching from a window.

'I bet he saw who was here on Monday evening.'

'Possibly, but is he going to tell us?' Edris gave a wave and a smile but got no response from Eddy. 'It doesn't matter anyway, it's not as if he would make a reliable witness.'

'He doesn't have to,' Meadows said. 'We just need a lead.'

* * *

They were met at the front door by Jane Pritchard. She wore a cream jumper over black trousers. Her arms were folded across her chest and her eyes moved swiftly over Meadows' attire.

'I expected you earlier. It'll be lunchtime for the residents soon and I would be grateful if you didn't disrupt their routine.'

'We shouldn't be long and we can break for lunch,' Meadows said.

'Good. Have there been any developments?'

'A few, but unfortunately we can't share any information with you at this stage.'

'I see. Well, I expect you'll want to get on with the interviews. I'll have the staff bring the residents to my office one at a time.'

So you can listen to what they tell me and then intimidate them? I don't think so.

'That won't be necessary, Ms Pritchard. We will interview the residents in their own rooms with their support workers.' Meadows gave her a tight smile. 'I'm sure it will be more comfortable for them. I have asked two of my female detectives to conduct the interviews with Nicole and Vanessa, as I understand they respond better to females.'

A look of irritation crossed Jane's face and her thin lips curled into a false smile. 'Right. I'll let you get on. You'll find most of the residents in the sitting room.' She turned to leave.

'One moment. I'd like to have a word with you first. I think it would be best if we used your office.'

'I don't see what more I can tell you,' she said.

'It won't take long.'

They followed Jane into the office and took their seats. Jane folded her hands together and placed them on her lap, her shoulders pulled back. Meadows waited for Edris to take out his notebook before addressing her.

'You told us yesterday that the last time you saw or spoke to Alan Whitby was Monday evening at 6 p.m.'

'Yes.'

'You didn't speak to him after that?'

'No.' Jane squirmed in her chair. 'I told you, I saw him before he left work for the evening.'

'I see. According to Alan's mobile phone records you called him Monday evening at 9 p.m.' Meadows nodded to Edris.

Edris flipped through his notebook and read out a phone number. 'Is that the right number for your mobile?'

'Yes, that's my number.' Jane paled.

'So you did speak to Alan late Monday evening?'
Meadows held eye contact.

'Yes.'

'And the nature of the call?'

Jane pursed her lips. She sat straighter in her chair. 'If you must know, Alan asked me to call him. He needed an excuse to leave the house.'

'Why did he need an excuse?'

'How would I know?'

'So did you arrange to meet him?'

'No,' she said and lifted her chin defiantly.

'You didn't find it odd that he would make such a request? Had you phoned him at home before?'

'On a few occasions.'

'And why do you think he needed an excuse to leave his home? You must have some idea?'

'I would assume to meet a woman.'

'What woman?'

'I don't know.'

'You must have some idea.' Meadows leaned forward.

'I wouldn't like to speculate.'

'Someone from work?'

Jane shrugged her shoulders. 'I really don't know. Alan was very flirtatious. It could be anyone, or maybe he just wanted to go to the pub.'

'Why didn't you tell us about this yesterday?'

'The man had just died. I thought I could save his wife the embarrassment.'

'That's kind of you. Is there anything else you decided not to tell us?'

'No.' Jane scowled.

'What about the abuse allegations four years ago? I understand two members of staff were struck off.'

'That was before I took the post of manager here.'

'You must have been informed of the situation? At the very least there would have been rumours.'

'I really don't take any notice of gossip. I prefer facts. I was only given brief details, the company wanted a fresh start, so I really can't help you.'

'I think that will be all for now,' Meadows said. 'In the meantime, if you think of anything else, no matter how embarrassing or inconsequential it seems, I would appreciate it if you would inform me or one of my officers.'

'How long are you going to keep that policeman standing guard at the door? I would like to get back to normal.'

'The officer is there for the safety of both the residents and the staff. I would've thought that would take priority over putting on a show of normality. We will see ourselves to the sitting room.' He nodded to Edris who closed his notebook and stood.

'Well, you put her in her place,' Edris said when they were at a safe distance from the office.

'Good. There's something dislikeable about that woman. She has a sneaky face.'

'A sneaky face?' Edris grinned. 'That's a new one, I don't think it's an arrestable offence though.'

'Well, she's definitely keeping something from us.'

'You think she is lying about why Alan asked her to phone?'

'Yes, she either knows who he was meeting, or–'

'She was the one having an affair with him.'

They entered the sitting room where some of the residents sat with members of staff doing various activities. Meadows scanned the room until he saw Kevin. He was sitting at a table next to Gemma. A half-completed jigsaw lay on the table and Kevin fumbled with a piece trying to fit it into place, his faced creased in concentration. He lifted his head for a moment and his eyes met with Meadows. A grin spread across his face.

'The Winter Man is here!' He leapt from his seat, knocking several pieces of jigsaw to the floor.

'Winter Man!' He stumbled towards Meadows, flung his arms around his waist and lifted him off his feet.

'Hi, Kevin, it's good to see you.' Meadows could feel his ribs crushing beneath the hug.

'OK, Kevin, you better put him down. You don't want to break him.' Gemma laughed.

Kevin released Meadows who resisted the urge to rub his ribs. He could hear Edris sniggering beside him.

'Do you want to do my jigsaw with me?' Kevin hopped from foot to foot.

'Maybe another time.' Meadows smiled. 'I thought we could go to your room and talk. I have something to give you.'

'A present?' Kevin's eyes lit up.

'Yes, a present. Come on lead the way.' He nodded to Gemma to follow.

They walked down the corridor with Kevin humming a tune as he ambled along, his large feet dragging across the floor.

'How long have you worked at Bethesda?' Meadows asked.

'Six years,' Gemma replied.

'And you enjoy your work?'

'Yes. I guess we all have bad days but most of the time it's a good place to work.'

'And do you get along with the other staff?'

'Yes, they're all friendly.'

'What about Alan?'

Gemma hesitated. 'He was OK. I guess as supervisor you're not meant to be too friendly with the staff.'

It was clear she hadn't liked him much.

'How long have you been Kevin's support worker?'

'Nearly six years. Just after I finished my training. We hit it off straight away, didn't we, Kev?'

'Hit it off.' Kevin grinned and stopped outside the room. 'My room,' he said and pushed open the door.

The plush snowman they had seen yesterday was now propped on a table strewn with paper and pens.

'Take a seat,' Gemma said.

Edris took the armchair and Gemma the sofa. Kevin stood facing Meadows, his body wiggling from side to side. Meadows put his hand in his pocket and took out a snow globe. He shook it and watched Kevin's eyes widen in delight as flakes of snow swirled around a house. 'It's for you.'

'For me!' Kevin took the globe and cradled it gently in his hands. 'A present for me.'

He shook the globe then held it out for Gemma to see.

'That's lovely, Kevin.'

'Yes, lovely,' Kevin agreed. 'Thank you, Winter Man.'

'You're welcome. Shall we sit down?'

Kevin plonked himself on the sofa next to Gemma, and Meadows pulled up a chair from the table.

'Kevin, I would like to talk to you about Alan. Do you know what happened to Alan?'

Kevin nodded and grinned. 'Frozen, frozen like ice cream.' He chuckled. 'Now he will have to melt.'

'Do you know who put him in the freezer?'

'No. It wasn't me. I didn't do it.' He hunched his shoulders and looked at Gemma.

'It's OK, Kevin,' Gemma reassured him.

'Don't worry, Kevin, you're not in any trouble. I just need you to help me again.' Meadows smiled. 'Is Alan a nice man?'

'No.' Kevin shook his head several times. 'Shouts at me.'

'Why does he shout at you?'

'Eating ice cream. I sneak into the kitchen.' Kevin giggled.

Meadows looked at Gemma who shrugged her shoulders.

'Was it dark when you sneaked into the kitchen?'

'No, the lights are on.'

'Was it dark outside?'

'Yes, night-time.'

'You were in your pyjamas?'

'Yes.' Kevin shook the snow globe again.

'It could have been any night,' Gemma said.

'Did Alan come in often during the night shift?'

'No, he usually left at six.'

'So it was probably Monday night that Kevin saw Alan, we know he was here.' He turned his attention back to Kevin. 'Do you like ice cream?'

'Yes, lots and lots of ice cream.'

'So do I.' Meadows sat forward in the chair. 'Who else did you see when you were eating ice cream?'

Kevin shrugged his shoulders and shook the snow globe, his eyes fixed on the dancing flakes.

'Did you see Gemma?'

Meadows noticed Gemma stiffen, she looked like she was about to say something when Kevin looked up and grinned. 'Gemma didn't see me.'

'I was probably in the laundry room. The residents' clothes are washed and dried each evening.' Colour rose in her cheeks.

'What did Alan say to you, Kevin?'

'Shouting.'

'About the ice cream?'

'Go to your room!' Kevin's face screwed up. 'You, you... words I'm not allowed to say.'

'Bad words?'

'Yes.' Kevin nodded.

'Did you go to your room?'

'Yes.'

'Did you see Alan again?'

Kevin looked blankly at Meadows.

'Did you stay in your room and go to sleep?'

'Peeked out.'

Meadows gave an encouraging smile. 'What did you see?'

'Liam out of bed. Alan called him bad words.'

'What did Liam do?'

Kevin shrugged.

'Did you see Jane?'

'No boss lady.'

'Thank you, Kevin. You have been a big help. You're a star.'

'A star.' Kevin beamed. He turned to look at Edris who was sat with his pen poised over his notebook. 'What are you drawing?'

'I'm writing.' Edris smiled.

'Why?'

'It's his job,' Meadows explained. 'He writes things down so we don't forget what people say.'

'Can I help you with your job?'

'Erm, yeah, OK.' Edris looked around then stood and grabbed a piece of paper and pen from the table. He handed it to Kevin and sat down.

Meadows turned his attention to Gemma. 'Did you see or hear Alan on Monday night?'

'No.' She shifted in her seat. 'I wouldn't have heard anything. The washing machine and tumble dryer go for a good few hours. I stayed in the laundry room to iron and fold the clothes.'

'So how do you know if a resident is up and needing attention?'

'I check all the rooms regularly throughout the night and I carry a monitor for Steven and Eddy. They are prone to fits.'

'You didn't hear anything on the monitors?'

'No, besides, Steven and Eddy sleep on the first floor.'

'What do you know about the abuse that took place here four years ago?'

Gemma looked uncomfortable. 'I don't think it is a good idea to discuss that now.' She looked pointedly at Kevin.

'I see, so I take it our friend was somehow involved.' Meadows looked at Kevin who was scribbling away on his piece of paper mimicking Edris' pauses.

'Yes, and Liam mainly. Will it all have to be dragged up again?'

'If it has any bearing on what happened here Monday then yes, I'm afraid we will have to look into it and those that were involved.'

'Then you should know that I was the whistle-blower. I would appreciate it if that piece of information didn't come out. It would make working here very difficult for me.'

'I can understand that. Who else knows about this?'

Gemma shrugged. 'No one here is supposed to know. I made my statement confidentially.'

'OK. There is no reason why your name should come into it but I would like to discuss it further with you at another time. Kevin, I'll let you get back to your jigsaw now.'

'Would you like to help?'

'I have to talk to Leah and Liam now but I will come and take a look later.'

'OK.'

Kevin handed the sheet of paper to Meadows. He looked at the illegible scrawls on the paper. 'Great job, Kevin, you would make a good policeman.'

Kevin chuckled.

'Leah isn't in today, she isn't very well,' Gemma said.

That's interesting.

'OK, we'll talk to Harry and Eddy then.'

'I'll find Harry for you. You can wait in the sitting room if you like.'

As they left Kevin's room, Meadows caught sight of a figure scurrying down the corridor and disappearing into Jane's office.

'Who's that going into Jane's office,' Meadows asked Gemma.

'Miles. He's Steven's support worker.'
So what's he got to tell Jane that's so urgent?

Chapter Fourteen

Jane sat at her desk, anxiety gnawing at her stomach. The door was flung open and Miles scuttled into the office, closing the door behind him.

'What the hell are you doing?' Jane demanded.

'Hush,' Miles hissed. He put his ear up against the door. Waited a few moments then turned to face Jane. 'They've gone into the sitting room.'

'Yeah, and they probably saw you coming in here, you bloody idiot.'

'Do you want to hear what was said or not?'

'Well hurry up and tell me then and get back into the sitting room before you raise their suspicion.'

'You're being paranoid.' Miles smirked. 'I told you we have to act normal. Staff are always coming into your office.'

Jane felt irritation grate her already frayed nerves. 'You're the only one that comes in here all the time.'

'Yeah, well, we've got bigger problems than that. Kevin saw Alan on Monday night.'

Jane laughed. 'Like anyone is going to believe that big oaf. Anyway, we would've seen him if he was lurking around the cellar. It's not as if he can play hide and seek.'

'He wasn't in the cellar, you stupid cow, he was in the kitchen,' Miles hissed.

'Who? Alan?'

'Yes, he caught Kevin eating ice cream.'

'But Alan was waiting in the car park when I arrived.'

'So? He could've been in the house before you arrived, he could have told someone what he was doing here. Security. Kevin said Leah saw him.'

'And that little bitch is off today.' Jane felt the anxiety coil around her chest and constrict her breathing.

'Why do you think that is?' Miles' eyes took on a dangerous glint.

'You're going to have to go and see her.' Jane pulled at her collar, she could feel the heat rising, it prickled her skin.

'Me? It's your problem. Why don't you go?'

'I can't leave here, in case it's escaped your notice the police are wandering around. It's not going to look good if I just disappear for a few hours. They won't notice if you leave. Anyway, you can go tonight.'

'Yeah, with Cillian there! Use your head. Besides, I'm on duty tonight. Best leave it. If she knew anything, she would have told the police by now.'

'For all we know she could be down at the station making a statement.' Jane noticed her own voice rising and fought to regain control.

'Then it's too late to do anything about it. Look, I'll keep an eye on Gemma. If Leah saw anything, she would've told her.'

'Or she could've seen something herself – she's been acting strange since the whole business started.'

'She's had her opportunity to say something and I don't think she is the type to keep quiet. Did you know she was the one who blew the whistle on Alex and Rhys?'

'Where did you hear that?'

'She just told the copper.'

'Did she now, sneaky little bitch. Maybe she has other plans. She could try and take Alan's place. Who are the police talking to now?' Jane asked.

'Harry and Eddy. I can't see any worries there.'

Miles perched himself on the edge of the desk.

'Except his bloody book. Fuck knows what he's written in there.' She clenched her fists and felt her nails dig into the palms of her hands.

'Yeah well, it's not like he is going to give it to them,' Miles said as he picked up a pile of documents and started to flick through them.

'No, it's unlikely but if they suspect there is something in the book then they could demand to see it. Get a warrant or whatever they do.'

'Will you listen to yourself?' Miles slammed the documents down on the desk. 'You're starting to lose the plot. Why the hell would they think there was something of interest in the book?'

'It doesn't matter what they think. You're going to have to get the book. Do it tonight when he's sleeping.'

'That bloody policeman is lurking around all night.'

'You're on night duty. You are supposed to go into the clients' rooms to check on them.'

'And I'll be the first person they'll blame.'

'Just put the book in my desk drawer and I'll get rid of it with the file.'

'You've still got it!' A vein pulsed in Miles' forehead. He leaned forward until he was inches from Jane's face. 'You stupid cow.'

'Don't you dare speak to me like that!' Jane hissed, pulling her shoulders back. 'What do you expect me to do? Have a bonfire on the front lawn?'

'I don't care what you do, just get rid of it,' Miles snarled as he stood up. 'I told you before, I'm not going down because of your stupidity.'

He turned on his heels and left the office, slamming the door.

Chapter Fifteen

Meadows sat at the table in the sitting room, helping Kevin with his jigsaw while he waited for Gemma to return with Harry. He could see Edris fidgeting in a chair opposite. He placed a piece of the puzzle and Kevin clapped. From his position he could see into the kitchen. A man with cropped brown hair stood at the cooker; Meadows guessed this was Cillian. Besides him the younger female resident, Nicole, was stirring something in a saucepan.

Miles entered the sitting room, his eyes darting around. He saw Meadows, nodded and walked into the kitchen, where he picked up the kettle and carried it to the sink. Meadows noted that he didn't acknowledge Cillian.

Gemma entered the room followed by another young woman. She had short red spiky hair and wore a lime jumper with a turtle printed on the front. They approached Meadows, both smiling.

'This is Harry,' Gemma said. 'Harry, this is Detective Inspector Winter Meadows.'

Meadows stood and shook her hand.

'I bet you were expecting a man.' Harry smiled.

She had sparkling sapphire eyes and full lips.

'Harry is short for Harriet,' she explained.

'I have a lot more problems with my name.' Meadows smiled.

'I can imagine.'

Meadows noticed that Edris had appeared at his side. 'This is DC Tristan Edris.'

'Nice to meet you.' Edris held out his hand and a flirtatious smile played on his lips.

Well, that's cheered him up. Meadows watched with amusement.

Harry turned her attention to Meadows. 'I'll take you to see Eddy. He's in his room. I'm not sure how he will react to your visit. He can be very unsociable when he chooses.'

'I understand, we've had the chance to read his file so are fully aware of his condition.'

They followed Harry up the stairs. Meadows noticed Edris' eyes travel up her long slender legs and resisted the urge to nudge him. They arrived at Eddy's room and Harry knocked the door before they entered.

Eddy stood gazing out of the window. He wore a purple shirt tucked into black trousers which were belted high on the waist. He kept his back turned to the visitors.

'Take a seat,' Harry said.

Meadows glanced around the room. Its design was similar to Kevin's room, but the furnishing was sparse. There were no pictures on the walls. A shelf held neatly stacked books ordered by the colour of their spines. He took a seat on the sofa and Edris sat down heavily next to him.

Harry walked over to the window. 'Eddy, you have visitors, remember we talked about it yesterday. I did tell you they were coming.'

Eddy turned around to face Meadows and Edris, his face expressionless. The first thing Meadows noticed was Eddy's lack of hair. His head had recently been shaved, leaving a shining pate; his face was clean of stubble and his eyebrows had been removed.

'Hello, Eddy, I'm DI Winter Meadows and this is DC Tristan Edris,' Meadows said.

Eddy walked towards the sofa his book clutched to his chest.

'Not a scheduled visit, infiltrators, cretins.' He opened his book and started scribbling notes.

'They are the police,' Harry explained. 'They just want to have a chat with you.'

Eddy swivelled his head towards Harry then back again to Meadows. His sharp eyes roamed the inspector's face, making Meadows feel a little uncomfortable.

'Black wavy hair,' Eddy said and wrote in his book before returning his gaze to Meadows. 'Green eyes' – he took a step closer – 'yes, definitely green eyes, six foot.'

'Six one,' Meadows said.

'Late thirties.' Eddy scrutinized Meadows' boots, then turned his attention to his jumper. 'Gipsy,' he announced.

'Close,' Meadows said.

Edris giggled. 'That's very clever.'

Eddy snapped his eyes towards Edris. 'Dark blond hair, too long. Too long for a man. Five foot nine.' He scribbled again in the book.

'Five ten,' Edris corrected.

'Blue eyes,' Eddy continued. He stepped closer, inspected Edris' shoes and clothes. 'Pretty boy, homosexual.'

'No, I'm straight,' Edris protested.

Eddy ignored him and wrote the details in the book. Meadows couldn't help the smile that came to his lips.

'He's very accurate with his assessments,' Harry said with a grin.

'Well, not this time,' Edris bristled.

'Do you write down all visitors in your book, Eddy?' Meadows asked.

'Unscheduled visitors.' Eddy started to pace the room.

Meadows sat back in his chair hoping that it would make Eddy feel more at ease. 'Eddy, do you know what happened to Alan?'

'Unscheduled termination.'

'Am I supposed to write that down?' Edris grinned.

Meadows nodded. 'Do you know who, um, terminated Alan?'

'Classified information.' Eddy clutched the book to his chest.

'Does that mean he knows something about what happened to Alan?' Meadows turned to Harry.

'Not necessarily. He could mean he doesn't have that information or it could mean he doesn't want to share that information with you.'

'May I see your book?' Meadows held out his hand and gave an encouraging smile.

Eddy recoiled, clutching the book tighter as he rocked back and forth.

'It's OK, you don't have to show me. Can you tell me what you've written in the book?'

Eddy continued to rock back and forth. Meadows fought back his frustration.

The whole case could be solved by what is in that book, or maybe there's nothing to be seen.

He stood, walked to the window and peered outside. Behind him Eddy let out a low guttural noise. Meadows turned to see him rocking harder as the noise grew louder and into a repetitive pattern.

'You're standing in his place,' Harry explained.

'I'm sorry, Eddy.' Meadows moved away.

Eddy took up his position by the window, after a few moments he ceased making a noise but continued to sway.

Meadows moved a little closer. 'What do you see when you look out of the window, Eddy?'

'Silver car, red car, black car, too many cars. Not in time slot.' Eddy kept his gaze fixed on Meadows' car. 'Unscheduled visitor, and unscheduled car.'

Meadows turned back to Harry. 'Does Eddy watch the staff arrive and leave every day?

'Yes, it's part of his routine.'

'So if there was a car parked outside that isn't usually parked there at that time it would upset his routine?'

'Yes, he knows all of the staff members' cars. So if someone changes vehicles it causes him anxiety.'

'And he would write it in his book?'

'Yes.'

'Have you ever read through the book?'

'No, and I'm Eddy's support worker, I'm with him most days.'

'Was Eddy unsettled on Monday?' Meadows asked.

'Not that I recall.'

'And what time did you leave work that day?'

'Eight in the evening, Eddy was in his room. He wouldn't usually leave his room after that. He reads or watches the television depending on the day. Night shift come in at around ten to tell him it's time to sleep. Although he can be quite restless so will pace his room, sometimes until the early hours of the morning.'

'So how was he Tuesday morning?'

Harry thought for a few moments.

'He was very elevated on Tuesday morning, ranting about cars. Then again, yesterday morning he was very unsettled with all the comings and goings.'

Meadows looked at Eddy, who was still gazing out of the window.

'I don't think we should distress him any further but it is important that we see his book,' Meadows said, keeping his voice low.

'I'm not sure that will be possible. I'll work with him over the next few days, see if I can persuade him to let me see it. I can't promise you.'

'If you can try, that would be great,' Edris added.

Meadows noticed the twinkle in the young man's eyes.

He just can't help himself.

'How did you get on with Alan?'

'OK, I guess. He liked things done his way. Liked to be in control.'

'In what way?'

Harry fidgeted in her seat. 'Sometimes he would change the residents' routine, said it was for their own benefit. He always had some justification, saying it was for their own good.'

'And you didn't agree with his ways?'

'Not always but it was difficult to argue against him. He was responsible for staff appraisals and could make things difficult if he wanted.'

'Was there tension between Alan and any of the other staff? Like Jane?'

'He spent a lot of time in Jane's office but I can't imagine he would've had any influence over her. As for the rest of the staff I didn't witness any tension apart from Gemma. I got the sense he didn't like Gemma. He always seemed to be picking on her for some reason or another. There were no major arguments so please don't read too much into it. I've probably said too much.'

Meadows smiled. 'I appreciate your honesty.' He stood and Edris put away his notebook.

'Thank you for talking to us, Eddy.'

Eddy kept his back turned and showed no sign that he had heard.

'We'll need to speak with Liam, I understand that Leah isn't in today.'

'I'll get Cillian for you. He also works with Liam. See you later, Eddy,' Harry called as they left the room.

They followed Harry downstairs and into the hallway where they waited while she went into the sitting room to find Cillian.

'I don't think we are any the wiser,' Edris said. 'I don't think we can learn anything here.'

'Oh, I don't know. You'd be surprised by what we have learned. You have to read between the lines. Think about it. Eddy talked about cars. He didn't mention unscheduled visitors. Whoever he saw Monday night was known to him.'

'Yeah like that narrows it down.' Edris shook his head.

'We really need to get hold of his book.'

Cillian appeared in the doorway.

'Hi, I'm Cillian, I understand you want to have a chat with Liam.'

Meadows shook his hand and looked into his pale blue eyes, and noted the younger man didn't hold eye contact for long. 'Yes, it shouldn't take long.'

Cillian was short, at a guess no more than five foot seven but muscular arms showed beneath his long-sleeved T-shirt. His brown hair was cropped short and one ear was pierced.

'Right I'll take you to see Liam. I'm afraid he isn't having a very good day. He's refusing to come out of his room,' Cillian informed them as they walked down the corridor.

'That's understandable, it must have been a shock for him finding Alan's body – and for Leah too,' Meadows said.

'Yes it was.' Cillian stopped outside the room and knocked the door before opening it. 'Hi, buddy, there are two gentlemen who want to have a chat with you.'

'No! I don't want to,' Liam shouted, his face screwed up in rage.

Meadows stepped into the room. 'It's OK.' He held up his hands. 'There's nothing to worry about, we just want to have a little chat with you.'

'Fuck off.'

'Now, Liam, that's enough.' Cillian's voice was stern. 'Calm down.'

Meadows glanced around the room hoping to find something of interest that he could use to distract Liam. His eyes fell on a blue-painted wooden hutch. Above the round entrance were the words *Hard Hat.*

'Is that a rabbit you have there?' Meadows approached the hutch.

'No,' Liam screeched. 'Leave him alone, he's sleeping.'

'He just wants to meet him,' Cillian coaxed. 'Why don't you show the visitors your tortoise?'

'Hard Hat's sleeping, he doesn't want to wake up,' Liam scowled.

'That's a great name for a tortoise.' Meadows smiled. 'I wish I could sleep through the winter.'

Liam eyed him warily.

'Does he go out into the garden in the summer?'

'Yes, when it doesn't rain.'

'Does he hide from you when he's out in the garden?'

'Yes, he's good at hide and seek.' Liam gave a small smile.

'Do you like to play games?'

'Not good at games.' Liam frowned.

'I bet you're good at hide and seek.'

Liam nodded. 'But not as good as Hard Hat.'

'Tortoises are very clever. Does Alan play hide and seek? Did you see him hiding in the house at night-time?'

'Mustn't talk about Alan.' Liam backed away from Meadows.

'Who says you mustn't talk about Alan?'

'Not telling, mustn't say.' Liam shook his head violently and drove his fist into his forehead.

'I think that's enough questions' – Cillian stepped forward – 'he's getting distressed.'

'It's OK, Liam, you don't have to get upset. You're not going to get into trouble,' Meadows continued.

'Get out! Get out!' Liam picked up a chair and hurled it towards Edris, who sidestepped it. It crashed into the wall. Cillian quickly ushered them out of the room and closed the door.

'It's best to leave him alone when he's like this. He'll calm down soon enough.'

'Do you think he might have seen something Monday night and that's why he is so upset by the mention of Alan's name?'

'I doubt it,' Cillian said. 'Liam can be unpredictable at times and like you said earlier, finding Alan's body has been an upsetting experience for him.'

'He seemed calm enough when we saw him yesterday,' Edris commented.

'Leah has a very calming effect on him. Perhaps it would be better to talk to Liam when she returns to work.'

'I understand that you and Leah are a couple,' Meadows said.

'Yes. There is no law to say that a couple can't work in the same place.' Cillian clenched his jaw.

A little defensive.

'We'll need to speak with her.'

'She isn't well at the moment.'

'I appreciate that, but it's important that we speak with her today.'

'Why?'

'We are interviewing all the staff and Leah was on duty Monday evening. She may have seen or heard something.'

'She didn't, she would've told me.'

Meadows could feel his patience slipping. 'That may be the case, but we still need to speak to her.'

'In that case I would prefer that you waited until I finished my shift. I would rather she wasn't alone when questioned. As I said, she isn't very well and had a terrible shock yesterday.'

'What time does your shift finish?'

'Six.'

'OK, it can wait until then. Can you tell me where you were Monday evening and the early hours of Tuesday morning?'

'At home, why?'

'We have to ask all the members of staff, it's routine at this stage. Were you alone?'

'Yes.'

'Did you leave the house at any time during the night?'

They had reached the entrance hall and Meadows stopped and faced Cillian.

'No, I finished my shift at eight, got home, made some beans on toast then watched a movie before bed.'

Meadows noticed Cillian stood still while he spoke. His hands were clenched by his side. He let the silence stretch until Cillian broke eye contact and looked towards the sitting room.

'Well, if there's nothing else I'd better get back to work.'

'OK, we'll see you later.'

Edris gave a heavy sigh as they left the building.

'Glad to be out?' Meadows asked.

'It wasn't too bad, apart from getting a chair chucked at me.'

As they approached the car park Paskin and Valentine pulled up. Edris' face lit up as Valentine exited the car.

'The residents are about to eat,' Meadows said. 'Perhaps it's best you wait in the office with Jane Pritchard. You can tell me what you make of her. I'm sure you can think of some leading questions.'

Paskin leaned into the car and took out a file. 'Blackwell asked us to pass this onto you. It's the information on the abuse case. He's gone off to interview Alex Henson.'

'Great.' Meadows took the keys from his pocket and handed them to Edris. 'You can drive while I read through this.'

'Where?'

Meadows opened the file and read out the address for Rhys Owens.

'See you two back at the station later,' he said as he climbed into the passenger seat. He caught sight of Edris winking at Valentine before he took the wheel.

Chapter Sixteen

Meadows' eyes scanned the file as Edris drove towards Bryn Mawr. He hated reading in the car and wished now that he had driven instead. 'Bastards,' he hissed as he absorbed the details of the case.

'That bad?' Edris asked.

'It's not pleasant reading. It wasn't an isolated incident, more like continued abuse and neglect over a period of time. Cold showers, unnecessary force when restraining, denial of food and water and the use of the toilet. That's just naming a few.' Meadows felt anger knot his muscles.

'Did they get sent down?'

Meadows flipped the page. 'Twelve months suspended.'

'What a crock of shit.'

Meadows saw Edris' grip tighten on the steering wheel.

'Looks like he hasn't worked since, at least that's something.'

'Yeah, dossing around and living off our taxes, some punishment,' Edris said with a scowl.

They drove into a council estate and Edris slowed the car to look at the numbers on the doors. 'This is Rhys

Owens' block,' he said as he pulled over and switched off the engine.

Meadows closed the file and put it in the footwell. 'I've seen enough,' he said before climbing out of the car.

The flat was on the first floor. Meadows rapped the door with his knuckles and tried to clear his mind from the words he had read on the case. He heard a shuffling sound from within and the door opened to reveal a scruffy man in his twenties. He wore a baggy T-shirt over sweatpants; his feet were bare. He peered suspiciously at the two visitors.

'Rhys Owens?' Meadows asked.

The man nodded.

'DI Meadows and DC Edris,' said the inspector, flashing his ID card.

Owens rubbed his hand across his stubbly chin. 'I thought you might come. I heard Alan Whitby got done in, I suppose you think I had something to do with it.'

'May we come in?' Meadows asked. Rhys turned and led them inside.

It was not as Meadows expected. Despite the sparse furnishings the sitting room was neat and clean.

'Sit down if you want.' Owens plonked himself down into an armchair.

Meadows sat and surveyed his quarry. Owens had soft brown eyes and an open face, with hair in desperate need of a cut.

'You guessed correctly. We are here concerning the death of Alan Whitby. Four years ago you were involved in the abuse against residents of Bethesda House, where you were employed as a support worker. Mr Whitby gave evidence in that case.'

'Well, thanks for getting straight to the point.' Owens sighed. 'So, because of that you automatically think I had something to do with it.'

'We're interviewing everyone who had a connection with Mr Whitby.'

'Well, don't expect me to shed any tears over him. He got away with it, even got his job back. Lying bastard.'

'I read all the case notes. Alan Whitby gave statements supporting the allegations against you and Alex Henson. There were no allegations of misconduct on his part. Are you saying different?'

'Yeah, he was the one giving the orders. Look, I was twenty-two at the time…'

'And that's supposed to excuse your behaviour?' Edris snapped.

'No, but you've no idea what it was like to work there. The residents can really try your patience. You work twelve-hour shifts and sometimes stay on for night duty. Alan was my boss. He ordered the sanctions when the residents played up.'

'And you just went along with it?' An image of Kevin stuck in a freezing cold shower flashed across Meadows' mind.

'Alan could be persuasive, he told us that the residents would respond better and if we lost control of the situation, we would be putting ourselves and other members of staff in danger.' Owens ran his hand through his hair. 'When you read it in one sitting it sounds pretty bad but it was small things over a period of time. You couldn't go against Alan's orders, he made it out like you were doing a bad job and not following procedure which was supposed to be for the clients' benefit.'

'Why didn't this come out at the time?'

'Alan denied he gave the orders. There was no paper trail. Each resident is supposed to have a care plan. According to Alan these rules were in the plan but we were never allowed to see them, only management had access. If you're told a resident has a limited fluid intake because too much will flush out the medication and cause behaviour problems, you go along with it.'

'Why didn't the other staff speak out against him?'

'I think they were frightened of coming under investigation themselves. Nearly all the staff that worked there then have left now. Only Gemma stayed, and they even put in a new manager. What does that tell you?'

Meadows glanced at Edris, who sat stony-faced with his pen gliding over his pad. He waited until the constable looked up then nodded for him to take over the questioning.

'Do you have a car?' Edris asked.

'Not anymore, I couldn't afford to run it.'

'When was the last time you saw Alan Whitby?'

'Not since the case four years ago.'

'So you didn't see him after that? Not even in the supermarket or the pub?'

'No.'

'What about Alex Henson?'

'I haven't seen him for years.'

'Where were you on Monday evening?'

'It was my sister's birthday so I went around for dinner.'

'What time did you leave?'

'About one in the morning, I think, I'd had a few drinks.'

'I think that will be all for now.' Meadows stood up.

'We'll be checking your story,' Edris warned as he shut his notebook.

'The family believed me,' Owens said as they were leaving.

'What family?' Meadows turned around.

'A girl came around a couple of years ago asking about Alan. She said the families of the residents were concerned.'

'What was her name?'

'Erm… Anna something. I don't remember – like I said, it was a couple of years ago. She was a pretty little thing. She wanted to know what happened during the time I worked there.'

'And what did you tell her?'

'Everything. It's not as if I had anything to lose.'

'Did she say which of the residents she was related to?'

'No, I don't think so… she could have. I thought there might be another investigation, a chance to clear my name, but nothing came of it.'

'Did she come back again?'

'No.'

'Right, well, if you do remember her full name or anything else she said during the visit, call the station.'

Meadows handed Owens a card.

'Did you believe all that crap?' Edris asked when they were back in the car.

'I believe he regrets his actions and he could be telling the truth about Alan.'

'It's still a poor bloody excuse if you ask me.'

'Knowing what you do about Rhys Owens, if I ordered you to rough him up a little during the interview would you do it? Or turn a blind eye if I did?'

'It would be tempting.' Edris grinned. 'But it's not the same.'

'Of course it is. You know it's wrong, yet it's possible you would go along with it because I'm your boss.'

'I don't know, maybe if I was with Blackwell.' Edris laughed.

'Maybe Alan was a bully and he did instigate the abuse. If so, and the families of the victims found out, that would certainly give some of them a strong motive.' Meadows started the car. 'We'll call back at the station and check out all the family members before we go to see Leah.'

* * *

It was dark and sleet was falling as Meadows drove towards Bryn Melyn. A look into the residents' family members hadn't revealed anyone called Anna or anything similar.

In the passenger seat Edris yawned and settled back.

'Tired, are we?' Meadows asked.

'It's because it's winter. I always feel tired this time of year. It gets dark so early it already feels like bedtime.'

'Well, unless we get a break in the case soon, we're in for a long weekend.'

'We've still got tomorrow.'

'Yes, but the relief staff come in on a Friday evening and I have a bad feeling. I'm sure one or more of the regular staff is involved somehow and we can't watch them all. If Gemma or Leah saw something, or even if the killer thinks they may have, those girls could be in serious danger.'

'Unless it was one of them.'

'Gemma definitely isn't telling us everything,' Meadows agreed. 'Liam is wound up and Leah is hiding at home.'

'They're all bloody dodgy if you ask me. Well, except Harry, she's alright. I wouldn't mind giving her–'

'Don't even go there,' Meadows cut in. 'She's a potential witness. Anyway, I thought you were after Valentine.'

'Gotta keep my options open,' Edris said rubbing his hands together.

Meadows shook his head in good humour. He pulled up in front of a row of terraced cottages. 'I believe that's Cillian's red Mini.'

They got out of the car pulling up their coat collars against the cold. Meadows pressed the doorbell and the door was promptly opened.

'You better come in.' Cillian stood back from the door. Leah was walking down the stairs as they entered.

'Hello again,' Meadows said. 'Sorry to bother you when you're not feeling well.'

Leah gave a weak smile and wrapped her robe tightly around her body. 'That's OK.' She stopped at the bottom of the stairs to catch her breath.

'Sounds like you've caught a chest infection. I'm not surprised in this weather,' Edris commented.

'Let's go into the sitting room,' Cillian suggested.

Meadows followed Leah. From his height advantage he could see white roots showing through her brown hair and wondered if it was more than a chest infection that ailed her. Cillian and Leah sat side by side on the sofa, arms and legs touching, leaving Meadows and Edris to take the armchairs opposite. Meadows gazed around the room. It was small and cosy, with an electric fire; a mantelpiece above it displayed photographs of the couple. Two large floor lamps illuminated the peach walls where modern canvases hung. He turned his attention to Leah. She had dark circles beneath her eyes and her hair hung limply on her shoulders. He caught a glimpse of a bruise on her wrist before she pulled down the cuff of her robe.

'I would like you to talk me through what happened yesterday morning, if you could.'

Leah took a shaky breath. 'I got Liam up at the usual time and we went down to the kitchen. Kevin and Gemma were already there. I gave Liam his breakfast then I checked to see if there was enough ice cream for the evening.'

'Is it usually your job to keep a check on the food stock?'

'No, well, yes, I mean it's all our responsibility to make sure the fridge is stocked.'

'OK, go on.'

'Most of the ice cream had been eaten so I told Gemma I would go to the cellar to get another tub. Liam wanted to come with me.'

'Was the cellar door locked?' Edris asked.

'Yes, I went into the office to get the key. We went down into the cellar and when I opened the freezer...' Leah's lips trembled.

'Is this really necessary?' Cillian took hold of Leah's hand.

'I'm sorry, we have to ask these questions. Perhaps a cup of tea would be a good idea. I know Edris here is dying for a cup.'

Edris smiled and nodded.

'I'll make it.' Cillian patted Leah's knee and stood, looking from Meadows to Leah and seemingly hesitant to leave.

'I'll be fine,' Leah said.

Meadows gave Edris a pointed look.

'I'll give you a hand.' Edris rose from the chair.

'I'm sure I can manage,' Cillian said, his eyes narrowing.

Edris ignored the comment and followed Cillian to the kitchen. Meadows turned back to Leah and gave her an encouraging smile.

'Was there anything that struck you as different in the cellar? Anything missing?'

'No, I don't think so, but I went straight to the freezer, I had no reason to look around.'

'OK, so then you called for help?'

'Yes.'

'What was Liam's reaction?'

'I don't think he really understood that Alan was dead. I tried my best not to frighten him. He just sort of stood there poking the body.'

'So, who came to the cellar first when you shouted for help?'

'Cillian, then Jane.'

'When was the last time you saw or spoke to Alan?'

'When he left work on Monday, at about six.' Leah pushed a lock of hair behind her ear.

'And you were on sleep-in duty on Monday night?'

'Yes.'

'Did anything unusual happen that evening?'

'No, I helped Gemma settle the residents down for the night, we had a cup of tea and I went to bed about ten.'

'Did you go straight to sleep?'

'Yes, I was tired, it had been a long day.' Leah smiled.

'Did you wake up during the night? Maybe hear a noise?'

'No, nothing.' Leah looked down and twisted her hands on her lap.

They were interrupted by Cillian walking into the room closely followed by Edris. Cillian handed Leah a mug of tea and sat down. Edris handed a mug to Meadows then took up his position in the armchair.

Meadows took a sip of tea. 'That's lovely, thanks.' He set the mug down on the coffee table then straightened up. 'From what we've learned so far it seems that both Liam and Kevin were up sometime during Monday night. They would've passed the sleep-in room.'

'I didn't hear anything,' Leah said. 'As I said, I was very tired.'

Cillian took Leah's hand in his and glared at Meadows.

'When we saw Liam today, he reacted badly to the mention of Alan's name. Do you know why that is?' Meadows asked.

Leah shrugged her shoulders. 'Perhaps he's still upset over finding Alan's body.'

'But you said you didn't think he understood that Alan was dead, and he seemed quite calm when we saw him yesterday.'

Leah looked to Cillian for help and Meadows saw the mug tremble in her hands.

'Liam can be unpredictable at times, he can fly into a rage for no reason,' Cillian said. 'What exactly are you trying to imply? That *Liam* put Alan in the freezer?'

Meadows ignored the comment. 'What do you know about the abuse that took place at Bethesda four years ago?'

'Nothing, we haven't been there that long,' Cillian said.

'But you've heard something. I understand you're friendly with Gemma, she must have mentioned it.' Meadows looked at Leah.

'Not really,' Leah said. 'She made some reference once but didn't go into any details.'

'Do you think it is possible that Alan could've been abusing the residents; Liam perhaps?'

'No, I would never let that happen.' Leah frowned.

Meadows noticed that Cillian's fists were clenched tightly. 'Did either of you have any problems working with Alan?' Meadows picked up his mug and drank deeply.

'No, he liked to have a weekly meeting and we would all have to write up daily reports which he checked. He didn't really involve himself in the day-to-day activities of the residents. His role was more administration so it's not like we worked that closely with him,' Cillian said.

'I understand that some of the residents receive regular visits from family members. Do you know of anyone named Anna who has visited?'

'No, no one by that name.' Leah seemed to shrink back into the sofa.

'Maybe you could ask Jane for a list of family members.' Cillian rubbed his hands down the top of his legs. 'Now, if that's all, I think you should leave Leah to get some rest. I have to go back into work.'

'And why is that?' Edris asked.

'I'm on sleep-in duty,' Cillian replied.

'Thank you both for your time, you've been very helpful.' Meadows stood up. 'Would it be possible to use your bathroom before I leave?'

'Up the stairs, and it's the door facing you.'

'I'm sure I can find it, thanks.' Meadows smiled and left the room. He could hear Edris making polite conversation as he walked up the stairs. The door to the right was ajar so he gave it a nudge and peered inside. There was a single bed against the wall with the covers pulled back. A pile of men's clothes were heaped on the floor next to a pair of discarded trainers and a towel dangled over a workout bench. A smell of sweat and stale socks lingered in the air.

Meadows pulled the door back, stepped over to the adjacent room and quietly opened the door. Another single bed, this time neatly made with a colourful throw and plush pillows. Beside the bed stood a metal cabinet. He was tempted to look inside but was aware that if he lingered too long it would arouse suspicion. His gaze swept the room, noting the dressing table laid out with make-up, perfume and hairbrushes. He closed the door and hurried into the bathroom, flushing the chain for the benefit of those downstairs before opening the cabinet above the sink. His eyes scanned the various bottles of pills. He picked one up and saw it was a prescription made out to Leah. After replacing the bottle, he washed his hands and made his way downstairs.

'We'll leave you in peace now,' Meadows said. 'I hope you feel better soon.'

As Edris thanked them for the tea and stood to leave, Meadows noticed Leah visibly relax.

* * *

'Did you get anything from Cillian when you were making the tea?' Meadows inquired as he started the engine and turned up the heating.

'Nothing much. They've been together six years and both enjoy working at Bethesda. I found him a little guarded. I take it you had a nose around upstairs. Find anything interesting?'

'I think Leah's ill, and not just a cold. There was a pile of prescription tablets in the bathroom. I had a quick look at the bedrooms, looks as if they sleep in separate rooms. There was a single bed in each, clearly a "his and hers".'

'Maybe he snores.' Edris grinned.

'No, it's more than that. There's something not quite right about those two. A young couple in separate rooms, yet they seem to be in love. He's very protective of her and you can tell by the way she looks at him that she adores him. Cillian is agitated by something. He looks like he's trying to hold his temper in. And I think that she's frightened.'

'Of Cillian?'

'I don't know. She knows more than she's telling us. She could be protecting him.'

'Or they could be in it together,' Edris said.

'But why? We need to do a bit more digging on Alan Whitby. Let's hope Paskin has found some discrepancy in his finances.'

When they arrived back at the station the team were still working despite the late hour. Meadows gathered them together for an update and exchange of information.

'Blackwell, how did you get on with Alex Henson?'

'Just some scrawny kid, came up with some bullshit story of how he was acting on Alan's orders.'

'We had the same story from Rhys Owens,' said Edris.

Blackwell raised his eyebrows. 'Do you think there's something in it?'

'Could be. Did he mention a visit from a family member of one of the residents?'

'Yeah, he did. Some girl called Anna, supposedly came around asking questions. There's no mention of an Anna in any of the files.'

'Owens had exactly the same story. No reason for them to make it up. It's worth following up. Any family member who visited Bethesda House would know the layout of the place. If Alan Whitby was abusing the residents, then that would be a strong enough motive to kill him. How did you get on with Steven?'

'No luck there, he was having a bad day so I'll try again first thing in the morning. I want to get there before Miles. Arrogant sod, that one. He claims he was away for an extended weekend and drove straight back to work on Tuesday morning. I've asked Traffic to check it out. If he's telling the truth then he would've been picked up on camera.'

'Good. I'm sure he was listening at the door when we interviewed Kevin. He went scuttling into Jane's office when we left the room.'

'Do you want me to dig a little into his background?'

'Yes. I think that'll be a worthwhile exercise.' Meadows turned his attention to Valentine and Paskin. 'How did you two get on at the home?'

'It was hard going, Nicole is non-verbal, and Vanessa, well…' Paskin shrugged her shoulders.

'She's quite a character,' Valentine added. 'I got my nails painted.' She held up her hand to show bright pink nail varnish covering both her nails and fingers.

'Very pretty.' Edris grinned.

'It seems she went to bed and slept through the night. She's a very heavy sleeper and as she sleeps on the first floor I doubt she would've heard anything.'

'Nicole's support worker, Danielle, was home all Monday night. She lives with her parents. I checked with them, all seems above board,' Paskin said.

'Cillian is Vanessa's support worker, he told us you had already spoken to him.'

Valentine looked at Edris.

'Yes, we have.'

'What did you make of Jane Pritchard?' Meadows asked.

'A bit of a bitch,' Paskin said, grinning.

'I think that's a fair assessment,' Meadows said.

'I've been going through Alan's financial records,' Paskin said. 'He's been paying in large sums of cash over the last two years.'

'How large?'

'It varies. The first payment was five thousand, then another three, then anything up from five hundred. The last payment was six weeks ago.'

'Drugs?' Edris suggested.

'Or blackmail.' Meadows ran his hand through his hair as he tried to come up with a theory.

Who would be in a position to pay that much money?

'How is Bethesda financed?'

'It's a private home,' Blackwell said. 'The residents receive high disability payments from the government and I would imagine contributions from the family.'

'We need to look into that, see who controls the finances. You better organise a warrant, I have a feeling Jane Pritchard isn't going to give up that sort of information easily. Let's call it a night. Tomorrow I want all the statements checked and cross referenced for inconsistencies. Both Gemma and Leah deny having seen or heard anything that night. I find that hard to believe.'

There was a murmur of agreement, then the team gathered their coats and left.

Meadows turned to Edris. 'Come on, I'll give you a lift home. Let's just hope that the killer doesn't get to those girls first.'

Chapter Seventeen

Whilst Meadows waited in front of Edris' house, he gazed into the rear-view mirror and saw two bloodshot eyes peering back at him. He had spent the night mulling over the case as he lay in bed chasing sleep. The feeling that the case was going to take a turn for the worse gnawed at his mind.

'Morning.' Edris climbed into the car with a blast of cold air. Today he wore a cream woollen jumper over black jeans. 'I'm sure it's colder than it was yesterday,' he said as he fastened his seatbelt.

'I thought we'd call in on my mother this morning before we go to Bethesda. She can be a good source of information. It'll be interesting to see what is being said around the village.'

'Great, I love seeing your mother. She's wicked. It won't be too early for her, will it?'

'It's fine, I called her to say we are on our way.'

And give her a chance to hide the plants.

Meadows smiled at the thought of Edris catching sight of the cannabis plants lining his mother's kitchen window.

* * *

Fern Meadows flung open the door as soon as they pulled up in front of the house. She wore a rainbow Baja over faded jeans and a warm smile.

'Morning, Mrs M,' Edris called out as he walked up the path.

Fern gave Edris a hug then stretched up to plant a kiss on Meadows' cheek.

'Come on in, boys, the kettle's on and I've just finished a batch of cakes.' Fern turned and led the way to the kitchen, her thick grey plait swinging across her back.

'You must've been up at the crack of dawn,' Edris said.

'I'm always awake early these days. Arthritis doesn't give me much rest.'

'Perhaps you should have a holiday in the sun, it would do you good.' Edris leaned over the kitchen counter. 'These smell delicious.'

'Oh, not those ones.' Fern moved the plate. 'That's a herbal cake, bit of an acquired taste.'

Meadows groaned inwardly as he plonked himself down in the chair.

'Here, have some carrot cake.' Fern placed a few slices on a plate and put it in the centre of the table. 'Sit down and I'll pour you some tea.'

Edris grinned and shoved a slice of cake into his mouth.

'So, what brings you here at this time of the morning?'

'Gossip,' Meadows said with a smile.

'As if I would.' She winked and placed the mugs on the table.

'What have you heard about Alan Whitby?'

'A prick by all accounts.'

Bits of crumbs flew from Edris' mouth as he choked on the cake.

'Excuse my mother, she likes to tell it as it is,' Meadows said. 'Go on.'

'He wasn't well liked. Had a few affairs over the years and it seems he favoured the younger ladies.'

'And his wife knew about this?'

'Apparently so. Put on a show of a happy marriage. I guess she stayed with him for the daughter's sake and now there seems to be money.'

'Any talk about where the money was coming from?'

'Just the usual, lottery win or a rich relative left it to him. I don't think anyone really knows, but a lot of money has been spent. A new car, caravan and a good few holidays. Nothing like a bit of good fortune to get the tongues wagging.'

'What about Jane Pritchard?' Edris asked.

'She's married to a bus driver, Huw; he's a nice guy. Jane grew up on a council estate, comes from a rough family. It's good to try and change your life for the better but you shouldn't forget where you came from.'

'So she pretends to be something she's not?'

'A bit of a snob is what I hear. There's also talk of how she got to be manager of Bethesda, if you know what I mean.'

Edris took a sip from his mug. 'What is this?'

'Lemon and ginger. It'll give you a bit of a boost,' Fern said.

'Have you heard any rumours about what happened to Alan?' Meadows asked.

'Just the usual crap. The residents of Bethesda shouldn't be allowed to live so close to the community, should be locked up, that sort of thing. The general view is that one of them is responsible.'

'Typical small-minded–' Meadows began.

'Now, you know what it's like around here, but it has its good points. People look out for each other,' Fern said.

Meadows took a sip of his tea. The ginger spread warmth through his chest. He could imagine the community starting a petition to get Bethesda closed down.

'So how are things with you, Tristan? Any new lady friends?' Fern picked up a slice of cake.

'I've got my eye on a couple.' Edris grinned. 'I met this really gorgeous girl yesterday. She works in Bethesda so I have to wait until the case is closed.'

'*And* he's after the young PC who is working with us at the moment.' Meadows shook his head.

'Well, he has a lot of love to give, nothing wrong with that.' Fern winked at Edris.

Edris' phone trilled and he reached into his pocket. 'Excuse me a minute. It's Daisy,' he said to Meadows as he left the room.

Meadows felt a warm sensation spread through his body at the mention of her name.

Fern raised her eyebrows. 'Who's Daisy?'

'The pathologist.'

'Pretty, is she?' Fern's eyes twinkled.

'Don't go there.'

'Why not? I just want to see you happy.'

'I am happy.'

'Really?' Fern folded her arms across her chest. 'Did you go to the court hearing?'

'No, but I've heard what happened. Five years.'

'That's not long considering the crime.'

'No, I'm just glad it wasn't my decision to make.'

'Time to put it all behind you and move on,' Fern said and patted his hand. 'When was the last time you went out and had some fun?'

'I'm busy.'

'Not too busy to get a bit of loving.'

Meadows' phone vibrated in his pocket. Grateful for the distraction, he pulled it out and saw Blackwell's name illuminated.

'Meadows.'

'I'm at Bethesda.' Blackwell's voice was barely audible over the background noise. 'Hold on a minute.'

Meadows could hear Blackwell moving on the other end of the line. The background noise faded to a babble.

'Sorry about that. They're all kicking off here. Someone has taken Eddy's book from his room. The poor bugger is in a right state.'

Meadows saw Edris walk back into the kitchen.

'I'm on my way. Make sure no one leaves,' he ordered and ended the call. 'Sorry, we've got to go.' He bent down and kissed his mother on the cheek. 'See you soon.'

'Thanks for the cake.' Edris gave Fern a hug.

'You're welcome.'

Fern walked them to the door and stood waving as they pulled off in the car.

* * *

'Someone has taken Eddy's book,' Meadows explained as he drove. 'What's the news from Daisy?'

'Sedatives were found in Alan's blood along with alcohol. Diazepam, about 30mg. He would have been fairly drowsy if not knocked out completely with alcohol thrown into the mix. Apparently it depends on the person's tolerance.'

'So he was drugged, hit over the head and then put into the freezer. It sounds like something went wrong. Maybe the killer miscalculated the dose and thought it would be enough to knock him out. Doesn't sound like a heat of the moment situation does it? This had to been planned.'

'Maybe he woke up when they were trying to get him in the freezer, and fought back so they hit him over the head,' Edris said.

'It's possible, but there were no signs of defence wounds, only the scratches. So he wakes up, lunges at whoever's in front of him – I think probably a woman – then the second person grabs the nearest object and hits him over the head.'

'There were no signs of any marks on any of the women we have interviewed.'

'Except Leah, she had a bruise on her wrist.'

Meadows took the turning to Ynys Melyn.

'And Cillian doesn't have an alibi for that night.'

'No, but then we're back to motive. Why would Leah and Cillian kill Alan?'

'How about Miles and Jane?' Edris swivelled in his seat. 'Yeah I can see that, but again, we need a motive.'

'So, do you think Harry has taken Eddy's book for us to read?'

'I doubt it, she wouldn't inflict that much distress on him.'

'Then it has to be Miles or Cillian.'

'Not necessarily. Any one of the staff could have taken it, they come in early, usually before the residents are awake.'

'Bit of a risk though, they would have been seen by Miles. Eddy's room is on the first floor.'

'Yes, but if Miles was in the sitting room someone could easily sneak past. Then again, with Cillian asleep Miles would have had plenty of opportunity. There's something in that book the killer doesn't want us to see and they are rattled. I'm sure Miles was listening to our interview with Kevin and possibly listening at Eddy's door. He always seems to be hanging around in Jane's office. It was Jane that made the call to Alan on the Monday evening and she gave a pretty lame excuse.'

'Yeah, those two look shifty,' Edris agreed.

They soon arrived at Bethesda House. 'You don't have a clear view of the car park from the house, it's only Eddy's window that overlooks the area. Whoever's inside wouldn't notice a car pulling up unless they were watching out for it,' Meadows said.

'Then it's just a case of entering through the cellar, it's easy to get a spare key cut.'

'Come on, we'd better get inside.'

Blackwell was standing at the front door. As they approached, he walked towards them.

'They're going to give Eddy a sedative to calm him down,' he said.

'Poor guy.' Meadows sighed. 'I want this place searched. Call in Paskin and Valentine to help. Once Eddy has calmed down, we'll make a start. Is Jane in?'

'Yeah, in her office. Do you really think the book is still here?'

'Yes, Matt Hanes was on guard all night, it would be too risky to try and sneak in during the night so it's either Cillian, Miles, or one of the other staff members when they came in this morning. The book has to be here somewhere.'

'Right I'll get onto it.' Blackwell pulled his phone from his pocket.

As Meadows and Edris entered the hall they could hear a high-pitched keening coming from upstairs. Meadows looked up towards the source of the noise and saw Harry coming down the stairs. She looked dishevelled and blood leaked from her bottom lip.

'You're bleeding.' Edris stepped forward. 'Are you OK?'

'Yeah, I'm fine.' Harry smiled then winced, putting her finger to her lip. 'Got caught by a backhander from Eddy. He didn't mean it, he's just in a bad way.'

'Anything we can do to help?' Edris asked.

'No, I've given him a sedative, it should kick in soon. Poor Eddy.'

'Poor you.' Edris smiled.

Harry gave him a coy smile and walked into the sitting room.

'Come on, Romeo, let's go and see Jane,' Meadows said.

As they walked towards the office they could hear a crashing sound followed by shouting from further along the corridor.

'Sounds like Liam's kicking off again,' Meadows said as he rapped on the office door. He turned the handle before waiting for an invitation to come in.

Jane was sat at her desk looking harassed. She quickly smiled but Meadows could see the anger bubbling below the surface.

'Bad morning?' Meadows asked.

'You could say that. This really isn't a good time. Perhaps you could come back later.'

'I am fully aware of the situation, that's why we are here. When the residents have calmed down, we will conduct a search of the premises for Eddy's book. More officers are on their way.'

'What? No, why would you want to search for Eddy's book? It's hardly a police matter.'

Meadows noted Jane's voice rising.

'We believe that Eddy may have witnessed what happened here on Monday night and recorded it in his book.'

'I doubt it, Eddy's book is just full of ramblings.'

'You've read it then?'

'Well, no.'

'Then you can't possibly know what's in there.'

Jane's eyes narrowed. 'I don't think I can authorise a search of the house, it will cause too much distress to the residents.'

'The book is Eddy's property. If you prefer, we can get a warrant. That will just delay the process and you'll all have to remain here until the search is complete. Either way, we will search for the book.'

'Fine,' Jane snapped. 'Do what you want, but please be aware that there are a number of confidential files on site containing sensitive information. I don't want you or your officers nosing in those files.'

What was she hiding in them?

'Our only concern is finding the book and I can assure you all my officers are trained professionals and will handle the search with sensitivity. Can you tell me who has access to the residents' medication?'

A puzzled expression crossed Jane's face. 'The medication is kept in a secure cabinet in a locked room. Only Harry, Miles and I carry keys. Why?'

'We need to check the medication, make sure it is all accounted for,' Edris said.

Jane opened the desk drawer and took out a bunch of keys. 'I'll take you.'

'No need, I'll ask Harry or Miles. I'm sure you have enough to deal with at the moment.' Meadows gave a tight smile. 'In the meantime, I would like you and all the staff members to remain on the premises until the search is complete.'

Meadows left the office before Jane had a chance to complain.

'You certainly put her in her place,' Edris said.

'I have a feeling she's used to getting her own way. She seemed very cagey about the files. I want to wait until the relief staff come in before we issue the warrant for the financial records. I would rather her not know what we are up to.'

It was quiet as they walked through the hall and into the sitting room. Miles was slouched on the sofa and Harry could be seen in the kitchen.

'Where is everyone?' Meadows asked.

'In their rooms,' said Miles. 'Jane thought it best until things calm down. They set each other off.'

'You were on night duty last night.'

'Yeah, what of it?' Miles' face darkened at the inspector's question.

'Eddy's book was taken at some point during the night,' Edris said.

'So you think I had something to do with it? What would I want with Eddy's book?' Miles sat up straight. 'Do you think I get some sort of kick out of distressing the residents?'

'Can you talk us through last night's shift?' Meadows asked.

Miles shrugged. 'Nothing to tell really. I settled the residents down at ten, watched a film with Cillian, and then did the rounds when Cillian went to bed.'

'Were all the residents asleep?'

'Eddy was up, staring out the window. The rest were asleep.'

'Any disturbances during the night?'

'Steve woke up and used the toilet. Liam was kicking off about someone waking his tortoise.'

'Why would Liam think someone was waking the tortoise?'

'I dunno, he probably had a bad dream. I told him to go back to sleep. I checked on him twenty minutes later. He was asleep.'

'Did you hear anything after that?'

'No, I would have checked if I had.'

'When did Eddy discover his book was missing?'

'When he woke up,' Harry said as she walked into the sitting room carrying a mug. Her lip had stopped bleeding but the swelling was still visible. 'I went to wake him up this morning, he was still in bed when I went into the room. The book is always kept on his bedside table. It's the first thing he noticed when he opened his eyes. I looked on the floor and under the bed thinking it may have fallen. Then we searched the whole room.'

'Was anything else disturbed in the room?'

'No, not that I could tell. Eddy's room is very well ordered. He would have noticed if something had been moved.'

'OK, we are going to search the house for the book when Eddy has calmed down.'

'Lot of fuss over a stupid book,' Miles huffed and picked up a newspaper from the coffee table.

'Eddy is calm now but is sedated so it's unlikely he will talk to you,' Harry said.

'I don't think we will need to bother him,' Meadows replied. 'I understand that you have a set of keys for the medicine cabinet.'

'We both do.'

Miles peered over the top of the paper. Meadows ignored him.

'If you can spare a few moments I'd like to take a look,' he said.

'I'll take you now.'

Harry set her mug down on the table then led them to the store cupboard which was located next to the sleep-in room. She took a set of keys from her pocket and unlocked the door.

It was a small room, with a sink set into a worktop, and shelving above. Meadows looked at the boxes of latex gloves, wads of cotton wool, plasters and antiseptic creams.

'Meds are kept in here.' Harry opened a metal cabinet.

'What is the procedure for administering medication?' Meadows asked.

'There are always two of us.' Harry took a hard-backed register from the cabinet and opened it. 'This is a list of each resident and their medication. The dose is checked, then the medication is checked and recorded in the register, timed and dated, with two signatures. Again, there are always two people present when the medication is administered.'

Meadows looked at the book his eyes scanning the entries for Monday evening. 'Do you keep diazepam here?'

'Yes, it's PRN, as needed.'

'How do you monitor the stock?'

Harry took the book back and turned to the back. 'Most of the meds are on repeat prescription but we still keep a record of the stock levels. We do a stock take at the end of each week, it's also a precaution to make sure the residents haven't missed any doses or been given too much.'

'Can you check the stock for diazepam please?'

'Do you think there's a problem with the medication?' Concern creased Harry's face.

'It's possible, we do need to check.'

Harry took three boxes from the cabinet and tipped the contents onto the worktop. She lined up the strips of tablets. Some of the strips had holes where the tablets had been removed. She counted the tablets then checked the book. A frown creased her forehead, she counted again then checked the log.

'Is there a problem?' Edris asked.

'Let me just check again.' She repeated the process and shook her head. 'There are tablets unaccounted for – about 60mg. There's no record of them being used.'

'Are you sure it's 60mg?'

'Yes, and that's a heavy dose.' Harry put the tablets back into the box.

'And it's just you, Miles and Jane that have access to the key?' Edris asked.

'Yes, we're the only ones trained to administer medication. You don't think that someone drugged Eddy so they could get his book, do you?'

'Was he very sleepy this morning?' Meadows asked.

'No, he woke and sat up in bed as soon as I went in the room.'

'Then I doubt the medication was used on Eddy. Like you say, it's a heavy dose and he would have been drowsy.'

'It wears off after four to six hours.'

'So he could have been given, say, 30mg and been fine this morning?' Edris asked.

'I guess.' Harry shrugged.

'You'd better lock this lot back up,' Meadows said.

'Should I put a note in the book about the missing pills?'

'Yes, it's probably best you do.'

'I'll counter-sign the book if you like.' Edris sidled up close to Harry.

Meadows leaned against the counter, his mind mulling over the missing tablets.

If Alan had 30mg of diazepam in his system then that leaves another 30mg unaccounted for. Would someone give that much to Eddy? Leah said she didn't wake up Monday night. If she had been drugged then that would account for her not hearing any noise. No, that doesn't make sense. Why drug Leah? Gemma was the one on night duty. Unless it was Gemma that drugged Leah.

'Sir?'

Edris' voice cut across Meadows' thoughts.

'Sorry I was trying to figure something out,' he said.

'Are we finished here?' Edris asked.

'Yes. Thank you, Harry, you've been a great help.' The three left the store. 'Is Kevin in his room?'

'Yes, he should be there with Gemma,' Harry said as she closed and locked the door. 'See you later.'

Meadows nudged Edris, who was watching Harry walk down the corridor. 'I think we should have a chat with Kevin again.'

'As long as he doesn't try to hug me!'

They reached Kevin's room and Meadows rapped on the door.

'I'm coming to open the door.' Kevin's voice boomed from the other side. The door opened and Kevin's face lit up. 'Winter Man!'

Meadows braced himself as Kevin enveloped him in a bear hug.

'Hi, Kevin, can we come in?'

Kevin released Meadows and turned to Gemma who was sitting on the sofa. 'Gemma, the Winter Man is here.'

'Yes, I see! Hi.' Gemma smiled.

'I'm beginning to think I'm invisible,' Edris teased as he closed the door.

'I need your help again, Kevin,' Meadows said as he sat down in the armchair.

'OK, Winter Man.' Kevin nodded.

'Do you know that someone has taken Eddy's book?'

Kevin frowned. 'A bad thing to do.'

'Yes, it is. We think that someone has hidden the book somewhere in the house. Do you mind if Edris looks around your room when we have a chat?'

'I didn't take it.' Kevin stiffened.

'I know you didn't take it, but someone could've come into your room when you were asleep and hidden it.'

'Sneaky.' Kevin's eyes widened.

'Yes. So it's OK for Edris to look for the book?'

'OK.'

'Thank you.' Meadows nodded at Edris. 'Kevin, do you remember the night you sneaked out of your room and ate the ice cream?'

Kevin nodded.

'You said you didn't see Gemma.'

'No, Gemma didn't see me.' Kevin put his hand to his lips and sniggered.

'Did you see Gemma?' Meadows leaned forward. 'Yes, Gemma fast asleep on the sofa.' Kevin giggled.

Gemma's cheeks flushed red. 'I didn't mean to fall asleep.'

'It's OK.' Meadows smiled. 'Just tell us what happened.'

'I'll lose my job.' Tears pooled in Gemma's eyes.

'Don't cry!' Kevin looked alarmed. He patted Gemma on the arm. 'It's OK.'

Meadows was touched by Kevin's concern. 'Don't worry, Kevin, Gemma will be fine.' He sat back in the chair. 'I think you may have been drugged. There's some diazepam missing from the medicine cabinet.'

'What? Who would want to drug me?'

'Whoever killed Alan, to make sure you didn't hear or see anything on Monday night. Tell me what happened on Monday night, everything please.'

Gemma took a tissue from her pocket and wiped away the tears that had escaped her eyes.

'Me and Leah settled the residents down. Eddy was in his usual place by the window so I told him I would come back to check on him later. The other residents were in their beds. I said goodnight to Kevin then joined Leah in the sitting room for a hot chocolate and a chat. We were watching something on the telly. The next thing I remember was waking up and it was daylight. I felt awful, I swear I've never fallen asleep on night duty. What if one of the residents had a seizure and there was no one to help?' Her bottom lip trembled.

'Who made the drinks?'

'I did.'

'Did you both have hot chocolate?'

'No, Leah had camomile tea, she doesn't drink any caffeinated drinks before sleeping.'

'Do you always drink hot chocolate in the evenings?'

'Mostly, yes.'

'Who would know that?'

'Everyone that works here. I've been on sleep-in duty with all of the staff members. We take it in turns.'

'OK, I think we should take the cocoa powder to be tested.'

'I've drunk it since and haven't fallen asleep.'

Meadows rubbed his hand across his chin as he thought of possible ways that Gemma could have ingested the diazepam.

'Do you make the hot chocolate with milk?'

'Yes.'

'Do you think it's possible there could have been something in the milk?'

'I suppose. There wasn't much left, I finished the bottle.'

'And Leah didn't have any milk at all that evening?'

'No, I don't think so, but I couldn't say for sure.'

'Kevin, did you see Leah asleep on the sofa with Gemma?'

'No, Leah didn't see me.' Kevin shook his head.

'But you saw Leah?'

'I was peeking out of my room.' Kevin smirked.

'You saw Alan and Liam?'

'Alan shouting at Liam, bad words.'

'Was Leah with Liam?'

'No, came out of the sleepy room. Leah says don't shout at Liam. Come on, Liam, back to bed,' Kevin sang.

'Thank you, Kevin, you have been a big help again.'

Edris walked out of the bedroom and shook his head.

'No sign of the book.'

'Will you have to tell Jane that I fell asleep on night duty?' Gemma asked.

'I don't see why that would be necessary at this stage. It will have to come out at some time but try not to worry. It wasn't your fault.' Meadows smiled. 'We'll leave you now.'

'How many days until it snows, Winter Man?' Kevin asked.

'Twelve days.'

If we manage to solve this case.

'Twelve days,' Kevin repeated and grinned.

Outside Kevin's room they met up with Paskin and Valentine.

'We've searched Kevin's room.' Edris gave Valentine a warm smile.

'We're about to see Liam so we'll search his room at the same time. Where's Blackwell?' Meadows asked.

'Searching the sitting room,' Paskin said.

'OK, perhaps you and Valentine can make a start upstairs. On your way can you tell Blackwell to search the office when he's finished with the sitting room?'

'He'll put Jane in her place,' Edris said.

'That's what I'm hoping.' Meadows grinned. 'Come on let's go and see Liam.'

Chapter Eighteen

Jane searched through the drawers of her desk, slamming each one as she went. She had already been through them once but frustration was making her doubt her eyes. She slammed the bottom drawer and marched over to the metal filing cabinet. She yanked open the top drawer and began rummaging through papers and scrabbling around under files.

The office door opened and she jumped away from the cabinet. Her heart thudded in her chest as she pulled back her shoulders and fought for composure before turning around.

Miles stood in the doorway, a bemused look upon his face.

'Where is it?' Jane demanded.

'Where is what?'

'The fucking book! I told you to put it in the top drawer of my desk.'

'I haven't got it.' Miles swaggered towards the desk. 'I thought you must've taken it.'

Jane felt a cold band coil around her chest. 'You'd better be joking,' she hissed.

'I fuck you not, I haven't got it.'

'Well if you haven't got it, who has?'

'I dunno. I went to Eddy's room at four, it wasn't there. I thought you had come in through the cellar and taken it.'

'Why would I come back here with that bloody policeman hanging around all night?' she shrieked, clenching her fists. She wanted to tear his face with her nails.

'Keep your voice down,' Miles snarled. 'In case you've forgotten, there are police all over the house.'

'Cillian must have it.'

'What would Cillian want with the book?'

'Well Harry then, she could've taken it. I don't trust that one. Eddy could have told her what he saw and now she's going to blackmail us.'

'If you think Harry sneaked in then it could easily be any one of them. Gemma knows something I'm sure of it. I asked her about Monday night, and she was evasive, couldn't wait to get away from me. Anyway, you have to keep your cool. Use your head. Whoever took the book isn't planning on giving it to the police. So we wait it out. Let them come to us and we'll deal with it.'

A cold shiver of fear ran down Jane's back. She didn't like what he was implying. 'We're just getting in deeper. We have to get rid of everything.'

'Yeah well good luck with that, they can still trace it back.'

'Not if they don't know what they are looking for. I'll delete the files from the computer. The paperwork can be burnt. Wait until the police have gone then you can deal with it.'

Miles' eyes blazed but they were interrupted when the door opened, and Blackwell stepped inside.

'I need to search the office.'

'We're in a meeting at the moment so you'll have to come back,' Jane replied tersely.

'The meeting's cancelled,' Blackwell growled.

'You can't talk to me like that.'

'I think you'll find that I can.' Blackwell fixed her with a steely gaze. 'Now you can either cooperate or I can cuff you and take you down to the station for obstruction.'

'Fine, go ahead and search.' Jane plonked herself down in the chair.

'I'll leave you to it.' Miles smirked and slinked out of the door.

Jane had the sudden urge to throw something. She watched Blackwell snap on latex gloves and move around the office. He reminded her of a pit bull. Thick neck and a triangular body on stubby legs. She glared at his back as he searched through every drawer of the metal filing cabinet.

He shut the last drawer and turned around. 'Can you move away from the desk, please?' His voice was clipped.

Jane stood abruptly, sending the chair coasting backwards on its wheels. She stepped back and folded her arms across her chest. Every muscle in her body screamed with tension as she watched him rifle through the drawers. When he reached the bottom one, she held her breath.

His meaty hands picked through the files until he reached the bottom. Jane felt the perspiration gathering on the nape of her neck; she had to remind herself to breathe.

He replaced the files, huffed and shut the drawer.

'Keys to the cellar?'

She slid open the top drawer and handed him the keys. He left the office without comment and Jane sank into the chair, her heart still thudding in her chest.

Chapter Nineteen

Meadows could hear voices coming from behind Liam's door. He knocked and the voices stopped abruptly.

'Keep him away from the chairs,' Edris whispered.

The door opened and Cillian stood there, looking from Edris to Meadows. Leah could be seen sitting at the table with Liam. They both had felt-tip pens in their hands and were jointly colouring a picture.

'We'd like to talk to Liam,' Meadows said.

'Right.' Cillian stepped back from the door, allowing them to enter.

Liam looked up from his colouring book, his small eyes darting between the two visitors.

'Hello again, Liam.'

Meadows smiled as he approached. Liam scowled.

'Liam,' Leah prompted.

'Hello.' Liam put his head down and continued colouring.

'Liam, did you know that someone has taken Eddy's book?' Meadows asked.

Liam threw down the pen. 'I didn't do it!' He jumped up from the table, sending the chair crashing backwards.

'No one is saying you took it, but we need to look around your room in case someone hid it in here.'

'No, get out!'

Leah stood and placed her hand on Liam's arm. 'Is this really necessary?'

'I'm afraid so, we are searching all the rooms.'

'It's OK, Liam,' Leah soothed. 'They are just going to have a quick look then they will leave. You want to help Eddy, don't you?'

Liam huffed. 'OK.'

'Perhaps we can sit down and have a chat while Edris has a look around.'

Meadows sat down in the armchair. He noticed a look pass between Cillian and Leah. He watched her take Liam's hand and lead him to the sofa where they sat side by side. She still looked unwell and there was a vulnerability about her. He glanced at Cillian who stood behind the sofa, his shoulders rigid.

'Cillian, can you talk me through last night's shift?' Meadows asked.

Cillian placed his hands on the back of the sofa.

'I settled the residents down with Miles, we watched a film and I went to bed about eleven.'

'Did you hear any disturbances during the night?'

'No, I was out like a light. Didn't wake up until my alarm went off.'

'Who was first in this morning?

'I don't know, Gemma, Leah and Harry were in the kitchen when I got up, Dani came in just after.'

Meadows looked at Leah.

'Harry and Gemma were already in when I arrived.' She turned her attention to Liam who was rocking back and forth as his eyes followed Edris around the room.

'When we spoke yesterday you said that after you went to bed Monday night you didn't see or hear anything.'

'That's right,' Leah said. She avoided Meadows' gaze and continued to soothe Liam.

'But you did get up during the night. You were seen talking to Alan, then taking Liam back to his room.'

'No I... I didn't get up.' Her eyes were wide as she looked at Meadows. 'There must be some mistake.'

'What is this?' Cillian demanded. 'She told you she didn't wake up. Whoever told you that is lying.' His fingers curled into fists.

'I don't think so. The witness has no reason to lie.' Meadows held Cillian's gaze.

'I don't remember getting up.' Leah looked panicked.

Doubt crept into Meadows mind.

Maybe she was drugged.

'Liam, Alan shouted at you sometimes, didn't he?' Meadows leaned forward in the chair.

Liam turned his head towards Meadows. 'Alan is a bad man, hate him.'

'Because he shouts at you?'

'Yes, and hurts Hard Hat, says he'll put him in the microwave and make me eat him.'

'I think he was teasing you, Liam.' A nervous laugh escaped Leah's lips.

Liam pouted. 'Not funny.'

'No, it's not funny,' Meadows agreed. 'Alan shouted at you because you were out of bed when you should have been sleeping. Did Leah take you back to bed?'

Liam put his hands over his ears. 'Stop asking questions, not telling, not telling.' He rocked back and forth.

Meadows turned to Leah. 'Tell me what happened on Monday night.'

Leah sighed. 'I've told you everything.'

Meadows could see her hands trembling. Cillian leaned over the sofa and put a hand on her shoulder.

'Tell me what happened before you went to bed.'

'Nothing happened. Me and Gemma settled the residents down then had a cup of tea in the sitting room, watched some telly then went to bed.'

'Camomile tea?'

'Yes.'

'What was Gemma doing when you left her?'

'Watching telly.'

'How did she seem to you?'

'She was OK, a little quiet.'

'She's told you everything she knows. You can't seriously think Leah had anything to do with what happened to Alan.' Cillian glared at Meadows.

'What I do know is the two of you are withholding information.'

'We've told you everything we know.'

'Did you drink anything other than tea on Monday evening?' Meadows asked.

'I had a glass of milk to settle my stomach, why?'

'It's possible that you and Gemma were drugged.'

Leah visibly relaxed. 'You think that's why I didn't hear anything?'

'There you go, if Leah was drugged then she wouldn't remember getting up to see to Liam, if that's what really happened,' Cillian said.

'No!' Liam leapt off the sofa giving them all a start. He charged at Edris, who was crouching down to look in the hutch. 'Get away or you'll wake him up.'

Edris stood up, 'It's OK. I won't wake him. I'll be very quiet.'

Cillian walked over to Liam who stood guarding the hutch. 'Are you going to let us look inside?'

Liam screwed up his face. 'No.'

'I'll see if I can persuade him to let you to take a look later.' Cillian patted Liam on the shoulder.

'I've checked everywhere else,' Edris said.

Meadows looked at Liam, who stared back with angry eyes. He felt his phone vibrate in his pocket. 'Excuse me a minute.' He walked to the far end of the room before answering. 'Meadows.' He listened with interest to the voice on the other end of the line. 'OK, on my way.' He signalled to Edris, who looked relieved not to have to battle Liam over the hutch.

Outside in the corridor they met with Blackwell coming out of Jane's office.

Blackwell grinned. 'Nothing in there, but she's wound up a treat.'

'Good. Keep an eye on her,' Meadows said. 'Traffic have found Alan Whitby's car, burned out up the mountain. I'm going up to take a look. The relief staff will be in soon; let the others go but search them on the way out. Try to use a bit of tact.'

Blackwell huffed. 'I'm sure I can handle it.'

'Good. After the staff leave, chase up the warrant. I want to get all the files and the computer checked without Jane knowing.'

'I would've had her in by now,' Blackwell commented. 'We have nothing on her other than the phone call. I want to know what she's hiding.' Blackwell grunted and walked off.

'Let's go and see this car, then I think we should pay Jane's husband a visit,' Meadows said to Edris.

'You think he's involved?'

'He gave Jane an alibi. I want to speak to him, see how reliable that alibi is. Most people would lie for the one they love.'

'I suppose.'

'With a bit of luck, he'll be in work and we can catch him on his break. See if you can get hold of his schedule from the bus depot.'

Meadows listened to Edris talking on the phone as he drove towards the mountain. They passed through the village of Bryn Melyn which proudly announced itself as the gateway to the Black Mountains. Once they passed over the cattle grid there were only a few scattered houses then the landscape opened to reveal the rolling hills. Meadows changed gear as he approached the first bend and pulled the car around. Crash barriers lined one side of the road to prevent cars going over the edge and plunging down into the river below.

Wild horses stood huddled together against the wind and sheep peppered the mountainside. The road twisted and turned until they reached the highest point where crags of limestone jutted from the mountain and the old quarry came into view. Farmland could be seen below as they made their descent. Meadows slowed the car as he rounded the hairpin bend and came to a halt behind a parked police car with its lights flashing. He pulled on his coat and stepped out of the car. The wind whipped around his head, biting into his scalp.

'It's bloody freezing,' Edris moaned as he zipped up his coat.

A uniformed officer approached and pointed down the side of the mountain. 'Down there.'

Meadows peered over the side and saw the burned-out car with its front end plunged into the river. A forensic team were inspecting the vehicle.

Edris frowned. 'We're not climbing down there, are we?'

'Yep.' Meadows grinned as he pulled up the collar on his coat. 'It's not that steep, just watch your feet, walk down sideways and you should be OK.'

Meadows started the decline. His feet slipped a few times and he struggled to keep his balance as the wind drove into him. Edris struggled behind him, a string of expletives, together with apologies flowing from his mouth. They eventually made it to the bottom, where there was some shelter from the wind, and walked over to a man who was taking samples from what was left of the boot.

'Found anything interesting, Mike?' Meadows asked.

He grinned. 'No body for you, I'm afraid.'

'We've already got the body, thanks,' Edris said as he checked his shoes for sheep droppings.

'Should have worn boots. Looks like a rag was pushed into the petrol tank and lit, would have been quite a show but I doubt anyone would have seen anything up here,' Mike said.

'Why burn it? Waste of a damn good car,' Edris said.

Mike rolled his eyes. 'Well, it's not likely we'll get any prints from it now.'

'They could have cleaned it, changed the plates and got rid of it. I'm sure there's more than one place to shift a stolen car and this one would have been worth a bit.'

'I'm not sure I like the way your mind is working.' Meadows laughed. His eyes followed the car tracks which were still visible on the mountainside. 'Looks like it was pushed over the edge and the fire set down here.'

'I'll agree with that,' Mike said. 'There's no evidence of the car being on fire as it came down. You would've seen some debris.'

'So you're saying he pushed the car over the edge, climbed down, set fire to it and ran like hell back up. He'd have to be fit,' Edris said.

'Doesn't have to be a man. It would've been dark so they would've needed a torch,' Meadows said.

'Most mobile phones have torches on them now,' Edris commented.

'Good point.' Meadows turned back to Mike. 'Anything else?'

'Lots of melted plastic in the boot and overdone sausages by the looks of it, a few chicken portions. Maybe they were trying to have a barbecue.' Mike laughed.

Meadows peered into the boot. 'It's probably the food taken from the freezer, they had to dispose of it somewhere.'

Mike carefully picked up some plastic and put it in an evidence bag. 'You could be right.'

'What's that?'

Mike reached in a gloved hand and held the charred object aloft for Meadows to examine. 'Looks like the remains of an iron.'

Meadows thought back to the meeting with Daisy. 'Can you get that tested? It could be our murder weapon. Edris, give Blackwell a call and see if there's an iron missing from the cellar.'

Meadows walked around the rest of the car while Edris was on the phone. There wasn't much to be seen. The interior had burned down to the metal and forensic officers were bagging melted compact discs. 'I don't think we're going to get much from this but I guess that was the point.'

'We'll give it a thorough going-over. I'll get the iron sent straight to the lab.'

'Thanks, Mike.' Meadows turned to Edris, who had finished his call. 'Anything from Blackwell?'

'Yes, he took Harry down the cellar to check. There is an iron missing, they keep a spare one down there.'

'It was probably the first thing to hand. Right, are you ready for the hike back up?' Meadows grinned.

'I'll race you to the top.'

'Challenge accepted.' Meadows took off, scaling the mountainside with ease. He could hear Edris puffing behind. He reached the top and stopped to catch his breath. Edris clambered the last steps and bent over, drawing in gulps of air.

'What kept you?'

Edris laughed. 'I'll give it to you, you're fit for an old guy.'

'Less of the old! I'm in my prime and not that much older than you.'

'Over ten years older, I reckon. It's all downhill for you now.'

'Cheeky sod!'

They reached the car, feeling grateful to get out of the wind. Meadows sat and gazed out of the window at the surrounding mountain. 'Why not just put the body in the car? They went to all this trouble to destroy the car. It doesn't make sense'

'Unless they wanted the body to be found,' Edris said.

'But why draw attention to Bethesda? If they dumped the body up here we wouldn't have connected it directly to the home. Yes, we would've questioned Alan's work colleagues, but we wouldn't have easily found the murder scene. Then there's the drugs, Gemma and possibly Leah were drugged sometime during the evening and Alan had enough to possibly knock him out. That would take some planning, yet the hiding of the body in the freezer and disposing of the car looks like it was done on impulse.'

'I can't feel my hands and I think my brain is frozen.' Edris rubbed his hands together. 'It just gets more complicated.'

Meadows started the engine and turned up the heater. 'Let's go and see Huw Pritchard. We'll get a cup of tea on the way to warm you up.'

* * *

They arrived at the depot as Huw's bus was pulling in. The manager had agreed to let them use his office so Huw grabbed a cup of tea and led them into the warm room.

'Is this about the business up at Bethesda? I worry about Jane working there now. I hope you're close to catching whoever is responsible.'

'We'll catch them, it's just a matter of time.' Meadows smiled. He watched Huw sip his tea. He had a boyish face with warm brown eyes that crinkled at the corners when he smiled.

'We're checking everyone's alibi for Monday evening. Jane said she was at home all evening,' Edris said.

'I've already given a statement,' Huw replied as he grabbed a biscuit from an open packet.

'Yes, but we need to go over a few things. It's just a formality.' Meadows watched closely to see if Huw showed any signs of discomfort but he remained relaxed.

'Sure.' Huw munched the biscuit and took a swig of tea. 'I got home from work about half seven. Jane was already home and had dinner ready. We ate then I went down The Bridge. I play darts on a Monday night.'

'Did Jane stay at home?'

'Yeah, she's not one for going to the pub. We go out for a meal sometimes but she's busy at work and tired on the weekends.'

Edris looked up from his notepad. 'What time did you get home from playing darts?'

'About eleven. Jane was in bed. She goes up about ten on work nights.'

'Did she wake up when you went to bed?'

'I don't think so. I went up quietly.' Huw shifted in his chair.

'Did you get a sense that she was awake?' Meadows asked.

'She didn't say anything.'

'Did she get up during the night?'

Huw hesitated. 'I didn't hear her get up.'

Meadows had a feeling that Huw was holding back so rephrased the question hoping to force the truth. 'Are you absolutely sure she was in bed? Did you talk to her? Switch the light on?'

'Well, no, I didn't go into…' Huw looked away and sighed. 'The thing is, when I go out for a drink, I snore, so I sleep in the spare room.'

'You didn't mention this in your statement,' Edris said.

'Well, that woman copper didn't ask. It's not the sort of information you volunteer. Anyway, it's not like Jane had anything to do with Alan's murder.'

'But you can't be certain that she was in bed,' Meadows added.

'Her car was parked in the drive. Where else would she be?'

Quite possibly murdering Alan Whitby.

Meadows felt sorry for Huw; he imagined Jane wore the pants in the house and her husband idolised her.

'How has Jane been over these past few days? Have you noticed any changes?'

'She's been a bit upset, not eating and sleeping well, but I expect she had a shock, working there with a killer on the loose.'

'I'd like you to come to the station tomorrow and change your statement. We may need to speak to you again.'

Huw stood up. 'OK, can I get back to work now?'

'Yes, thank you for your time.'

'Bloody idiot,' Edris said as they walked back to the car. 'I think he was embarrassed about the separate rooms. I'm guessing it's not only when he has a drink. I don't think he was deliberately withholding information and he obviously has no reason to think that his wife is involved.'

'But you think she is?'

'Alan was getting money from somewhere. If it was from Bethesda then I'm betting Jane knew about it.'

Chapter Twenty

When they arrived at the station, they found the team unpacking boxes.

'Any problems getting these?' Meadows asked.

'No.' Blackwell put a stack of files onto his desk. 'I warned the relief staff not to have any contact with Jane or any of the regular staff concerning the removal of files.'

'Good.' Meadows stood at the enquiry board and addressed the team. 'I want us to split the files and search for any inconsistencies. Check signatures on any withdrawals and receipts. We need to look at the overall finances of Bethesda as well as individual residents' accounts and personal files. Also I want to be sure that all the medication over the last four years is accounted for. Jane Pritchard's alibi is shaky, her husband can't confirm that she was in bed all night. We still don't have confirmation of Miles' alibi and Cillian doesn't have one. Alan was getting money from somewhere and someone knew about it. Any questions?'

There was a general shaking of heads and the files were divided among the group. Paskin took charge of the medication, cross-referencing the log against the client files. Blackwell huffed his way through the house expenses while Valentine checked the computer taken from Jane's office. Meadows and Edris were left with the residents' personal accounts. Each time money was withdrawn there was a corresponding expense form with two signatures, which was then matched to receipts. It was slow going, and despite the copious amounts of coffee the team drank, Meadows could sense the enthusiasm and energy waning.

'I think we need to get one of the tech guys to check out the computer,' Valentine suggested. 'There doesn't appear to be anything incriminating but files may have been deleted.'

'That's a good idea, Valentine. Take it over to them then call it a night,' Meadows said.

'Thanks.' Valentine smiled and began packing up the computer.

'How come she gets to go home?' Blackwell grunted.

Meadows looked at his watch. *No wonder Blackwell was grumbling.*

'You can go, you too, Paskin. It's late, go home get some sleep and we'll start early in the morning.'

'I'm happy to stay a bit longer,' Edris said.

'No surprises there, golden boy,' Blackwell said as he shut his file.

Meadows ignored the comment.

Sergeant Folland walked into the office. 'Still at it then?'

Meadows looked up and noticed that Blackwell had paused at his desk. 'Looks like it's going to be a long weekend.'

'I've got something that will cheer you up.' Folland approached Meadows' desk. 'That vehicle travelling from London you asked to be checked out? Traffic picked it up on the M4 cameras, but not on the day your boy says. Last camera picked it up on Monday at 7.05 p.m.'

'Now that is good news. No alibi and Miles lied about his whereabouts.'

'We should bring them in now,' Blackwell said.

'We still don't have a motive. I want to go through this lot first to see what we turn up.'

'If you find anything,' Blackwell sneered.

'Why don't you have a dig around, see what you can find out about Miles' last employment?'

'Yeah, first thing in the morning,' Blackwell grunted. He picked up his jacket and sauntered out of the office.

'What's up with him?' Folland asked.

'It's Blackwell, he doesn't need a reason to be a dick,' Edris said.

'Right I'll leave you to it, I'm off home. Have a nice weekend,' Folland said with a wink.

Meadows returned his attention to the bank statement. There appeared to be a regular income, what looked like a disability payment from the government. Payments were made for various items which coincided with receipts and expenses forms. Some money was gifted for birthdays and Christmas, possibly from family members. He paused at an entry for a payment to Guardian Holdings, which was followed by a receipt from the same company for the same amount a few weeks later. He checked through the rest of the statements and found more entries of the same nature.

'Whose bank statements have you got?' Meadows looked across to Edris.

Edris looked up, keeping his finger marked on an entry. 'Eddy's.'

'Are there any entries from Guardian Holdings?'

Edris looked through the statement. 'Yes, in and out for the same amounts.'

'They go back at least two years. I want to check the other residents' accounts, see if they have the same entries.' They split the pile between them and methodically worked through each statement. Each one showed similar entries, the amount increasing each month. He picked up Vanessa's file and was shocked by what he found.

'Look at this.' Meadows pointed the entries out to Edris. 'Whoa, she's minted!'

'Was.' Meadows shook his head with disgust. 'I would imagine she inherited this money from her parents. They're both dead and she is an only child. These entries to Guardian Holdings go back three years. The first payment is for ten thousand, then it's paid back in a month later. This goes on until the payments increase to a hundred thousand – there is no receipt, and the account is almost cleared out.'

'So, what is Guardian Holdings?'

'That's what I would like to know.' Meadows turned to his computer and searched the company. There wasn't a lot of information available so he put in a request for full company information. He sat back and rubbed his hands over his face. 'Let's call it a night. We'll look at the other files in the morning and calculate how much money is missing. With a bit of luck I'll have the company report back and we can see who is behind it.'

'I'm betting Jane Pritchard,' Edris said.

'I think you might be right, and if Alan Whitby was a part of it that would give her a strong motive for getting rid of him.' Meadows grabbed his coat and flipped his desk calendar to December. 'Twelve days until the Lapland trip, let's hope we can wrap it up over the weekend so Kevin can build his snowman.'

Meadows left the station and drove towards home. He passed in and out of villages, each with its own shop, church, and pub before arriving in Bryn Bach. There he stopped at the shop to pick up milk and tobacco and spent a few minutes talking to Jay, the shopkeeper.

The farm track was in darkness and with the moon hidden behind thick cloud there was no light once he parked and turned off the car engine. Inside the cottage the heating was on and once he turned on the lamps and radio, the sitting room felt cosy and welcoming.

In the kitchen Meadows cooked up some scrambled eggs and gobbled them down. He washed the plates and left them in the rack to dry. What he really wanted was hidden in the sitting room. After brewing a cup of camomile tea, he changed into tracksuits bottoms and an old T-shirt then turned off the radio. The cottage fell silent.

In the sitting room three shelves with neat rows of books lined the wall above the television. Meadows stretched up and plucked a book from the top shelf. He flipped open the book, the inside was hollow and hid a grinder and bag of weed. This was his only vice and he knew it could cost him his career. It was one reason he was happy to live alone.

Meadows sat back in the armchair and lit the freshly rolled joint. He inhaled deeply and felt the smoke coat the back of his throat. With each puff he felt his body relax and he sank back in the chair.

We really need to find Eddy's book. I'm sure it's in the building somewhere. Where would you hide a book? A place where no one would look?

Meadows eyes came to rest on his bookshelves.

Eddy has a lot of books in his room. No, he would notice if one was out of place. Too risky.

He stubbed the remainder of the joint in the ashtray then rested his head on the back of the armchair.

I'm sure Cillian said something important. I'll have to ask Edris to go through his notes in the morning.

This was his last thought before he fell asleep.

Chapter Twenty-one

*Leah and Cillian have been whispering to each other all day. I hate it
when they do that – not supposed to whisper, it's rude. It's all the
policeman's fault, he keeps asking questions. It hurts my head. Too
many pictures, words and noise pushing inside my head. I want to let
them out, make more room, but I promised Leah, promised I would
keep them hiding in my head.*

*Leah's gone home now, home with Cillian, and the Saturday
woman is here. I don't like Saturday, only when Leah comes to visit
but she won't come, she says, not this time. It's because of the
policeman. She was crying when she left. I don't want Leah to be sad.
My tummy feels funny again, like there's a fish swimming around,
wiggling against my skin. It's because Leah says we have to go away
to a place where we will be safe. I want to take Hard Hat but
Cillian says he can't come where we are going. I don't want to go if
Cillian is going to be there. I want to stay here with my friends and
Leah but Cillian says I won't see Leah again if I don't go. Leah is
afraid.*

'Liam, time for bed.'

*How did she get in here? I don't like people sneaking into my
room.*

'You didn't knock. You're supposed to knock.'

'I did knock, Liam, you didn't hear me. Come on, time to get into bed.'

The Saturday woman is making a face at me.

'I don't want to get into bed.'

Too many pictures in my head.

'Come on, Liam, you are not going to give me a hard time, are you?'

I suppose I better get into bed, she will go away then. She's pulling down the covers and smiling. I take off my slippers and get into bed.

'Goodnight, Liam.'

It's dark, Saturday woman has turned off the light. I have to think nice things, that's what Leah says, but I can't. I should've told the policeman the answers, we could stay here and Leah will be safe.

Chapter Twenty-two

All thoughts of Eddy's book were pushed to the back of Meadows' mind when he entered the station the next morning and found the report on Guardian Holdings in his mailbox. He clicked open the mail and his eyes scanned the information with growing interest. The company directors were listed as Jane Pritchard and Miles Flint.

So that's what you've been up to.

'What have you got?' Edris asked as he walked over to the desk followed by Blackwell and Paskin.

'Guardian Holdings is owned by Jane and Miles,' Meadows told them. 'There isn't much information with regards to trading. The last financial statements were filed in April and looks like they were doing well. Both have been drawing large dividends out of the company.'

'That explains how she gets to drive around in that flash car,' Edris said.

'What's this got to do with Alan Whitby's death?' Blackwell asked.

'Money has been taken from the residents' accounts to finance the company,' Edris explained. 'If you had stayed around last night you would know about it.'

Blackwell's lips turned up into a snarl. 'I was here when your mother was still wiping your arse. I already knew those two were up to their necks in it, it's all about experience. I said we should've brought them in.'

'And we will,' Meadows said. 'First I want all the information on Guardian Holdings before we interview them. Where's Valentine?'

'Gone to pick up the computer from the tech guys,' Paskin said.

'Good. Blackwell, I suggest you do some more digging into Miles Flint's background. Paskin, Edris, I want to collate information from the residents' financial records. I want to see exactly how much money has been embezzled and when the transactions were made.'

They worked through the files feeding the figures into a spreadsheet. In the background Blackwell could be heard on the phone, his voice rising as he demanded private numbers for contacts in London.

'Well, that makes over a hundred and fifty thousand pounds.' Meadows leaned back in his chair and stretched his arms. 'Most of it from Vanessa's account.'

'Why keep putting the money back in?' Edris asked. 'The money is obviously moved to finance some other activity. The money was moved in and out, so if anyone was to check the balance, it would be correct. They started small and when they got away with it, increased the amounts. Something went wrong because they haven't been able to pay the money back in.'

'Drug money or laundering?' Paskin suggested.

'Could be, let's hope Valentine comes back with some information,' Meadows said.

'So finally I got hold of the manager from Miles' last employment.' Blackwell perched on the edge of the desk. 'He worked at a residential home for the elderly. Questions were raised about missing money but no charges were brought, he left of his own accord.'

'And before that?'

'Stockbroker. Haven't been able to get hold of anyone yet but I'll keep trying.'

'Morning all.' Valentine walked into the office with a large grin and waving a flash drive. 'Tech guys managed to retrieve some deleted files, some interesting stuff.'

'Guardian Holdings?' Meadows asked.

'Yes.' Valentine's face fell. 'Don't tell me you've already found the files.'

'No, only the entries on the residents' bank accounts. Let's see what you've got.'

Valentine plugged in the flash drive and pulled up the files for Guardian Holdings as they all gathered around the computer.

'The money's just going in and out of the account again,' Edris said.

'Yes, but look, there are payments to H D Baines.' Meadows pointed to the screen. 'Then larger sums are paid back into the account before the original amount is returned to the residents' accounts. The remainder is divided between J Pritchard and M Flint. Then the whole process starts again but with larger amounts. It stopped a few months ago, no money received from H D Baines.'

'So, who is H D Baines?' Paskin asked.

'Possibly a stockbroker. I think Jane and Miles have been using the residents' money to trade on the stock exchange. It makes sense, Miles knows the business. Looks like they made quite a bit until their luck ran out.'

'And they couldn't pay back the residents' money,' Paskin added.

'Or the broker ran off with the money,' Blackwell suggested.

'So you think that Alan was in on it?' Edris asked. 'There are no payments direct to his bank account, but there are cash withdrawals. He could have found out about it – it was only a matter of time before someone picked up on the missing money. Alan would've had access to the information as supervisor. He could've asked for a piece of the pie or for money to keep quiet.' Meadows pushed back his chair. 'Right, I think we have enough to bring them in.'

Blackwell grabbed his jacket. 'I'll pick up Miles, it'll give me great pleasure to wipe that smirk off his face.'

'OK, take Paskin with you. Edris, we'll pick up Jane. Valentine, can I leave you to check out H D Baines, see if they are still trading?'

'I'll get right on to it.' She gave Edris a coy smile before returning to her desk.

Meadows noticed the glow in Edris' face. 'Come on, let's get going before the jungle drums relay the news that Miles has been picked up and Jane makes a run for it.'

Chapter Twenty-three

Meadows pulled up behind Jane's convertible. 'Looks like we're in luck.'

'Probably doesn't have any money left to go shopping,' Edris said. 'I bet her old man is going to have one hell of a shock.'

'Poor sod.' Meadows looked towards the house. 'Maybe we're doing him a favour.'

The house was a newly built semi-detached on a smart estate. Meadows imagined that Huw Pritchard must have worked constant overtime to keep up with the mortgage payments.

'I bet the neighbours are hiding behind the nets. We'll soon give them something to gossip about.'

'You really don't like her, do you?' Edris said. 'It's unlike you, you usually always see the best in people, even Blackwell.'

'Yes, well, taking money from vulnerable people. That money is supposed to be making their lives easier. Vanessa's account is almost cleared out.'

'Yeah, I guess you can't sink much lower.'

They walked up the path and knocked on the door which was opened by Huw.

'Oh, hello.' He smiled. 'I was just about to come down the station to alter my statement. I didn't realise I had to be there at a certain time.'

'We're not here about the statement,' Edris said. 'Although we would appreciate it if you wouldn't leave it too long.'

'We're here to see Jane. Is she in?' Meadows peered over Huw's shoulder.

'Yes, come in. She's just watching a film. She likes to have some time to relax on her day off.'

They followed Huw into the sitting room. It appeared to be freshly decorated, and jacquard floor-length curtains draped the windows. The room was dominated by a cream leather corner sofa where Jane sat with her feet up.

'You have visitors, love,' Huw said.

Jane turned her head away from the television and looked from Edris to Meadows. 'It's my day off. Can't you wait until Monday?'

'I'm afraid not,' Meadows said. 'We would like you to come down to the station to answer a few questions.'

Jane's eyes narrowed. 'It's not convenient.'

'It's not a request.' Meadows turned to Edris and nodded.

Edris stepped forward. 'Jane Pritchard, I am arresting you on the suspicion of the murder of Alan Whitby–'

'What!' Jane sprang up from the sofa, eyes wild. 'You can't do this.'

Confusion creased Huw's face. 'There must be some mistake…'

Edris continued with the caution which was drowned out by Jane's protests.

'Don't just stand there like a fucking idiot, do something,' Jane shrieked at Huw.

Huw stepped in front of Jane. 'You're making a mistake. Jane didn't have anything to do with what happened to Alan. She's been very upset by the whole thing.'

'If you would please step away, sir,' Meadows said. 'It would be better for both of you if your wife doesn't make this difficult. I'm sure you don't want to cause a scene in front of the neighbours.'

Jane's nostrils flared and her face creased with hate. 'Fine, I'll come with you, but I will be putting in a complaint for wrongful arrest. Get hold of a solicitor, Huw.'

She turned on Edris who had placed a hand on her arm. 'Get off me.'

'I'll cuff you if you don't behave,' he warned.

'Can I come with her?' Huw asked as Edris led Jane outside.

'I'm afraid not,' Meadows said kindly. 'You can ring the station later and they'll inform you of your wife's status. Best call that solicitor.'

Tears welled in Huw's eyes. 'I don't understand.'

'Did you not wonder where the money came from? Jane's car must have cost a fair bit and it looks like you've had new furniture for the house.'

'She's the manager of Bethesda and she's had a few large bonuses to thank her for her work.'

Meadows followed Edris to the car. Jane sat in the back scowling, her arms folded across her chest, but fear was evident in her eyes.

They drove back to the station with Jane keeping up a stony silence. Meadows hoped she was going to be a bit more cooperative when they got her into the interview room. She kept her head held high as they led her to reception and handed her over to the custody sergeant.

They grabbed a cup of tea from the canteen before taking the stairs to the office. Blackwell, Paskin and Valentine were sat at their desks when Meadows walked in.

'Any problems with Miles?' Meadows asked.

'No, I cuffed the little swine and chucked him in the car.' Blackwell grinned. 'He mouthed off a bit.'

'Let them stew for a while. Valentine, how did you get on with Baines?'

'Still trading and seems all above board. Stockbroker, as you correctly guessed.'

* * *

The interview room felt warm and stuffy and Meadows had to resist the urge to loosen his tie. Edris sat next to him with a serious expression on his face. Opposite sat Jane and her solicitor, Roger Thomas, a small bespectacled man with a receding hairline.

Meadows placed a file on the desk, opened it then smiled at Jane.

'I would like you to tell us about Guardian Holdings.'

Jane looked at Roger and arched an eyebrow.

'It is my understanding that you arrested my client in connection with the death of Alan Whitby. My client has already provided you with an alibi. What evidence do you have to justify detaining my client?' Roger asked looking over the top of his spectacles.

So that's how they're going to play it. Still, he has a point, we have no evidence to tie her to the murder.

'We'll come to that shortly. I assure you that your client's involvement in Guardian Holdings is connected to the death of Alan Whitby.'

Roger turned to Jane and nodded. Jane looked furious.

'Guardian Holdings is my own private business and has nothing to do with Alan, so I don't see how it is relevant.'

'You're a director along with your co-worker Miles Flint. Is that correct?'

'Yes.'

'And can you tell me the nature of the business?'

'It's a trading company.'

'Really. From what I can see money is moved in and out of the company with no actual trading.'

'That's because we employ a broker.'

'And how is the company financed?'

Jane fidgeted in her seat and glanced briefly at Roger who was looking mildly interested. 'I put up capital from my savings.'

Meadows took the statements from the files and laid them on the table, pushing them towards Jane and Roger.

'Money has been taken regularly from the accounts of the residents of Bethesda House. Bethesda has joint power of attorney, together with some of the family members, over these accounts.'

Roger leaned forward and perused the accounts.

'I don't know anything about that.' Jane's thin lips were set in a grim line.

'Files were retrieved from your computer. Not so easy to delete them,' Edris said. 'These files clearly show payments to and from the residents' bank accounts. Accounts you are responsible for, as well as approving any withdrawals.'

Jane's eyes darkened. 'I don't know anything about that. I'm not the only one to use the office computer.'

'No, I would imagine Alan Whitby had use of the computer as supervisor. Only you and Miles have an interest in Guardian Holdings. Why would anyone else move money into that account?'

'How would I know? Perhaps to set me up. You're the detective.'

Meadows glared. Her eyes were hard and her lips drew into a sly smile. He couldn't believe that even with the evidence before her, she could continue to lie.

She's going to blame it all on Miles.

'Don't you regularly reconcile the residents' accounts, check the balances? Surely it's your job to make sure the accounts are in order.'

'Well, yes, but I didn't see any inaccuracies with the balances.'

'When was the last time you checked the accounts?'

Jane folded her arms across her chest. 'I can't be sure.'

'Last week? A month ago? The residents are due to go on holiday in just over a week.'

'Yes.'

'Who financed the holiday?'

'The residents.'

'And was it you that organised the booking and payment?'

Colour rose in Jane's cheeks. 'Yes.'

'Then you would've had recent access to the residents' accounts. I would imagine a hundred and fifty thousand pounds missing from the accounts wouldn't be that easy to miss.' Meadows noticed the solicitor raise his eyebrows.

I bet she didn't mention that.

Jane wriggled in her seat. 'The bank didn't alert me to a withdrawal of that amount.'

'No, they wouldn't have. As you know, they would have been used to seeing money transferred in and out of the accounts. Was Alan part of Guardian Holdings?'

'No, just me and Miles. It had nothing to do with Alan, why would it? As I said, it's my personal business.'

'Financed by the residents of Bethesda House,' Edris said.

'We know that Alan Whitby received large amounts of cash over the last year. Was he blackmailing you?' Meadows asked.

'No. If he was concerned about the residents' accounts then he didn't bring it to my attention.'

'Oh, I think he did, and he wanted a slice of the pie. What happened, did you lose all your money and Alan still wanted his share to keep quiet?'

Meadows leaned forward.

Jane's nostrils flared. 'I told you, I don't know anything about the missing money or what happened to Alan. Perhaps you'd better speak to Miles.'

'We will,' Edris said.

Meadows leaned back in his chair and let the silence fill the room for a few moments until he sensed Jane's discomfort. 'Your husband was out last Monday evening.'

'Yes, what of it?'

'So you decided to call Alan and arrange to meet him at Bethesda. We have a record of that call.'

'I already told you, he asked me to call so he would have an excuse to leave the house.'

'You called him to meet you and Miles. Was he expecting payment? When he got there, you and Miles were waiting but you had other plans.'

'No.'

'You drugged him, then what went wrong? Did he wake up before you could carry out your plan?'

'What? No!'

The shock on Jane's face raised a spectre of doubt in Meadows' mind.

She turned to the solicitor in panic. 'Are you listening to this?'

'Do you have any evidence to connect my client to the murder of Alan Whitby?'

'She had both opportunity and motive.'

'I was at home all night with my husband, ask him.'

'Your car was there all night, but as you and your husband have separate rooms, he cannot say with certainty that you were in bed all night,' Edris said.

Jane reddened. 'This is ridiculous. If my car was parked at home all night, then how do you suppose I got to Bethesda?'

'I would imagine Miles picked you up,' Edris answered.

'We found Alan's car,' Meadows watched for signs of distress from Jane but she didn't react to the news. 'Forensics are combing through it now. It's only a matter of time. They will find the evidence. You can't burn away all traces.'

'You won't find anything because I have never been in his car.'

She appears very confident. Maybe Miles disposed of the car.

'Are you going to charge my client?' The solicitor's voice cut through Meadows' thoughts.

'We will be charging your client with misappropriation of funds. We have enough evidence. All the transactions are timed. You received statements from Guardian Holdings detailing the payments and receipts from the residents' accounts. There is no doubt in my mind that you knew where the money was coming from. You could be looking at four years, maybe more considering the vulnerability of the persons you stole from.'

Jane paled. 'Can I go now?'

'No, you will remain in custody until the court hearing. A judge can decide if you will be granted bail until the trial.'

'You can't do this! I have to be in work on Monday morning.'

'You better get your solicitor to inform Bethesda that you won't be in, and if I have my way you will never set foot in that place again.' Meadows stood and beckoned for Edris to follow.

'Charge her with misappropriation of funds and put her in a cell, give her some time to think. I'll interview Miles with Blackwell. Let's see how he tries to worm out of this.'

Edris grinned. 'Probably blame it on Jane.'

'No doubt he will, but it'll be interesting to see his reaction when I tell him that Jane is laying the blame at his door. I'll update you later.'

Meadows left Edris to deal with Jane and went in search of Blackwell, he found him drinking coffee at his desk and chatting to Paskin. Meadows watched the two for a moment and realised that he knew little about the lives of his team outside of work.

Maybe DCI Lester is right, I should socialise more, get to know them.

'How did it go with Jane?' Paskin asked.

'As we expected.' He gave a brief account of the interview.

'Lying bastards, the pair of them,' Blackwell growled.

'Well we've got them both for theft, that's something at least. We still don't have any physical evidence to tie them to the murder,' Meadows said.

'Yet. I reckon I can get a confession.' Blackwell cracked his knuckles.

Good luck with that.

'Right, let's go and see what Miles Flint has to say for himself. I'll let you lead.' Meadows saw Blackwell smile as he stood up from his desk.

'He's refused legal representation,' Blackwell said as they made their way down the stairs. 'He reckons we have nothing on him so doesn't need it.'

'He'll probably change his mind,' Meadows said. 'I'd prefer it if he had counsel, it looks better on us when it goes to court.'

They entered the interview room where Miles was sat with his legs stretched out under the table and hands behind his head.

'About bloody time, I've got better things to do than hang around here all day.'

The young PC that sat in the corner of the room rolled his eyes.

'You can go and take a break now, thanks, Ryan,' Meadows said.

Once the PC had left the room Meadows pulled up a chair in front of the table and recorded the time, date and those present for the interview.

Blackwell plonked himself down in the chair and slammed the file down on the desk, causing Miles to sit up in his seat.

'Guardian Holdings. You've been screwing over the residents of Bethesda House. It's all here.' Blackwell tapped the file. 'Perhaps you should reconsider legal representation now.'

Well, I suppose he gets straight to the point.

Miles smirked. 'Don't need to, mate, there's nothing in that file that isn't above board.'

Blackwell leaned across the desk, his eyes glinting dangerously.

'You're a director of Guardian Holdings along with Jane Pritchard. Money has been transferred from the residents' accounts into Guardian then to Baines the brokers. Made quite a bit from the scheme, didn't you? Enjoy taking money from vulnerable people, do you? You piece of shit.'

Meadows coughed to alert Blackwell that he was going too far.

Blackwell's nostrils flared and he leaned back in the chair.

'I don't know anything about residents' money. Jane asked me to set up the company and she provided the capital. I assumed it was from her personal savings.'

'Funny, she said the same about you,' Meadows said.

'Don't take me for an idiot,' Blackwell growled. 'The transactions are clear on the account. You knew where the money came from.'

'I told you, Jane provided the money. I had no reason to think it wasn't above board.' Miles leaned back in his seat.

'I've been talking to your old employers. Looks like you make a habit of misappropriating client's funds.'

'I think you'll find that was a misunderstanding,' Miles drawled. 'No charges were made.'

'You were fired.'

'Voluntary redundancy.'

'So you left a well-known brokers on 60K plus bonuses to work looking after little old ladies for 15K a year?' Blackwell chuckled. 'That's because no one would touch you, the stench followed you around, eh?'

Meadows saw Miles' eyes darken and his fists clench.

'So Alan found out about your little scheme,' Blackwell continued. 'Did he want in or money to keep his mouth shut?'

'I don't know what you are talking about. How many times do I have to repeat myself? Jane asked me to set up the company and provided the money. If she had something going on the side with Alan, she didn't mention it.'

'Your sticky fingers are all over this.' Blackwell waved the file. 'My guess is that Alan wanted more money and he didn't care where you got it from. You were already 150K down with no way of getting the money back. You had to keep him quiet. So Jane calls him and arranges to meet him at Bethesda. You drug him, intending to set it up so it looks like one of the residents attacked him. What happened? Did Alan wake up and you had to finish him off.'

Not a bad theory.

Meadows watched Blackwell stare Miles down.

Miles leaned forward, anger twisting his lips into a snarl. 'This is bullshit!'

'Where were you Monday evening?' Meadows asked.

'In London. I already made a statement.'

'What time did you get back?' Blackwell relaxed his shoulders.

'I drove straight from London to work on Tuesday morning. Had to get up at a bitch of a time. Got into Bethesda about nine. Made good time.'

'Yet your car was picked up on camera on the M4 Monday evening, the last sighting at seven.' Blackwell grinned. 'Enough time to get to Bethesda for your meeting with Alan.'

Miles ran his hand through his hair. 'OK, you got me there. I lied. I told work I was away for a long weekend and wouldn't be back until Tuesday. It was supposed to be my turn to do the night shift on Monday. If Jane knew I was back I would have been called in to do the shift.'

'So where did you go Monday night?'

'Home to bed. I was knackered after the drive.'

'And I suppose you were alone,' Blackwell snapped.

'Like I said. I was tired.' Miles pushed back his chair and stood. 'Well if that's all, I think I'll go. I've answered all your questions.'

'Sit down!' Blackwell barked. 'I haven't even started.'

'You don't have anything on me.' Miles shrugged his shoulders. 'I don't see what more I can tell you.'

'You will be charged with the misappropriation of residents' funds and remanded in custody until the court hearing,' Meadows said.

'To start with,' Blackwell said with a malicious grin.

Meadows stood and nodded to Blackwell to continue. He didn't think there was any more information to be gained from Miles at this stage. He left the interview room and called for the PC to go back in to watch over the proceedings.

Meadows found Edris sat at his desk completing the paperwork for Jane's arrest and charge. 'Get any more from her?'

'No, just kept denying the theft charges. How did it go with Miles?'

'Much the same story, they're just going to try and shift the blame onto each other. With a bit of luck they'll both be tried and found guilty.'

'It's just a shame we've got no evidence to place them at the murder scene.' Edris turned back to the screen and continued typing.

'We might have if we can find Eddy's book.' Meadows pulled off his tie and put it in his pocket.

'We searched the whole place, they probably shredded it.'

'No, I don't think so. I'm sure we're missing something. What did Miles say when we asked him about Thursday's night shift?'

'Hold on a sec.' Edris' hands skimmed across the keyboard, his eyes shifting across the screen. He hit the save button then took his notebook from his jacket pocket and flicked through the pages. 'Settled residents down, watched a film with Cillian, Liam woke up complaining about the tortoise—'

'Stop there.' Meadows held his hand up. 'Didn't he say that Liam complained that someone had woken Hard Hat?'

'Something like that.'

'Come on, I think I know where we'll find the book.'

Chapter Twenty-four

The first thing that struck Meadows as he entered Bethesda House was the silence.

'Where is everyone?' Edris peeked into the sitting room.

'Maybe out on a day trip,' Meadows said. 'Let's see if there's anyone in the office. They would have locked the door if they were all out.'

'Maybe not, I can't see anyone trying to break in here.' Edris grinned. 'You might never come out.'

As they approached the office they could hear muffled voices from behind the door. Meadows knocked and opened the door. Harry stood next to the desk where a man sat writing in a notebook. They both looked up at the visitors.

'Hello,' Harry said, smiling at Edris. 'This is our new supervisor, Jason.' She introduced the detectives.

Edris' eyes twinkled. 'I thought you were off for the weekend.'

'I'm just giving Jason a hand to settle in,' Harry explained.

'We have no computer or files at the moment so Harry kindly agreed to talk me through the running of Bethesda, the background and needs of the residents,' Jason said.

Meadows noted there was no accusation in Jason's voice. 'I'll get the files back to you as soon as I can.'

'Thank you. I'm sure we can manage in the meantime.'

'We had a call to say that Jane and Miles have been arrested, is it true?' Harry asked Edris.

'Yes, it looks like you'll be a bit short of staff for a while.'

'I'm sure we'll manage. Jason can step into Jane's position until she returns.'

I don't think she will be coming back, not if I can help it.

'Where is everyone?'

'They've gone out for the day and are seeing a show this evening so I guess they will be worn out when they get back. Liam and Eddy are here, they're both in their rooms. Liam didn't want to go and Eddy has barely left his room since he lost his book.'

'Poor fellow,' Jason commented.

'It was Liam that I was hoping to see,' Meadows said, turning to Jason. 'Perhaps you can spare Harry for a few moments.'

'Yes, of course, and if there is anything else I can do, let me know. Terrible business.' Jason shook his head. 'I understand the residents have planned a trip to Lapland. I do hope this is not going to delay the trip.'

'I hope not, we're working to get things cleared up in time.'

They left Jason in the office and walked the corridor to Liam's room. Harry called out and knocked before opening the door. Liam was pacing the sitting area, muttering. He wore blue cotton pyjamas and his feet were bare.

'You not getting dressed today then, Liam?' Harry asked.

'No, don't want to.' Liam stopped pacing and frowned at Harry.

'Oh well, it will be time to get changed for bed soon anyway. You can have a pyjama party in the kitchen later. I have cake. Chocolate cake,' Harry said.

'Chocolate cake?' Liam's eyes lit up. 'A big one?'

'Yes, a big one.' Harry laughed. 'Jason bought it. He thought it would be a nice treat for you and Eddy as you didn't go on the trip.'

'Can we eat it all?'

'I think we should leave a little bit for the others.'

Liam scowled. 'Can I have a big bit?'

'Yes.'

Liam grinned and it struck Meadows how easy it was to make him happy.

'I've brought some visitors for you,' Harry said.

Liam looked from Edris to Meadows as if he had only just noticed them in the room. 'I don't want visitors.'

'We won't stay long,' Meadows said. 'Why didn't you want to go on the trip today?'

Liam pouted. 'Don't want to go.'

'Because Leah didn't go on the trip?'

Liam nodded. 'Leah isn't here today.'

'You like Leah, don't you?'

'Leah is my friend.'

'Yes, Leah looks after you. I'm sure you want to look after Leah. I think Leah is afraid.'

Worry creased Liam's face and he started to rock back and forth.

'It's OK, Liam.' Meadows held up his hands. 'I think you can help Leah. Do you want to help Leah?'

Liam's eyes darted around the room, he looked at Harry who nodded her encouragement.

'Yes, Leah is my friend.'

'Do you remember that someone took Eddy's book?'

Liam's eyes darkened. 'I didn't take it.' He clenched his fists.

Edris stepped forward but Meadows put up a hand to stop him. He stepped back and stood quietly next to Harry.

'I know you didn't.' Meadows moved towards Liam and perched on the arm of the sofa. 'Eddy wrote something in the book that will help Leah. We have to find the book, so I need you to help me.'

'To make Leah safe?'

Meadows nodded. 'Yes.' He wanted to ask why Leah needed to be kept safe but he didn't want to risk upsetting Liam. Now that he had his trust, he had to keep him calm. 'I think Hard Hat is trying to help, I think he is keeping Eddy's book safe.'

'Hard Hat reading Eddy's book.' Liam laughed.

'Shall we take a look?'

'No.' Liam's face creased. 'You'll wake him. He mustn't wake up until the sun is warm.'

'How about you take a peek? I'm sure you can look without waking him. I won't come near. I bet you are really good at checking on him,' Meadows coaxed.

Liam shuffled over to the hutch and put his finger to his lips. 'Hush.'

Meadows nodded and smiled.

Liam got down on his knees, opened the latch on the hutch and pulled open the door. He put his hand in and gently felt around.

Meadows sat on the edge of the chair, not daring to move. He watched Liam withdraw his hand with the book clutched in his fingers. He turned and grinned at Meadows before closing the door.

'Well done, Liam, I bet he's still asleep.'

'Fast asleep.' Liam stood up and shuffled back to Meadows.

'Can I have the book?' Meadows held out his hand.

Liam paused for a short while. 'Keep Leah safe.' He placed the book in the inspector's hand.

'Thank you.' Meadows felt a twinge of excitement as he held the book in his hand. 'Liam, why is Leah afraid?'

Liam shook his head and stepped back.

'Why do you need Leah to be safe?'

Liam put his hands to his ears. 'Mustn't tell, mustn't tell.'

'It's OK, Liam, you don't have to tell me,' Meadows soothed. 'You've been a great help and I think Harry is going to give you a big slice of chocolate cake.'

Liam took his hands from his head and looked at Harry.

'I'm going to make the drinks now then we can have cake. Would you like to help me?' she asked.

'No.' Liam shook his head.

'OK, you relax here and I'll come and get you when it's ready.'

Meadows stood. 'Thank you, Liam, enjoy your cake.'

Liam grinned. 'Chocolate cake.'

'How did you know?' Edris asked as they had left Liam's room.

'Miles said that Liam complained that someone was trying to wake his tortoise on Thursday night. The only reason he would say that is if there was someone in his room. I doubt he would make it up for attention.'

'That's right,' Harry said. 'Liam and most of the others don't have that sort of imagination. They tell it as it is. I think Eddy is going to be thrilled to get his book back.'

'I need to take a look first,' Meadows said. 'Do you have a photocopier?'

'Yes, there's one in the office.'

Edris talked with Jason and Harry as Meadows flicked through the book. His heart upped tempo as his eyes scanned the information and he found what he was looking for. He turned to Edris and nodded before returning his attention to the book. An entry that he wasn't expecting caught his eye but he didn't want to discuss his findings in front of Harry and Jason so set about photocopying the relevant pages.

'That should do it.' Meadows picked up the pile of papers.

'Best put them in this.' Jason handed him an A4 envelope.

Meadows put the papers inside.

'Shall we take Eddy his book? Thanks for your help, Jason, and good luck with the new job.'

'I still can't believe that Jane and Miles had something to do with Alan's death,' Harry said as they walked up the stairs. 'Still, I guess you don't really know the people you work with that well. Surely now that you have arrested them we can go on the trip. You don't think that anyone else is involved, do you?'

'We haven't charged them yet, they are just helping us with our inquiries,' Meadows said.

Harry grinned. 'Short for you can't discuss the case with me.'

'I'll do my best to make sure that the residents don't miss out on their trip but my priority is their safety and that of the staff of course.'

'If you need someone to keep an eye on things, I don't mind going,' Edris offered. 'I'm due some leave.'

'Or we could send Blackwell,' Meadows teased.

They reached Eddy's room and Harry knocked and called out as she entered.

Eddy stood by the window rocking back and forth as he emitted a low humming noise.

'We've good news for you, Eddy,' Harry said. 'Your book has been found.'

Eddy turned to face the visitors, his expression neutral.

Meadows stepped forward and held out the book.

'There you go, I bet you'll be glad to have it back.'

Eddy snatched the book with a high-pitched squeal. Meadows took a step back, not sure if Eddy was about to attack him.

'Give him a minute,' Harry said.

Eddy opened the book and flicked through the pages, his eyes dancing over the words. He took a pen from his pocket and began writing furiously.

'I guess that means he is pleased,' Meadows said. He was about to turn to leave when Eddy sprang forward.

'Classified information.' Eddy thrust the book at Meadows.

Meadows opened the book and read a page. 'Thank you, Eddy.' He handed the book back. Eddy took it and walked to the window, keeping his back turned.

'That's his way of saying thank you,' Harry explained. 'He's never let anyone read the book before.'

They stepped out of the room with Meadows feeling touched by Eddy's gesture. 'It's very rewarding when you make a connection,' he commented.

'It is,' Harry agreed. 'I love working here, it feels like I'm making a difference to their lives. You become their family and they yours.'

'I think it takes a special kind of person, you must have more than your fair share of patience,' Edris said softly. Meadows noticed the glow in Harry's cheeks.

'Well I'd better get back to work, Liam will be waiting for his cake.'

'Nice seeing you again,' Edris said.

'You are incorrigible.' Meadows laughed as they walked to the car.

'What?' Edris raised his eyebrows.

'You know what, flirting with the poor girl. Getting her hopes up.'

'You never know, she might get lucky.' Edris winked. He slid into the passenger seat and buckled his belt. 'So I take it Miles and Jane were featured in Eddy's book.'

'Yes, and someone else, take a look for yourself.' Meadows passed the envelope to Edris and started the car.

'Cillian's Mini was there Monday night,' Edris said. 'And he said he was home all evening. I think we should pay him a visit.'

'So, according to Eddy's log, Alan arrived at 10 p.m., Jane five minutes later, then Miles at ten past. They drove off half an hour later, first Miles, then Jane and finally Alan. Alan's car is back at eleven, then there's an entry for Cillian's car but no time is logged.'

'Maybe Eddy didn't see Cillian arrive,' Meadows said. 'He could've moved away from the window, used the bathroom or even went to sleep and got up later.'

'He doesn't mention Jane or Miles coming back.'

'No, but they could have moved to a different location, drugged Alan then drove back in his car. Blackwell had a theory that they planned to set it up so it looked like one of the residents were responsible.'

'Not a bad theory, and that's why they needed to drug Leah and Gemma. Do you think they called Cillian to help?'

'It's possible, but I can't see why they would've involved him, unless he was in on it.' Meadows kept his eyes on the road as his mind whirred with possibilities. 'Let's see how he manages to explain his car being there. Liam seemed to be concerned for Leah's safety but I think he's been instructed not to tell.'

'Do you think Leah is frightened of Cillian?'

'He has a temper. If you watch the way his fists curl, it's like he's fighting for control. We should let it be known that we've found Alan's car. See what reaction we get. If he's involved, then Liam has good reason to worry about Leah's safety.'

Chapter Twenty-five

Meadows pulled up behind Cillian's Mini and looked at the house. The curtains were drawn but the window was illuminated by a soft glow from within. He looked at the parked cars as he left his.

'Looks like they're both in.' He indicated Leah's blue Fiesta, then knocked on the door.

A few minutes later the door was opened by Leah, who looked surprised to see them. Meadows noticed there was a little more colour in her cheeks and her grey roots had been covered.

'Oh, hello.'

Cillian appeared behind Leah and laid a hand on her shoulder. 'It's a bit late to be calling, we're just about to watch a film. We don't get a lot of time together.'

'Sorry to disturb you on your evening off but it's important we talk to you,' Meadows said.

'You better come in then.'

They gathered in the sitting room where an open bottle of wine stood next to two glasses and a half-eaten box of chocolates. Meadows watched Cillian take a seat on the sofa; he sat with his legs apart, hands resting on his knees. Leah sat close with her arm touching his.

Meadows sat down in the armchair and Edris took the other taking out his notebook.

'We heard about Jane and Miles getting arrested. Shocking news,' Cillian said with a ghost of a smile.

They looked more relaxed and there was a lighter atmosphere than the last time he had been there. Maybe they feel safer with Jane and Miles locked up. Meadows sat forward in the chair.

'We haven't charged either of them yet. We still haven't finished with our inquiries and need to clear a few things up.'

'Well I don't see how we can help. We've told you everything we know,' Cillian said.

'We've found Eddy's book.' Meadows looked at Cillian trying to gauge his reaction.

'I bet he was pleased.' Cillian's expression remained neutral.

'Yes he was.' Meadows smiled. 'He recorded a lot of information from last Monday night. Among the cars he noted was your red Mini. You told us you were in all evening.'

Cillian sat forward in the chair. 'I was in all evening.'

Meadows noticed a glimmer of anger in his eyes.

'Then how do you explain your car being at Bethesda at around 11 p.m.?' He was taking a chance on the time.

Leah looked at Cillian, concerned.

'Monday night?' Cillian ran his hand through his hair and bit his bottom lip in concentration.

'I'm sure you would remember going out at that time of the night and given that it was the night that Alan was murdered,' Meadows prompted.

'Oh yes, Leah had my car because hers wouldn't start. Sorry I forgot about that.' Cillian gave a forced smile.

Meadows turned to Leah. 'But your car was parked in Bethesda all night.'

'I… well… It was parked in Bethesda because it wouldn't start. I needed to go home to get a change of clothes because I was doing the night shift. I dropped Cillian off then drove back.'

'At 11 p.m.?'

'No, it was earlier than that. Maybe Eddy didn't notice Cillian's car until later.'

'The car was gone when Eddy awoke in the morning.'

'Because she had to pick me up for work,' Cillian said.

'You can check with Gemma,' Leah said. 'I had to leave her on her own when I picked up Cillian.'

'Well, that clears things up,' Meadows said. 'We have to make sure we cover every detail. It doesn't look good if we didn't check out every car that was in Bethesda that evening.'

'It all comes down to collecting as much evidence as we can,' Edris said. 'We've found Alan's car, which is a real breakthrough in the case.'

'Where was it?' Cillian asked.

'Burnt out up the mountain,' Meadows said. 'What people don't understand is that you can't destroy all traces of evidence with fire.'

'Forensics are really clever now, aren't they? I was watching a documentary the other day. Fascinating.' Cillian smiled.

Either he's telling the truth or he is arrogant enough to think he left no trace.

'Well, I think that's about all.' Meadows stood. 'When we spoke to Liam he seemed to be very concerned about keeping you safe. Why do you think that is?' He looked down at Leah.

Leah shifted in her seat. 'Who knows with Liam, the world is a dangerous place to him. He keeps safe by routines. Finding Alan's body has been difficult for him to process. He's very unsettled and sometimes he sees me as an extension of himself.'

'I see. Thank you for your time. We might have to speak with you again. There are certain aspects of the case that we cannot disclose at the moment.'

'I'll see you out.' Cillian stood and ushered them outside where he stood and watched them climb into the car.

'Do you think he's in on it?' Edris asked.

'I'm not sure, there's definitely something not right with those two.' Meadows watched Cillian close the door, and started the engine.

'Maybe it's just that they knew about Jane and Miles and were too afraid to say anything?'

'They did appear more relaxed today and if Cillian was involved in any way Jane would have been first to point the finger. Let's see what happens when she knows we have the book.'

* * *

The team gathered around Meadows' desk. Blackwell stood flanked by Paskin and Valentine, all three eagerly reading the copy of Eddy's book.

Blackwell's eyes skimmed across the pages. 'Got the bastards,' he said. 'Did you believe Cillian and Leah's story about the car?' He looked over the top of the page at Meadows.

'I'm not sure. Edris is trying to get hold of Gemma to see if she will corroborate Leah's story.'

'Let's hit Jane and Miles with this.' Blackwell waved the papers.

'It's getting late, maybe it's best to let them stew in the cell overnight and talk to them in the morning.'

'I'd rather do it now. They've already fucked up my weekend, if we interview them now and charge them we can all have a day off tomorrow.'

'I think you're being a bit optimistic,' Meadows said. 'Besides, I can't see Jane's solicitor being too happy about coming in this late.'

'I'll sort him out,' Blackwell barked.

Meadows looked at the rest of the team. They'd worked non-stop since Monday. They could all do with a day off. 'OK let's see what they have to say.' He turned to his computer and updated the case notes. 'You can go now if you want, Valentine,' he called over the top of the computer.

'I'll stay a bit longer, see if Blackwell gets a confession and I get a Sunday morning lie-in,' Valentine replied.

The notes were typed up and Meadows was checking through the statements when Folland rang to say that Jane's solicitor had arrived. Blackwell and Paskin were already interviewing Miles, who was still refusing legal counsel.

'Right, let's do this,' Meadows called to Edris.

Edris yawned loudly as they approached the interview room.

'Just how I feel,' Meadows said. He pushed open the door and took his seat behind the table.

The solicitor made a show of looking at his watch, which Meadows ignored. He looked at Jane, whose confidence seemed to have bolted. Mascara was smudged beneath her eyes which were swollen from recent tears.

'I'll get straight to the point,' Meadows said. 'We now have a witness that places you in Bethesda at 10 p.m. last Monday evening.'

'They've got it wrong.' Jane's voice was small.

'It's a reliable witness. Miles has been interviewed and made a statement that you asked him to set up Guardian Holdings and that you provided the capital. You've had plenty of time to think things over. As I said before, you're looking at maybe four years for misappropriation of funds. It will be a lot more for murder, so I suggest you start telling us the truth.'

Jane looked at her solicitor who leaned over and whispered in her ear. She nodded and turned her attention back to Meadows. 'I didn't kill Alan,' she stated.

'You were in Bethesda on Monday evening.'

Jane nodded.

'Is that a yes? For the record,' Edris said.

'Yes.' Jane glared at Edris, then sighed. Her shoulders slumped. 'It was Miles' idea that we set up the company, he said he'd done that sort of thing before. I honestly didn't see anything wrong in it. All that money sat in the accounts, it's not like they need it and they don't care about money, it means nothing to them.'

'You were in a position of trust. The money is to make their lives easier. The families of the residents trusted you.' Meadows made no effort to hide his disgust.

'We only took a little to start with,' Jane whined.

'So that made it alright?' Edris said.

'We put it all back, we only kept the profits. It's not like we stole from them. It was just an investment.'

'From which the residents didn't receive any benefit,' Meadows said.

Jane squirmed in her seat. 'Miles said we needed to invest more, so I transferred a bit more, we made a profit again, I put the money back and no one noticed, so we just kept increasing the amount each time. Then Alan found out and he wanted a cut, we paid him a monthly sum but he kept wanting more. I told Miles I wanted out. I was worried we'd get found out. Miles agreed but wanted to have one more go, this time we transferred a hundred and fifty thousand. The profit would have seen us alright for a long time. We invested in high risk high yield bonds but the issuer defaulted and we lost the lot.' Jane ran her hands through her hair and took a sip of water from the plastic cup on the table.

'I didn't know what to do, Alan still wanted his share of the money and the residents would need spending money for the holiday; it was only a matter of time before someone would notice. Miles said he would go up to London to see if he could get a loan from his parents. I went to the bank to see if I could increase the mortgage but I needed Huw's signature. If we could've just got enough money together to try again, we would have made the money back.' Jane's voice cracked.

'Go on.' Meadows felt no sympathy for her.

'Alan still wanted his money so I told him he had to wait for Miles to get back from London. I arranged to meet him in Bethesda car park. Miles thought we could persuade Alan to put up some money. I got to Bethesda at about ten, then Alan arrived and we waited for Miles. Alan went mad when Miles turned up without the money. He said he was going to grass us up. Miles said to go ahead as he was blackmailing us and was up to his neck in it. Things got out of hand then.'

Jane rubbed her hands over her face before she continued.

'There were a lot of accusations. Alan pushed Miles against the car. I thought Miles was going to hit Alan but he just laughed and said there wasn't anything Alan could do about it, he got in the car and drove off. He left me there. Alan turned on me. I didn't hang around. I got in the car, locked the doors and drove home. That was the last time I saw Alan until Leah found him in the freezer.'

Meadows sighed. 'You have continually lied, why should we believe you?'

'I'm telling the truth.'

'So how do you think Alan got into the freezer?'

'Miles. He must have gone back. When Alan was found Miles told me I had to keep my mouth shut. I was frightened. I thought I would end up the same way.' A tear trickled down her cheek.

'I think when you were left alone with Alan you persuaded him to go into the house and have a drink. You drugged him and called for someone to help, or maybe you called Miles back.'

'No, I drove home. I never went into the house.'

Meadows leaned forward. 'You knew Gemma and Leah would be asleep, you made sure of it.'

'What? I don't know what you are talking about.' Jane's face creased with confusion.

'You had access to the drug cabinet, you know the different types of medication and the effects. What did you do, mix up the cocoa powder with the meds or dissolve it in the kettle?'

Jane shook her head. 'I really don't know what you are talking about. Why would I put drugs in the kettle?'

Meadows sat back and folded his arms across his chest. 'Who else was with you that night?'

'No one, just Miles, Alan and myself. Alan was alive when I left him. Why would I kill him?'

'To keep him quiet about the money,' Edris said.

'It wouldn't have mattered, he couldn't have told anyone without getting himself in trouble, and besides we were going to get found out anyway. We had no way of getting that sort of money.'

'You could've been buying yourself some time. Did you plan on running away?' Meadows asked.

'No, where would I go?'

The solicitor made a show of looking at his watch again.

'My client has explained why her car was at Bethesda House, so if there is nothing else I think we should call an end to the interview, given the late hour.'

'I've told you everything,' Jane added.

'I doubt that,' Meadows said. 'Perhaps you will have a clearer mind in the morning.' He nodded to Edris who called an end to the interview.

Jane was led back to the cell and Meadows and Edris returned to the office where the team were waiting.

'So, did you get a confession?' Paskin asked.

'No, not to the murder. She admits to being involved in the misappropriation of the residents' funds. She claims she met with Alan in the car park on Monday night, left him there alive and drove home. She did seem genuinely confused about the drugs. What about Miles?'

'Same story,' Blackwell said. 'Well rehearsed.'

'I don't know,' Meadows said. 'Something isn't right.'

'So are you going to charge them with murder?' Valentine asked.

'I'll sleep on it. Let's call it a night, it's been a long day.' He looked around at the team. 'No point in coming in tomorrow, you all deserve a break and those two aren't going anywhere. Good job, thanks.'

They all filtered out of the office leaving Meadows alone at his desk. He updated the notes on the computer before grabbing his jacket and heading out the door. A feeling of foreboding followed him.

Chapter Twenty-six

Tara Lane sat at the bar of The Crown Inn gazing at her reflection in the mirror behind the rows of glasses. A melancholy cloud settled over her as she thought of all the times she had sat in bars and attracted male attention. She used her fingertips to push up the skin at the corner of her eyes. The effect was comical. It straightened the wrinkles but did nothing to the bags under her eyes or lines around her cracked lips.

'You OK there, Tara?' The barman drew her attention.

'Yeah.' She pushed the empty glass towards him. 'Same again.'

The barman frowned. 'Are you sure? You don't want to go falling on the way home.' He chuckled.

'I'm not pissed,' Tara retorted.

'OK, but this is your last one, I'm calling time in five.'

'Better make it a double then.'

The barman shook his head as he picked up the glass and turned to the optic.

Tara returned her gaze to the mirror. She could see a group of young men playing pool behind her. She pulled her top down to reveal a little more cleavage as the barman placed the drink in front of her. She paid for the drink then turned on the stool, wobbled and cursed as the contents of the glass spilt over her hand.

One of the men looked over and laughed. Tara licked the alcohol from her hand, running her tongue seductively along her finger.

'I think you're in there, Bryd.' The young man was nudged playfully by his mate.

'Ugh, fuck off! I wouldn't touch that munter with your dick, let alone my own.'

The words stung and Tara felt her cheeks burn. She knocked back her drink. An arm snaked around her waist and hot breath tickled her neck.

'Hello, darling.'

Tara turned her head and saw Joe grinning at her, a regular at the Crown. 'Get off,' she shouted out as she wriggled free.

'Oh don't be like that, I'll buy you a drink.' He stood next to her and leaned against the bar.

Tara could see his stomach hanging over his jeans and wrinkled her nose. 'And what do you want in return?'

'Just a bit of company.' Joe signalled the barman. 'Another pint, and stick a double in for Tara.'

'I think Tara's had enough,' the barman said.

'Go on, I'll walk her home, make sure she gets in safely.'

'Like hell you will,' Tara protested, 'but I'll have the drink.'

'So, what do you think of this business at Bethesda?' Joe took out his wallet and handed a note to the barman. 'Bloody loonies, next thing they'll be breaking into our houses, killing us in our beds.'

'Shut up, you don't know what you're talking about!' Tara said.

'They shouldn't be allowed in the community,' the barman commented.

'Yeah, there's places for people like them, I've heard they aren't even locked in, free to wander around,' Joe said.

Tara tried to block out the conversation but it was too late. Guilt gnawed at her stomach and she felt bile rise in her throat. She slid off the stool and landed unsteadily on her feet. She reached out her hands to steady herself on the bar, letting out a loud belch.

'You alright there? Don't go puking in here.' The barman barely hid his disgust.

'I need a piss,' Tara said. She made her way to the bathroom, using the wall as a prop. She reached the bathroom in time to vomit in the sink. She stood clutching the side of the basin as she waited for the spasm in her stomach to subside. A few minutes passed before she was able to look up at her reflection in the mirror. Mascara had run down her face, washing away a track of foundation. She took a tissue from her bag and rubbed at her face but it only served to smear the dark marks. Fresh tears leaked from her eyes, she wiped them away and staggered out of the bathroom.

Joe was still propping up the bar, talking to the barman. He turned and grinned when he noticed Tara. 'There you are, we thought you'd fallen asleep.' He walked towards her and grabbed her arm. 'Come on I'll take you home.'

'Get off.' Tara pulled her arm free. 'I can walk myself home. I don't want company.'

'No need to be like that.' Joe's eyes narrowed. 'Just looking out for you.'

Tara ignored him and grabbed her coat. Her head was spinning and she suddenly felt tired. All she wanted to do was climb into bed and block out the world. It was freezing outside with frost already glistening on the windscreens of parked cars. Tara didn't bother putting on her coat. She wanted to feel the cold bite at her skin and freeze out the guilt she felt.

At her front door she rummaged in her bag looking for her keys. Her fingers were numb with cold and she dropped the key twice before managing to insert it into the lock. As she pushed the handle down, she felt a hand clamp over her mouth. The alcohol had dulled her thoughts and reactions. She felt no fear. She tried to talk but the leathered fingers pushed her lips against her teeth.

She tried to claw at the hand that covered her mouth but her captor grabbed her by the wrist and twisted her hand behind her back. Pain shot through her arm, sharpening her senses. Joe. I'll kill the fucker when we get inside, she thought as she was shoved through the doorway.

Chapter Twenty-seven

Meadows arrived at the station early on Monday, had a quick chat with Folland then grabbed a cup of tea before heading for his desk. He had spent all day Sunday going over the case notes and reading through the statements and had finally made his decision on charging Miles and Jane for murder. The team hadn't arrived yet so he used the time to gather his thoughts and think of the best way to address them.

He stood and walked over to the incident board.

What are we missing?

'Morning.'

Meadows turned to see Edris plonk himself down at his desk.

'Good day off?' he asked.

'Boring.'

'So I take it you didn't have company.'

'I don't have a black book full of girls to call up, despite what everyone thinks. It would be handy though!'

Blackwell was next to saunter into the office. 'So, are we closing the case?' He leaned against the desk with his arms folded across his chest.

'And good morning to you,' Edris said.

Blackwell shot him a dirty look then turned expectantly to Meadows.

Meadows was about to speak when Paskin and Valentine walked in, chatting together as they removed their coats. He waited for them to settle then called the team to gather around the board.

'I have been over the case notes and statements and I've also received a preliminary report from forensics on the car. As it stands, we don't have enough evidence to charge Miles and Jane with murder.'

There was a general murmur of discontent.

'The iron found in the car has been matched to the weapon that caused the injuries to the back of Alan's head. Forensics have been unable to get any prints. Bloodstained clothing was found in the vehicle, the blood is a match to Alan's. The items were badly burned, and they are still working on identifying them. The material appears to be flannelette, common to pyjamas.' Meadows paused and looked around the group.

'The residents would have been wearing pyjamas,' Edris said.

'So, what, are you now saying that one of the residents killed Alan and the staff covered it up?' Blackwell frowned.

'Not necessarily, but one of them could have been present, witnessed the attack, which would have made things complicated,' Meadows said.

'Still puts Jane and Miles in the frame. They were there, had motive and opportunity. I think there's enough circumstantial evidence to charge them,' Blackwell said.

'There are still some inconsistencies. We know that Miles was in London until Monday evening so he wouldn't have had the opportunity to drug Leah and Gemma. Jane left the office at six and her husband said she had dinner with him that evening so she wouldn't have had time to go back to Bethesda House. Although we know her husband is an unreliable witness, we still don't have a sighting of her in Bethesda after six. It would be a big risk to drug the girls that early, there would be no one to settle the residents. The girls drank something between six and nine-thirty, so the drugs must have been added later than six.'

'Maybe she drugged the lot of them,' Valentine said. 'Then she would be sure that no one was awake.'

'There aren't enough drugs unaccounted for to have drugged all the residents and staff. We know that Kevin, Liam and Eddy were awake. Jane appeared puzzled when I mentioned the drugs. I'm inclined to believe her.'

'She's lied all the way along,' Blackwell huffed. 'So she slipped back into the house before Alan arrived. What does it matter?'

'We're not going to get a conviction unless we have a stronger case. We still haven't found Anna, the so-called relative that was asking questions.'

'If she even exists,' Paskin said.

'According to Eddy's book there was no one else there on Monday night,' Blackwell said.

'He didn't note any unusual cars but someone could have walked.'

'So, what are you saying? You think someone else is responsible?'

'No, I say we should keep asking questions, find the evidence. For the most part this looks like a carefully planned murder, the drugging of the girls to make sure there are no viable witnesses, but why drug Alan? The manner in which he was killed wasn't well planned. Hit over the head and bundled into the freezer. So, what went wrong?'

At that moment the door opened and Folland rushed in.

'Another suspicious death in Ynys Melyn.'

Images of the staff and residents flashed through Meadows' mind in quick succession and the feeling of foreboding that had hovered all weekend shrouded his body. 'Bethesda House?'

'No, the council estate. Hanes called it in.'

The team had fallen quiet and all eyes were on Meadows.

Blackwell broke the silence. 'We don't know that it is related yet?'

'A bit of a coincidence, though,' Paskin said.

'Let's see what we find when we get there.' Meadows picked up his jacket and signalled Edris to follow.

* * *

'I don't know what's worse, an unconnected murder or us getting it completely wrong,' Edris said as they sped towards Ynys Melyn.

'Two murders, the same village. I'm inclined to think the latter.'

'And you already had doubts about Jane and Miles.'

'Some. Like I said, it doesn't add up.'

As they approached the council estate, they could see two police cars and an ambulance parked outside a house, while a crowd had gathered on the opposite side of the road.

'Why do people have to do that? Are they hoping to see a body?' Edris said.

'Morbid curiosity. It's just human nature.'

They parked behind the ambulance where a woman wrapped in a blanket was being attended to by a paramedic. Meadows stepped out of the car and was met by PC Matt Hanes.

'What have you got for us Hanes?'

'Tara Lane, forty-eight years old, lives alone, found by her friend, Sarah Higgs.' He indicated the woman in the ambulance. 'She's had a bit of a shock. Came to pick her up for work, the door was unlocked, no sign of a break-in. Doc's in there now.'

'OK, we'll talk to her later.'

At the front door they covered their shoes and snapped on latex gloves before crossing the threshold and following the path laid down by forensics. The first thing Meadows noticed was the stale smell of alcohol mixed with an acrid smell of urine. They stood in a small entrance hall with stairs to the left and an open door leading to the living room on the right. His stomach tightened with tension.

He turned to Edris. 'Are you OK?'

'Yeah.' Edris wrinkled his nose. 'It's just the thought of what's behind that door.'

Meadows nodded and walked forward. The room was cluttered and untidy. Light streamed through the window, falling upon the body of Tara Lane which lay on the sofa, with the doctor leaning over it. Her eyes stared, glazed and lifeless. One hand trailed the floor while the other clutched an empty bottle to her chest. Another bottle was tucked at the side of her head and various wine and spirit bottles were lined up on the floor.

'Looks like a hell of a party,' Edris commented. 'Probably drank too much and choked on her own vomit.'

'Not far off.' The doctor straightened up and turned towards them. 'But my guess is she had some help.'

Meadows stepped closer and peered at her face. There were marks on both cheeks and vomit had trickled from her mouth and dried on her chin. 'Mouth forced open?'

'Looks that way,' the doctor said. 'And there's this.' He grabbed her forearm and pointed to the marks around her wrist.

'Tied up, so looks like she was moved after she died. Laid out for show,' Meadows said.

'Or to make it look like she passed out and choked on her own vomit.' The doctor dropped the dead woman's hand which fell with a thud. 'She emptied her bladder at some point.' He pointed to the stains on her trousers. 'Dead about eight hours.'

Meadows turned to Edris. 'Give Daisy Moore a call, I'd like her to take a look before we move her.'

'I don't see what more she can tell you without the post-mortem,' the doctor said.

'Puts things in context,' Meadows replied. 'Better than looking at photographs.'

'Right, there's no more for me to do here.' The doctor picked up his kit and walked out.

'Is that man ever cheerful?' Meadows asked.

'Not that I've seen. Guy needs to get laid once in a while.' Edris chuckled.

While Edris made the call to Daisy Moore, Meadows looked around the house. In the kitchen SOCO worked silently gathering prints and bagging various items. The sink was filled with dirty dishes and the kitchen table was smeared with crumbs.

'Anything interesting, Mike?'

'Not much. There's a stain on one of the kitchen chairs.' He pulled it from under the table.

Meadows peered closely. 'Urine?'

'Yes, looks like it.'

'Likely she was tied to the kitchen chair, poor woman.'

'Moore is on her way,' Edris called through the door.

Meadows felt a tingle brush his skin at the mention of her name. 'Thanks, Mike.' He walked back into the living room. 'We'll have a look upstairs then have a chat with Tara's friend while we wait for Daisy.'

Upstairs was in the same disarray. In the bedroom, clothes were strewn on the floor and drawers were half-open, the contents spilling out.

'Not one for housework,' Edris said.

'I guess not.' Meadows opened the bedside drawer, which held several packets of condoms and a vibrator.

Edris peered in the drawer and smirked. 'That explains the lack of cleaning.'

'Looks like she had a boyfriend,' Meadows said. He moved into the bathroom and checked the cabinet. 'Not a regular boyfriend though, only female products in here. Let's talk to the friend.'

They walked outside. Meadows inhaled the fresh air, trying to eliminate the smell of death. Sarah Higgs sat in the ambulance, a blanket around her shoulders, clutching a cup.

'I see someone has brought you a hot drink.' Meadows smiled and sat next to her.

'One of the neighbours,' Sarah croaked.

'Are you feeling up to answering some questions?'

Sarah nodded and looked into the cup.

'Can you talk me through what happened this morning?'

'I... I came to pick Tara up for work. I beeped outside as I usually do. When she didn't come out, I thought maybe she'd overslept.'

Sarah shivered and pulled at the blanket. 'I knocked on the door then tried the handle, the door was open.' She drew a shuddering breath. 'I went inside and called upstairs then went into the sitting room, that's when... she was... just lying there, eyes open.' She covered her mouth as a sob shook her body.

Meadows laid a hand on her arm. 'It must have been a terrible shock for you.'

Sarah nodded and wiped her tears with the back of her hand.

'Do you often pick Tara up for work?'

'Yes, she doesn't drive.'

'Where do you work?' Edris asked.

'BM Packing, Coopers Hill.'

'Have you known Tara long?' Meadows asked.

'About eight years.'

'Does she have a boyfriend?' Edris said, looking up from his notebook.

'No, her husband died a few years ago. I don't think there's been anyone since.' Sarah's hands shook as she sipped from the cup.

'Just a few more questions,' Meadows said kindly. 'We need to contact Tara's next of kin, do you know who that might be?'

'No.'

'Children? Siblings? Are her parents still alive?'

'Tara didn't have any children. Her mother's in a nursing home in Cardiff. She took the train to visit her some weekends.'

'OK, thanks. We might need to talk to you again.' Meadows stood. 'One more thing: did Tara ever mention Bethesda House?'

'No, I don't think so.'

Meadows stepped out of the ambulance leaving Sarah in the care of the paramedic. He noticed that the neighbours had come out despite the cold and stood on their doorsteps either side of Tara's house. He turned to Edris. 'Let's see if they saw anything.'

'I'll take the one on the left,' Edris said.

Meadows studied the young woman on the left. Her long blond hair was tucked to one side; she stood with a toddler balanced on her hip watching the activity. 'Now why doesn't that surprise me? Go on then use your charm.'

'Oh I will.'

Edris walked off.

Meadows joined Hanes who was talking to a man he guessed to be in his late forties. He was unshaven, dressed in jeans and a hoodie and leaned heavily on a walking stick.

'This is Colin Evans,' Hanes said.

'Hello, Mr Evans,' Meadows said. 'Did you see Tara last night?'

'I saw her about seven, I was putting out the bins.'

'Did you talk to her?'

'No, not really. Just said hello.' Evans took a pack of cigarettes out of his pocket.

'Do you know where she may have been going?'

'Up to the Crown, I would think. She goes most nights.' He pushed a cigarette between his lips and lit up.

'How long has she lived next door?'

Evans drew in a lungful of smoke and blew it out slowly. 'Must be about ten years. She moved down from Cardiff.'

'With her husband?'

'Yeah, Wayne. Died of cancer a few years ago. Tara took it bad, started hitting the bottle.'

'Did you see or hear her come back last night?'

'No, I would've been in bed. Tara didn't usually come back until closing time.'

'Did Tara have many visitors?'

'You mean men?' Colin smirked.

'Not necessarily, but go on.'

'She sometimes brought company back from the pub.'

'Anyone in particular?'

'Not really. So, what's going on in there?' Colin took another drag of the cigarette pulling it down to the tip. 'Her friend is in a hell of a state, I took her a cup of tea. You must think someone has done her in or you wouldn't be here.'

'It's too early to tell,' Meadows said.

'Do you think it's one of those lot?' He inclined his head in the direction of Bethesda.

Meadows felt a prickle of irritation. 'No, we have no reason to believe that the residents of Bethesda House have any involvement. Why would you think that?'

'Well, after what happened last week, we've all been a little worried.'

'Did Tara have any connection to Bethesda? Work or visit there?'

'No, I don't think so.'

'OK, thanks. PC Hanes will take your statement.'

As Meadows turned away, he saw Daisy Moore approaching and felt a warmth spread through his body. Her hair was pulled back with small tendrils coiling behind her ears. As she neared, she smiled, illuminating her face.

'Nice to see you again.' Meadows struggled to hold his poise.

'Nice?' She raised an eyebrow. 'Most greet me like the Grim Reaper.'

Save my soul, I'm going to have to get lessons from Edris.

'Well, I… I appreciate you coming out here.'

'No problem, it's good to get out.'

'Hiya.' Edris joined them. 'Neighbour didn't see or hear anything. Doesn't sound like she was particularly friendly with Tara, so couldn't tell me much.'

'I got much the same, it's seems that she frequented the local most nights maybe we'll have better luck there.' The sky darkened and there was a rumble of thunder. He turned to Daisy. 'Shall we go in before the rain comes?' An image of removing his coat and draping it over Daisy's shoulders flashed across his mind. He groaned inwardly as he followed her into the house.

Get a grip.

'Right then, sweetie, let's take a look at you.' Daisy knelt beside Tara. 'Forty-eight you said,' she addressed Meadows.

'Yes, she looks a lot older.' He stepped closer.

'A hard life perhaps,' she picked up Tara's right arm with care and examined it closely. 'Old scars, looks like she was a user in the past, but nothing to indicate any recent use of drugs.' She moved a gloved finger over the marks on Tara's wrist before gently placing the arm back to its original position. She repeated the same process on the left arm. 'No rope burns or residue from tape on her wrists. Cable ties?'

Meadows was touched by the way Daisy examined the body. She continued to talk to Tara as she made her examination, making notes and instructing the photographer.

'You should take a look at this,' Daisy called over her shoulder.

Meadows peered into Tara's mouth where Daisy pointed to a swelling at the back of throat. 'It looks like something was forced down her throat.'

'Do you think a bottle?'

'No, I don't think so. Something with a sharper or thinner edge. Whatever it was scraped the side of her throat.'

'Maybe they tried to force pills and alcohol down her throat to make it look like suicide,' Edris suggested.

'A poor attempt,' Daisy said. 'The bruising on her cheeks? Marks from fingers prising her mouth open. I don't think she died quickly. See these tiny spots – burst blood vessels consistent with asphyxiation. Then the marks on her wrist. I don't think your killer was trying to cover their tracks. It looks like they chose this method to kill her. I'll know more when I carry out the post-mortem.'

'Did she die on the sofa?' Meadows asked.

'No, she was moved after death.'

'There's some staining on one of the kitchen chairs.' Meadows rubbed his chin. 'I think she died in the kitchen and was moved in here. The killer wanted her found like this, surrounded by empty bottles.'

Daisy stood and snapped off her gloves. 'I'll carry out the post-mortem as a priority. I'll call you as soon as I have something for you.'

'Thank you.' Meadows smiled. He was aware of Edris watching him closely. 'We'd better get back to the station and brief the team.'

He picked up a picture of Tara before leaving the house.

* * *

'You should just ask her out,' Edris said as they climbed into the car.

'I don't know what you are talking about.'

Meadows started the engine.

'Come off it! The air was thick with sexual tension. I could barely breathe,' Edris said with a laugh.

'She probably already has a boyfriend, and besides we are in the middle of an investigation. It wouldn't be professional to go asking out the pathologist.'

'She's single.'

'Is she?'

'Well, it's not as if she gets a lot of dates. Who'd want to date someone who works with dead bodies all day?'

I would.

'It's not going to happen. I'm not about to make a fool of myself.' Meadows stretched out his hand and turned on the stereo. The music vibrated through the car as he tried to chase away thoughts of Daisy.

Chapter Twenty-eight

'Chief is in,' Folland called out as Meadows walked through the station doors.

'I'd better start calling you *sir*, then,' Edris said. 'Do you think he's come to take over?'

'It's unlikely, he has enough to deal with, can't be easy covering as many stations as he does. He does have a right to be concerned though. Two murders in one week.' Meadows hurried up the stairs. 'Don't look so worried, he's just a man doing his job like the rest of us.'

'No he's not, he's the chief. Our careers are in his hands,' Edris said. 'I don't know how you're staying so cool.'

'You worry too much.' Meadows laughed as they walked into the office.

DCI Lester stood talking to Blackwell. He was dressed in a dark grey suit with a crisp white shirt. His expression was serious as he listened intently.

Meadows stepped forward. 'Good morning, sir.'

'Morning.' Lester turned his slate grey eyes to Meadows. 'Blackwell has just been filling me in on the case. I expect you want to brief the team so I won't delay you. We can talk after.'

'Thank you, sir.'

Meadows walked to the incident board and pinned up a picture of Tara as the team gathered around. Lester took a seat and sat with his hands folded on his lap.

'Tara Lane. Found this morning at her home by her friend Sarah Higgs who had come to pick her up for work. Lives alone, no family apart from a mother in a residential home somewhere in Cardiff, who we need to trace. She was killed sometime after midnight – initial examination suggests asphyxiation, she was tied up, her mouth forced open and an object forced down her throat, possibly to pour down alcohol or pills until she choked.'

'Nasty,' said Lester.

'Yes. We'll know more when the post-mortem is carried out, hopefully later this afternoon. There was no sign of a break in, so either the killer caught her unaware as she opened the door or she knew her killer and let them in. The body was moved and placed on the sofa with several empty bottles of vodka and absinthe.'

'Absinthe! That stuff is lethal,' Blackwell said. 'They certainly meant business.'

'Why kill her in this way, and what's the connection to Alan Whitby and Bethesda House?' Meadows looked around the team.

'You think they're connected?' Lester asked.

'I'm fairly certain. Two murders, the same village, a week apart. Too much of a coincidence. It looks like Tara was seeing someone, not a regular boyfriend. Perhaps Alan Whitby – he was known to have had several affairs. We need to speak to everyone that knew Tara, find out if she had been seeing Alan or anyone else at Bethesda. She may even have worked there at some time.'

'Perhaps she witnessed something on Monday night. She lives close to Bethesda,' Paskin suggested.

'Good point,' Meadows said, 'but the nature in which Tara was killed and laid out suggests something more personal. The killer wanted her to suffer. Blackwell,

Paskin, can I leave it to you two to carry out the search of the house when forensics have finished? Go through everything. I don't think she was well off, judging by the way she lived, but there may be an insurance policy. We also need to find her mother, she needs to be told before she sees it in the news, and she may be able to provide some valuable background. Better check Alex Henson and Rhys Owens, see if they have any connection with Tara.'

'What about Miles and Jane?' asked Blackwell.

'They're due in court in an hour, but yes, talk to them again.'

'My pleasure,' Blackwell said with a grin.

'Edris and I will talk to the landlord at The Crown Inn. Tara was there last night and I want see if she left alone. I'll meet you at the house. Valentine, could you make a few copies of Tara's picture then talk to Sarah Higgs and Tara's work colleagues. Thanks, everyone.'

As the team set about their tasks Meadows followed Lester into the office and closed the door.

Lester took a seat behind the desk. 'You seem to have everything under control. Do you need any extra personnel?'

Meadows knew Lester was referring to outside help, a move that neither man wanted. 'I don't think that would be beneficial at the moment. Uniform are carrying out house-to-house and will follow up on any leads. Further enquires at Bethesda House need to be handled delicately. The residents have met the team. Any new faces will cause unnecessary upset.'

'I quite agree.' Lester smiled. 'I'll handle the press, and of course clear all overtime. I'll work from here for the next couple of days.'

'Thank you, sir.'

Meadows stood, he was keen to get out of the office and on with the investigation.

'Blackwell seems more settled. He actually smiled,' Lester said. 'It's good to see the team working together. I miss it sometimes. I must confess I was a little concerned bringing you in over Blackwell but I think it's worked out for the best.'

'It's a good team,' Meadows said. 'Valentine has worked well in the unit, perhaps it may be time to move her out of uniform. Blackwell would be happy to have a DC.'

'I'll have a word with her, and perhaps with Edris. It's time he thought about taking his sergeant exams. At least you would be paired with a DS – unless of course you want to reconsider working with Blackwell.' A smile played on his lips.

'Oh, I think Edris is ready – and Blackwell is better working on his own initiative.'

'I'll trust your judgement. Right, I'll leave you to get on.'

Meadows grabbed a photo of Tara before calling Edris and heading out of the station.

* * *

'Eifion Roberts is the landlord of The Crown Inn,' Edris said as Meadows started the car.

'Well, if Tara frequented his pub as often as the neighbours say then hopefully he'll be able to tell us a little more about her. So far we don't have a lot.'

A sudden hail shower beat down on the windscreen and Meadows reached out to turn up the blowers.

'They're forecasting snow tomorrow,' said Edris.

'That will please Kevin,' Meadows said.

'I don't get it.' Edris fidgeted in his seat. 'Why kill Tara when Jane and Miles are in the frame? Surely the killer would want to lay low for a while.'

'I think our killer is rattled and this is far from over.'

'You think there'll be more killings?'

Meadows glanced across at Edris and nodded, and turned his attention back to the road. 'I think it likely. If we can find a motive for Tara's murder, then I think we'll have the case solved. Until then I think the residents and staff at Bethesda House could still be in danger. I don't think this is about money.'

'Someone else could be involved with Miles and Jane,' Edris said.

'I can't see it. Jane would have thrown suspicion on anyone to shift the blame. She would've told us if there was a third party. She isn't going to take the rap alone.'

'I guess so; so that leaves us with Cillian. I can't see it being one of the women.'

'Why not? Just because you have the hots for one of them? A pretty face doesn't make you any less capable of murder. If Tara had been drinking heavily last night she could have easily been overpowered. There was no sign of a break-in, maybe she didn't feel threatened and let the killer in.'

'But you thought two people were responsible for Alan's murder.'

'I didn't say it couldn't be two women, and don't forget Rhys Owens and Alex Henson. They aren't out of the frame yet. Then there's the mysterious Anna.'

The inspector pulled up outside The Crown Inn and zipped up his coat before stepping out of the car. Cigarette butts littered the pavement outside the front door. The windows were encrusted with grime and blue paint peeled from the sills.

'So much for the nightlife,' said Edris.

Meadows knocked on the door which was opened a few moments later by a middle-aged man wearing black joggers and a T-shirt.

'Eifion Roberts?' Meadows asked.

'Yeah?' The man yawned.

Meadows showed his identification as he introduced himself and Edris.

'This about Tara? Colin next door to her phoned a few moments ago. Can't believe it. You better come in. I was just about to make a cuppa. Want one?'

'Oh yes,' Edris said.

They followed Eifion into the kitchen where he placed two extra mugs on the counter, flicked the switch on the kettle and turned to the stove.

'Mind if I carry on with my breakfast?'

'Go ahead,' Meadows said. 'Was Tara here last night?'

'Yeah, Tara was in here every night.'

Eifion placed a frying pan over the hot ring, then picked up the kettle and poured boiling water into the mugs.

'Was Tara a heavy drinker?' Meadows asked.

Eifion stirred the tea thoughtfully. 'I guess so, she drank every night but I wouldn't say that she was an alcoholic. She held down a job and was usually sober when she came in, unlike some. You see them come in here as soon as the doors open, already tanked up. Sugar?'

'Two please,' Edris said.

'Not for me, thanks.'

Meadows accepted the offered tea. 'Anything different about Tara last night or the past week?'

'She seemed a little down, knocking them back a bit.'

'Did she say why?'

'No, she wasn't one to talk about herself.'

Eifion returned to the stove where he put a couple of rashers of bacon into the pan.

'If anything, she was quieter than usual. She got upset before she left last night. Joe offered to walk her home but she wasn't having any of it.'

'Joe?' Edris eyed the bacon.

'Joe Morgan, another regular, lives down the road. Number eighty-seven I think.'

'Did he leave with Tara?' Meadows asked.

'Just after.'

'And Tara argued with him?' Meadows took a sip of his tea.

'Not really an argument. We were talking about the murder up at Bethesda. It's all that's been talked about for a week. Tara got upset then went staggering off to the toilet, came back, grabbed her coat and walked out.'

'Why was she upset by the conversation? Was she worried about living so close to Bethesda or was it something else? Did she know the victim, Alan Whitby?'

'I don't know.' Eifion slid the bacon from the pan onto a slice of bread and added brown sauce. 'If anything she seemed to be defending the inmates.'

'You mean residents.' Meadows didn't bother to hide his irritation.

'Yeah if you want to call them that. Maybe she felt sorry for them.' He bit into his sandwich. 'Who knows what she was thinking, she was well gone when she left here.'

'Was there anyone else here last night?'

'Just a couple of the local lads playing pool, it was quiet.'

'Does Joe work?'

'No, he used to work down the pits. Hasn't worked since they closed – like a lot of men his age.'

Meadows drank the remains of his tea and laid the cup on the counter. 'Ok, well, thanks for your time, we'll see ourselves out.'

* * *

'He could have offered us a bacon butty,' Edris complained as they drove the short distance to Joe's house.

'Hungry are you?' Meadows laughed.

'Yeah, it's past lunchtime – and the smell of frying bacon, even *you* must find it irresistible.'

'I can resist, doesn't do anything for me.'

'You veggies don't know what you are missing,' Edris said.

'But my arteries do.'

Meadows grinned.

They pulled up outside Joe's terraced house and climbed out of the car.

'It's bloody freezing.' Edris pulled the collar up on his coat.

'You're in a right whinging mood today,' Meadows teased as he knocked the door.

'You need to feed me once in a while.'

The door opened to reveal a man with receding grey hair and a pot belly straining his jumper.

'Joe Morgan?' Edris asked as he showed his identification. 'We'd like to ask you a few questions.'

'It's not convenient at the moment.' Joe moved backwards.

Meadows stepped closer and caught the pungent scent of cannabis.

'It's important that we speak to you. How about we give you a minute to dispose of the joint then you can invite us in.'

'I don't… well, I…' Joe stuttered. 'I have arthritis.'

He turned away from the door.

'You should've nicked him for possession then asked questions,' Edris said.

'Is it worth the paperwork? Unless you think he has a factory in the attic we have more important things to worry about.'

'You're too soft.'

'I like to see the best in people.'

Joe appeared in the doorway looking sheepish. 'You better come in then.'

He led them into the sitting room where a chat show played on the television. Joe picked up the remote control, muted the sound and plonked himself down on the sofa.

'What's this about then?'

Meadows perched on the armchair. 'You were in The Crown Inn last night.'

'Yes.'

'You talked to Tara Lane.'

'Yeah.' Joe frowned. 'Has something happened to Tara? I saw an ambulance go past this morning.'

'Tara Lane was found dead at home this morning.'

'Tara, dead? No.'

Meadows was surprised to see Joe's eyes fill with tears. 'I should've insisted on walking her home. She was well gone, even Eifion was worried she would fall.' Joe rubbed at his eyes.

'Tara didn't have an accident,' Edris said. 'She died in suspicious circumstances.'

'You mean someone… no, who would want to hurt Tara?' Joe sniffed.

'Eifion said you left after Tara last night,' Edris continued.

'Yes, but…' Joe shook his head. 'You don't think I had anything to do with it. I'd never hurt Tara.'

'You and Tara had an argument last night,' Meadows said.

'Not really, she was in a pissy mood, that's all. I offered to walk her home but she didn't want me to.'

'Did you follow her home?' Edris leaned forward.

'No, she was walking ahead of me when I left the pub. I called out to her but she ignored me so I came home. I can't believe it, Tara gone.'

'Did you see anyone else as you walked home?'

'No, no one.'

'Did Tara have a boyfriend?' Meadows asked.

'No, I don't think so. I never saw her with anyone.'

'Were you in a relationship with Tara?'

'I wouldn't call it a relationship. We were friends. Kept each other company now and again.'

'You mean you had sex,' Edris said.

'Yes, nothing wrong with that. We were just two lonely people.' Joe wiped away a tear. 'Tara was alright, a good laugh.'

'Eifion thought that something was bothering Tara, that she had been quiet this past week. Do you know what had upset her?' Meadows asked.

'No. She had been a bit funny since the murder up at Bethesda. She didn't want to talk about it, which was odd because Tara liked a bit of gossip.'

'Did she know Alan Whitby?'

'I don't think so, she never mentioned him. I can't see Tara having anything to do with him. Wasn't her type.'

'What do you mean?'

'He'd drive by in that Jag of his, stuck-up, both him and that woman who runs the place. Tara was down to earth.'

'Did she ever talk about Bethesda House, the staff or residents?'

'Not that I remember.'

'Could she have worked there in the past?'

'No, she would have said, especially after what happened there.'

'OK, we'll need to take a statement from everyone that was in the Crown last night. So expect a call.' Meadows stood. 'Did Tara talk about her mother?'

'Yeah, the old lady's in a home. Tara used to go and visit.'

'Do you know her mother's name or the name of the residential home?'

'No, she didn't say.'

'Well, if you think of anything that may be important please call the station.'

* * *

'So what now?' Edris asked.

'Grab some lunch, then go and see how they are getting on with the search in Tara's house. Maybe you'll be in a better mood after you've eaten.'

Edris was stuffing down a bar of chocolate as Meadows parked outside Tara's house where Matt Hanes stood hopping from foot to foot.

'You have no luck.' Edris laughed as they approached the front door.

'Tell me about it! I can't feel my toes,' Hanes complained.

'As soon as they've finished the search, secure the house then get back to the station to warm up,' Meadows said.

'Thanks.'

Hanes stood aside for them to enter the house.

Blackwell's voice could be heard drifting down the stairs. They followed the sound and found Blackwell barking into his phone while Paskin shifted through a box of paperwork.

'Found anything interesting?' Meadows asked.

'Yes, we found an insurance policy and a will,' Paskin replied.

'Go on.'

'Looks like she left everything to Bethesda House.'

'Who is the executor of the will?'

'Sarah Higgs. Blackwell is just checking with the insurance company now.'

Meadows waited for Blackwell to finish the call. 'Policy's still in force and paid up to date. Looks like Bethesda House is 100K richer,' he said.

'That's some policy! There's our connection, but why? Was the money bequeathed to anyone in particular?'

'No, sounds like it was the home.'

'Maybe she had a relative there,' Paskin said. 'According to Sarah Higgs she had no relatives other than her mother.'

'Maybe she had a soft spot for the place. Some people leave money to dogs' homes,' Edris said.

'Yes, but Bethesda isn't a charity.'

'Well, if Miles and Jane knew about the policy, then Tara's death would have solved their little problem,' said Blackwell.

'Yes,' Edris said, 'but as they were safely locked up last night, they couldn't have had anything to do with Tara's death.'

'Yeah, but there could be someone else mixed up in their scheme. There's Jane's husband, he was pretty desperate yesterday to get her released, or they could have paid someone.'

'A hit man in Ynys Melyn?' Edris laughed.

'You got any better ideas?' Blackwell growled.

'I think it's worth following up,' Meadows said. He turned to Paskin. 'Talk to Huw Pritchard. Have you found out any information about Tara's mother?'

'Nothing yet,' Paskin said. 'Valentine's looking into it.'

Meadows looked around the bedroom where all that remained of Tara's life had been upturned and laid bare for all to see. He shook off the gloomy thoughts and turned to Edris.

'Come on, let's go to Bethesda.'

Chapter Twenty-nine

'Winter Man!'

Kevin leapt up from the floor, where he was playing Twister with some of the other residents.

Meadows braced himself for the hug. 'How's it going, Kevin?'

'I've been shopping.' Kevin grinned.

'What did you buy?'

'I'll show you.' Kevin shuffled out of the room.

Meadows turned to the rest of the group. Liam was tangled with Nicole, Harry and Leah while Danielle sat with Vanessa spinning the Twister wheel. Eddy stood scribbling in his book and Jason sat at the table playing cards with Steven and Cillian.

'Sorry to interrupt your fun,' Meadows said, 'but I would like each of you to look at this photograph and tell me if you have seen this lady.'

Danielle stood and took the photograph, shook her head and showed it to Nicole who wasn't interested in looking, then she handed it to Gemma.

Gemma stared at the photograph. 'I think I've seen her before.'

'Has she visited the home?' Meadows asked.

'No, I saw her outside on the pavement a few times.'

'Did she say anything to you?'

'No, she seemed to be passing by and just stopped to look at the house. Some people are curious.'

Meadows took the photograph and handed it to Cillian. 'No, never seen her.' Cillian gave the picture a cursory glance before handing it to Leah.

'Who is she?' Leah asked.

'Tara Lane, she was found dead this morning,' Edris said.

'Dead?' Leah's hand shook as she passed the photograph back to Meadows.

'Are you OK?' Meadows asked.

'Yes… it's just–'

'It brings it all back,' Cillian interrupted. 'It's only been a week since she found Alan.' He took hold of Leah's hand. Meadows noticed that Leah snatched it away before she moved next to Liam who was spinning the Twister wheel.

What's going on with those two?

'Do you think she has some connection with Bethesda?' Jason asked as he looked at the photo.

'We believe the two deaths are connected.'

'I thought this was over now that Jane and Miles have been arrested. Are you saying there's someone else involved?' Harry asked as she took a copy of the photo from Edris.

'We're looking into that possibility. We haven't charged Jane and Miles with Alan's murder,' Edris said.

'We're going to need each of you to give an account of your whereabouts last night,' Meadows said.

'Winter Man, look!' Kevin shuffled into the room dragging a suitcase behind him. He picked up the case and held it out to Meadows.

Meadows examined the case and smiled. It was bright pink with large white spots. 'I don't think I have ever seen such a magnificent suitcase!'

'With snow.' Kevin pointed to the white spots and beamed.

'He chose it himself, didn't you, Kevin,' Gemma said.

'And now we put in our clothes,' Kevin said with a grin.

'Not yet, in nine days.'

'Nine days, nine days!' Kevin jumped up and down waving his hands.

'Shut up, Kevin,' Liam yelled and put his hands over his ears.

'Kevin, can you look at this photo for me?' Meadows asked. 'Have you seen this lady? Maybe outside.'

Kevin held the photo close to his face his eyes narrowing in concentration.

'No. Do you want to come on holiday with me?'

'I would love to come, Kevin, but I have to work.'

'Poor Winter Man.' Kevin frowned.

'Don't worry about me, you can show me photos when you get back.' Meadows turned to the rest of the group. 'As I was saying, we need you all to account for your movements last night.'

'Surely you don't think any of us is involved?' Harry said.

'I'm afraid we have to look at every possibility. You all have a connection with Alan Whitby, so yes, we have to ask so we can eliminate you from our inquiries.'

'Well, I was at home last night,' Harry said.

'Alone?' Edris asked, his eyes twinkling.

'Yes, I had an early night. I'm on night duty tonight.'

'I was at home,' Danielle said. 'I live with my parents so you can check with them.'

'Same here,' Gemma added.

'We were both home all night,' Cillian said.

Leah nodded.

'I went out to dinner with my wife, it was her birthday. Afterwards we went home and finished off a bottle of wine,' Jason said.

'Thank you.' Meadows looked around at the group. 'I will have an officer present overnight, it's just a precaution. In the meantime, I would ask you all to be vigilant. If you see or hear anything out of the ordinary then please call the station–' His phone vibrated in his pocket. He took it out and saw Daisy's name flash across the screen. 'Excuse me one moment.' He walked out into the hallway.

'Meadows.'

'Hi, I've finished the PM and sent samples to the lab.'

Her voice sent a warm tingle through his chest. 'OK, we will be with you shortly.'

'I haven't written up the report yet, but I can talk you through it now on the phone if you're busy.'

'I'd prefer to do it face to face.'

'Great, I'll see you soon.'

Meadows walked back into the sitting room, where the game of Twister had resumed and Edris stood talking to Harry, his body angled towards her and a flirtatious smile on his face.

'We have to go.'

'Catch you later.' Edris winked at Harry before following Meadows outside.

'I can't leave you alone for five minutes!'

'Just passing the time,' Edris said.

'Daisy called. She's finished the post-mortem so we need to get over there to see what she's found.'

Edris laughed. 'Ah, so that's why you're in such a hurry.'

'No, well, yes, I'm eager to see her findings.' Meadows opened the car door and slid behind the wheel.

'If you say so,' Edris said as he clipped on his seat belt. 'It's about time you put yourself out there.'

'I have no intention of putting myself out there.'

Meadows switched on the stereo and turned up the volume.

'What are you assaulting my ears with now?' Edris complained.

'Thin Lizzy. Music helps me think.'

'No one can think with that racket, you need to update your collection.'

'Nothing wrong with my collection. I also like Bob Marley and I've got some country music.' Meadows pulled out into the road. 'What would you prefer?'

'If I could connect my phone I'd show you, but even the stereo is outdated.'

'Cheeky sod! Maybe I should swap you with Blackwell, at least he only grunts now and again.'

'I don't think he'd like your choice of music either.'

'Maybe not, I think he's more the classical type.'

Edris laughed. 'Yeah, I can see him chilling out to opera. Seriously though, when were you last out on a date?'

'It's been a while. I'm out of practice.'

'You haven't tried. There is plenty on offer, I've seen the way women look at you. You're a tidy-looking guy, you're just oblivious to the signs.'

'Thank you.' Meadows laughed. 'I wouldn't know where to start, it's been so long since I asked a woman out.'

'It's easy, just ask someone out for a drink.'

'Someone?' Meadows glanced at Edris.

'Daisy.'

Meadows snapped his eyes back to the road. 'No, I'm not making a fool of myself.'

'You wouldn't, she likes you. Poor woman is just waiting for you to rip off her clothes and make love under the watchful eyes of the corpses.'

'Bloody hell, there's something seriously wrong with your imagination!' Meadows laughed. 'I'm not listening to you anymore, I need to get that image out of my head.' He reached out and turned up the volume as they sped towards the hospital.

* * *

They found Daisy in her office, music playing as she tapped away at the keyboard. Her hair was loose and cascaded over her shoulders. Meadows was horrified as an image of Daisy removing her clothes flashed across his mind.

Bloody Edris, he's damaged my mind! Think about the case.

'Hi.' Daisy looked up from the screen and smiled. 'Give me a sec and I'll be with you.' She finished typing and saved the document. 'Right, I'll take you through.'

She stood and pulled on a gown before twisting her hair into a knot and securing it with a band.

'Thanks for rushing the PM through,' Meadows said.

'I didn't have a heavy schedule today and nothing that couldn't be pushed back.' She opened the door.

'No date to hurry off to then?' Edris said.

'No, funnily enough the job doesn't provide me with many dates,' Daisy replied.

'I'm sure you're fighting them off.' Edris turned to Meadows and winked.

'You're such a flirt,' Daisy said. 'I bet no woman is safe in the station.'

'No woman is safe in the whole valley,' Meadows said with a grin.

Daisy pushed open the double doors that led into a sterile room. The atmosphere became serious. Tara lay on a metal gurney, covered up to her neck with a sheet.

'There were no signs of a sexual assault,' Daisy began.

'At least she was spared that,' Meadows said.

'Large quantities of alcohol were found in her stomach and some in her lungs.'

'Does that mean she drowned in alcohol?' Edris asked.

'That was quite possibly the intention, but she vomited and inhaled. I've sent off blood samples and would guess that she ingested enough to cause alcohol poisoning – perhaps sufficient enough to kill her anyway if she hadn't choked.'

Meadows studied Tara's face. 'I think she would have been a pretty woman when she was younger.'

'I think you're right.' Daisy smiled. 'But years of abuse have ravaged her looks. She was a heavy drinker, evidenced by cirrhosis of the liver. Other than the marks on her face there are no other signs of violence. There's an old fracture on her right arm and a caesarean scar.'

'A caesarean? According to Tara's friends and neighbours she didn't have any children,' Meadows said.

'Well, she was pregnant on more than one occasion. She also gave birth naturally at some time.'

'So you're saying she had at least two children?' Edris asked.

'Yes.'

'Why lie about it?'

'Maybe, as she was a drinker and a drug addict, they were taken away,' Meadows suggested.

'Or they could be estranged,' Daisy offered. 'It happens.'

'Yes, but most mothers wouldn't hide the existence of their children. She didn't even mention them in the will,' Edris said.

'Perhaps she felt guilty. If they were taken into care, she may have been too ashamed to tell anyone. Maybe she didn't know where they were.' Meadows turned to Daisy. 'Can you let me know as soon as the blood results come back?'

'Of course.' Daisy smiled. 'I'll call you straight away.'

'Thanks.'

Meadows' mind was whirring with questions as he said goodbye and headed for the car.

'I think one of Tara's children may be a resident of Bethesda House,' he said as he started the engine. 'It makes sense. Why else leave all her money to Bethesda? Let's get back to the station, we need to go through all the residents' files again.'

'But if you are saying one of the residents is Tara's child, does that mean you think they left the home last night and killed her?'

'No, I don't think that at all. Think about it. Daisy said Tara had been pregnant at least twice. What if one of the children ended up in Bethesda and the other is protecting their sibling?'

'Protecting them from what?'

'Alan Whitby was part of the abuse. Rhys and Alex were brought to justice whereas Alan still worked there and was a threat.'

'I don't know,' Edris said. 'The children could be anywhere, adopted, moved away or even dead.'

'That's what we need to find out.'

* * *

Valentine jumped up from behind her desk as soon as Meadows entered the office.

'I was just about to call you,' she said. 'I've managed to track down Tara's mother. Her name is Joan O'Leary, she's in Riverview residential home in Cardiff.'

She handed the details to Meadows.

'It's too late to go now, it will have to wait until morning, poor woman. Good work, Valentine. Can you see what you can find out about Tara's father?'

'Yes, I'll get on to it.'

Meadows called Blackwell and Paskin to join the group as Edris handed around mugs of tea.

'Did you get anything more from Tara's house?' Meadows asked sipping his tea and taking a biscuit from the packet Edris had placed on the desk.

'Not much, we've been through all her bank statements. She didn't earn that much, and after bills and the insurance payments there was only pocket money left, no savings,' Blackwell said.

'She probably spent what was left over on booze,' Edris added.

'There weren't many photographs,' Paskin said. 'A few of Tara and her friend Sarah and one or two that could be her mother. No old family album. Quite sad really.'

'The post-mortem confirmed asphyxiation and showed large amounts of alcohol in her system. No signs of sexual assault. At some time Tara had at least two pregnancies. We need to find those children. Well, young adults now, I would imagine. I'll put in a request for Tara's medical records, maybe that will shed some light on things, at least give us some dates. Meanwhile I want to go through all the residents' files, see who has an absent mother.'

'You think one of her children is a resident at Bethesda?' Paskin asked.

'I think it is a strong possibility.' Meadows thought for a moment. 'It could also be a staff member or both. Two children, one protecting the other.'

'And you think one or both of Tara's children killed her?' Valentine raised her eyebrows.

'It's not unheard of,' Meadows said. 'But why? Alan Whitby was involved in the abuse case. We know that questions were asked. Both Alex and Rhys reported a relative called Anna and the descriptions match.'

'A relative that we haven't found,' Blackwell huffed.

'Doesn't mean she doesn't exist. Let's say she does exist, and her brother or sister is in Bethesda. She finds out about the abuse and takes revenge on Alan and Tara,' Meadows said.

'Why Tara?' Valentine asked.

'Because she's the one responsible for putting her child into a home. A mother is supposed to protect her children. We need to look at all the relatives again.'

'Someone would have seen this Anna going in and out of the house,' Edris said.

'Not necessarily, she could be using a different name. The residents get family visitors and they would know the layout of the house. She could also be a member of staff, regular or relief staff.' Meadows ran his hands through his hair. 'It could be any of them. Gemma is very close to Kevin, as is Leah to Liam and Harry to Eddy. Harry actually said to us that the residents become your family. What if one of them *is* family.'

'It couldn't be Gemma,' Edris said. 'She was working there the same time as Rhys and Alex, so she couldn't pretend to be this Anna.'

'I don't see it myself,' Blackwell said. 'You're saying one of those girls killed Alan and shoved him in the freezer. Have you seen the size of them? They'd never lift him.'

'I agree, but it doesn't mean they didn't have help.'

'I still think this is about the money. Miles and Jane killed Alan and had already arranged to have Tara killed by a third person.'

'And why would they keep quiet about a third person's involvement?'

'Because we haven't got anything on them for Alan's murder. They're sitting tight and hoping they only get done for the theft. Let's face it, they'll be out in a few years.'

He's got a point. Am I over-thinking this, making it more complicated?

Meadows looked around at the team.

'We still need to find Tara's children. We've got nothing else to go on at the moment.'

'I think it's worth a try,' Edris agreed.

'You would,' Blackwell barked.

'Well I agree,' Paskin said. 'She left her money to Bethesda, didn't talk about her children. I don't think I'd be happy if my sister was left in the hands of abusers.'

'Fine,' Blackwell said and picked up a file before plonking himself down at his desk.

Meadows picked up Kevin's file and read through the notes.

'Do you have the name of the social worker assigned to that resident?' he asked Edris.

Edris flicked through the pages. 'Martin Hughes.'

'Same here,' Blackwell grunted.

'Yep,' Valentine and Paskin chorused.

'Well he should know more about the residents and their families. See if you can get a number for him. According to Kevin's file he has a brother that visits, there's a mention of his father but none at all of his mother.'

'Both of Vanessa's parents are dead,' Valentine said.

'Liam has been in care all his life,' Blackwell added. 'I remember from when I read the files last week. Steven's parents are alive and still come to visit him.'

'Eddy's sister and parents visit him,' Paskin said.

'So we have at least two possibilities so far,' Meadows said. 'Kevin and Liam. We still need to check out the other family members to make sure there is no divorce or adoption.'

'I have a number and address for Martin Hughes,' Edris said.

'Good, give him a call and tell him we are on our way. Blackwell, Paskin, you can go and see Kevin's father and brother. See what you can find out about Kevin's mother. Valentine, can you make a start on the other families? Check for divorces or adoptions.' Meadows checked his watch and was surprised at the time. 'It's getting late, the families may get concerned if we call on them at this hour. Best not to cause any unnecessary worry. It can wait until tomorrow. I'll let you all know if I get any information from Martin Hughes.'

'I'll check in with Bethesda before I clock off,' Blackwell said. 'Make sure everything's OK.'

The gesture surprised Meadows. 'Thanks, that'd be great. Edris and I will interview Tara's mother in the morning. We'll meet back here for a briefing in the afternoon. Let me know of any developments in the meantime.'

* * *

Edris rang ahead, so Martin Hughes was expecting them and had the kettle boiling by the time they arrived.

'Thank you for seeing us,' Meadows said. 'I appreciate it's late.'

'It's no problem. I'm not sure how much help I'll be.' He placed three mugs on the coffee table and sank down on the sofa.

Meadows took an instant liking to Martin, with his receding ginger hair, open face and kind eyes.

'How long have you worked with the residents at Bethesda House?' Edris asked as he leaned forward and picked up a mug of tea.

'About ten years, it's not a large part of my work. I mainly work with families with young children that are having difficulties. Most of the residents are settled and are doing well. I get involved in the assessments, monthly checks to make sure their needs are being met and that they are generally happy and not showing signs of deterioration.'

'Do you work with the relatives of the residents?' Meadows asked.

'Sometimes.'

'You were working at Bethesda at the time of the abuse case?'

'Yes, although I never witnessed any abuse first-hand. I did assess the residents and give evidence at the trial.' Martin shook his head sadly. 'It never fails to shock me that those in a position of trust abuse the most vulnerable.'

'I expect you've seen some horrors in your line of work,' Edris said.

'Yes, too much.'

'So you have no doubt the abuse took place?' Meadows asked.

'None at all. You'll find that the majority of the residents don't make up stories. They have no guile. Yes, they can throw a tantrum and be difficult but there is also an innocence about them.'

'What did you make of the allegations against Alan Whitby?'

'The residents didn't like him very much and I got the sense that some of them were afraid of him. Unfortunately, I couldn't isolate any one incident. I did voice my concerns at the time of the investigation. No charges were brought against Alan so other than keep an eye on the situation, there wasn't much I could do.'

'Did you discuss the case with the families?'

'Yes, naturally they were very distressed and concerned.'

'Any particular member of the families stand out as being threatening or display anger against those accused?'

Martin took a sip of his tea. 'Well, there was plenty of anger and who can blame them. If I recall, Kevin's brother, Adam, was very verbal at the trial.'

'Have you ever met with someone called Anna?' Edris asked. 'She'd be one of the relatives.'

Martin ran his hand over his chin thoughtfully. 'No. I don't think so.'

'What about Tara Lane?' Meadows asked.

'No– oh, hang on, wasn't she the woman found dead in Ynys Melyn this morning?'

'Yes, although officially we haven't released her name.'

'You don't need a newspaper around here.' Martin smiled. 'Was she a relative of one of the residents?'

'That's what we're trying to find out. We have reason to believe that she was the mother of one of the residents. We know that Liam has been in care all his life and there is no mention of Kevin's mother in his file. We are looking into the backgrounds of the other families. We were hoping you might be able to help with this.'

'Well you're right about Liam. He was transferred to Bethesda from Bristol, it wasn't his first move. I'm afraid I can't help you with his early life. I'll make some enquiries when I get into the office in the morning but it may take some time.'

'That would be great,' Meadows said. 'And Kevin?'

'Kevin the gentle giant, he's quite a character.' Martin smiled. 'Kevin's mother left when the boys were young. It's not unusual in cases like this. It can be very difficult and frustrating raising a child with Kevin's disabilities. Then there is the guilt, especially when a decision has to be made about full-time care.'

'Do you remember the mother's name?'

'No, sorry, the family never talk about her and Kevin has forgotten. I'll look it up for you. As for the others, Vanessa's parents have passed away and I don't think there are any other absent mothers but I can't be certain.'

'That's OK, you have been a great help.' Meadows stood and put down his mug. 'Thank you for your time this evening.'

'You're welcome,' Martin said. 'I'm sorry I couldn't be more help. I hope you find what you are looking for.'

'So do I,' Meadows said.

Before it's too late.

Chapter Thirty

Meadows zipped in and out of the lanes as unfamiliar music played on the car stereo. The team were out interviewing relatives of the residents of Bethesda House and Valentine had made arrangements for him to meet Tara Lane's GP later that day. He was hoping that Tara's mother, Joan, would shed some light on the absent children.

'Looks like it's going to snow,' Edris commented.

They had just passed Port Talbot steelworks where plumes of smoke rose to meet grey, leaden skies.

'Well let's hope it doesn't. I don't want to get stuck in Cardiff.' Meadows reached out and turned down the volume on the stereo. 'What is this rubbish?'

'It's just a compilation CD I made up for you, to bring you up to date. It's club music.'

'I can't think with this constant beat, it all sounds the same to me!' Meadows said.

'Fine, I'll put another one on.' Edris changed the CD and sat back in the seat. 'Try this.'

'That's a bit better, who's this?'

'Red Hot Chili Peppers. *Californication*.'

'I can live with this.'

Meadows tapped the steering wheel as he drove. The traffic was light and soon they were passing Castell Coch, perched on a hilltop, with its fairy tale turrets peeking out of the trees. They took the slip road and joined the traffic from the A470. Meadows was grateful they didn't have to drive into the city centre. The second turning led them to Riverview retirement home. A newly built complex with wide paths and benches dotted around a lawn.

Inside, they were shown into the matron's office where a plump woman with a cheery smile greeted them. 'Irene Jones,' she said and held out her hand.

Meadows made the introductions and took a seat.

'Joan is just finishing her breakfast, then she'll return to her room. She had a bad morning so she's running late today.' Irene smiled. 'I'll get one of the staff to take you up shortly. We were all very sorry to hear about Tara.'

'Have you told Joan about her daughter?'

'Yes, although how much she has taken it in I can't be certain. Joan suffers from dementia. It started in her mid-sixties. She's one of our youngest residents. Most are in their eighties.'

'How long has Joan been with you?' Edris asked, pen poised over his notebook.

'Five years.'

'So she's about seventy?'

'Yes, she celebrated her seventieth birthday a few months ago. Tara took her out for the day and bought her a huge birthday cake.'

'Did she live with Tara before she came here?' Meadows asked.

'No, she lived alone. When she became ill there was no one to take care of her. Tara worked and lived too far away to check on her mother every day.'

'Was Tara upset moving her mother into residential care?' Edris asked.

Good question.

Meadows gave his constable an encouraging nod.

'It's always a difficult decision to make for any family member and Tara was an only child so had no support. If I remember correctly, she said she thought her mother was better off with us.'

'Did Tara visit often?' Meadows asked.

'Every two weeks on a Saturday; sometimes she came in between. I know she caught the train and I had the sense that she would've come more often if she could afford the journey.'

'Does Joan have any other visitors?'

'Her old neighbour Liz. She comes now and again but finds it difficult. Sometimes Joan doesn't remember her. There were even days she didn't recognise Tara. There's been no one else.'

'Has Joan ever mentioned grandchildren?' Meadows asked.

'No, from what I understand Tara didn't have any children.'

There was a knock on the door and a woman with cropped brown hair and various piercings on her face and ears entered. 'Joan is back in her room now.'

'Thanks, Sally, would you mind taking these gentlemen to see her?'

They followed Sally down the corridor and into a light cosy room which housed a single bed and table, where a jigsaw was laid out. An armchair was positioned next to the window where Joan stood looking out.

'Some visitors for you, Joan,' Sally said.

Joan turned around and eyed the detectives. She was a petite woman with wiry grey hair, wearing a pair of jeans and a blue woollen jumper. It was clear from her expression that she was struggling to recognise them.

'Hello, Joan.' Meadows stepped forward. 'I'm Detective Inspector Meadows and this is Detective Constable Edris. Do you mind if we ask you a few questions?'

Joan turned to Sally. 'I don't know these people.'

'Policemen, Joan, they have come to talk about Tara.'

Sally said. 'Do you remember we talked about Tara yesterday?'

'Tara?' Joan looked at her watch. 'Tara's in school. Has she been bunking off again?' Joan shook her head. 'I don't know what I'm going to do with that girl.'

'Come and sit down, Joan,' Sally took her arm and guided her into the armchair. 'Tara is grown up now.' Sally knelt and took hold of Joan's hands. 'I'm sorry, Joan, Tara died yesterday and the police need to ask you a few questions.'

'No, not my Tara. There must be some mistake.' Her lips quivered.

Poor woman.

'Perhaps a cup of tea,' Meadows suggested. He placed a chair in front of Joan. 'I'm really sorry about Tara,' he said as he sat down.

'I keep forgetting things, sometimes everything just blurs together.' Joan took a tissue from her sleeve and dabbed her eyes.

'How about we talk about what you do remember,' Meadows said. 'It sounds like Tara was full of mischief. Did she often bunk off school?'

'Oh yes.' Joan gave a watery smile. 'She didn't like school very much. She was such a sweet little thing but he spoilt things.'

'Who spoilt things?'

'Her father. Bastard. I should've left him when she was a baby.'

'Where's Tara's father now?'

'I don't know and I don't care. Dead with a bit of luck. We were better off without him. The only good thing he did was leave us.' Joan turned her gaze to the window.

'Did Tara get on with her father?'

Joan returned her gaze to Meadows. 'No, he beat her. I tried to stop him, but it only made things worse for both of us.' She looked down at her hands. 'There wasn't the help then. I know what people thought, if she has a black eye she probably deserves it, can't keep her man happy. It wasn't like that and I was ashamed to go to my parents.'

'I understand,' Meadows said kindly. 'Tara must have been very unhappy.'

Joan looked up. 'She was full of hell, smoking, drinking and boys. I think she did it to get back at her father. She's a pretty girl.'

'Yes,' Meadows agreed. 'She had a baby, didn't she?'

'She was still a baby herself, too young to be a mother.'

'How old was she when she had the baby?'

'Barely sixteen.'

'A boy or a girl?'

'Lovely baby boy,' Joan smiled. 'And she loved him.'

'What did she call him?'

'She called him… she called him…' Joan's face creased with concentration. 'I can't remember now' – she put her hand to her head – 'I should remember.'

'It's OK, it doesn't matter, I'm sure it will come back to you,' Meadows said.

'I think this might help.' Edris plucked a photograph from the shelf and handed it to Joan. 'Is this Tara and her baby?'

Joan rubbed her fingertips over the photograph. 'Yes, Tara and Dean.'

'Dean? Is that the name of Tara's baby?' Meadows asked.

'No, Tara's boyfriend.' Joan pointed to the young man in the photograph.

'Is Dean the baby's father?'

'Yes, he's a nice boy.'

'What's Dean's surname?' Edris asked.

Joan shrugged her shoulders.

'What happened to the baby?' Meadows asked.

'She lost him.' Joan handed the photo to Meadows.

'You mean the baby died?'

'No, the baby didn't die.' Joan frowned.

'Was he taken away?'

'Here we go.' Sally entered the room carrying a tray which she set down on the table. She took a cup and handed it to Joan. 'Help yourself to milk and sugar,' she said to Meadows, smiling.

Meadows stood and poured milk into a dainty cup. 'Was the baby taken away?'

'What baby?' Joan looked at Meadows as if he had only just stepped into the room.

'Tara's baby.'

'Tara doesn't have a baby,' Joan snapped. 'What's he talking about, Sally?' Joan sipped her tea. 'That's lovely. Is the lady coming to do my hair today?'

'No, she comes on Friday,' Sally said.

'Do you know where we can find Dean?' Edris asked.

'Dean? I don't know anyone called Dean.'

'Tara's boyfriend,' Meadows prompted.

'No, Tara doesn't have a boyfriend. Her man died. She'll be coming on Saturday. She always comes and stays the day. She's a good girl.'

Meadows nodded. 'Well thank you for talking to us, Joan.' He drained his cup and placed it on the tray.

'Has Joan ever told you about her grandson?' Edris asked Sally.

'I didn't know she had one.' Sally lowered her voice. 'As far as I know Tara was the only family she had.'

* * *

'Maybe her illness is a blessing,' Edris commented as they drove back to Bryn Mawr. 'At least she can live in the past and not have to deal with the death of her daughter.'

'Oh, I don't know,' Meadows said. 'When she remembers that Tara comes to visit she will have to be told what happened. Imagine reliving that pain every time. No moving through the grieving process.'

'Yeah, I didn't think of that. It wasn't worth upsetting her today, we didn't really learn anything.'

'We know Tara had a son and the father of the baby is called Dean. We also have a rough idea of when the baby was born. If Tara was sixteen at the time then we're looking at 1988 or '89. Narrows it down a little.'

They arrived at the station and Edris headed to the canteen while Meadows briefed the team.

'We still don't know where the child was born, it could be Cardiff or she may have been living somewhere else at the time,' Paskin pointed out. 'It's a hell of a job to go through every baby boy born in those years on the registers of births and deaths.'

'I'm hoping to get some more information from Tara's medical records. I have to wait until the end of the doctor's surgery to see him but we should get an exact date of birth.'

'You should just walk in there and flash your warrant card. Demand he sees you straight away,' Blackwell growled.

'I find that gets people's backs up,' Meadows said. 'At least the doctor is happy to disclose the information on a voluntary basis. He has no obligation to do so, if we have to make a formal request it could set us back. Did you talk to Kevin's family?'

'No, they're away on holiday according to the neighbours,' Blackwell huffed. 'Waste of time.'

'No adoption or divorce with the other families,' Valentine said.

'OK, we need background checks on all the staff, including relief staff. I want to know previous employment, references, family background.'

'I brought you a sandwich, cheese.' Edris handed the package to Meadows.

'Where's mine?' Valentine teased.

'I thought you lot would have had lunch by now,' Edris said.

'We've been too busy for lunch.'

Meadows took some money from his wallet and handed it to Edris. 'Go and get a plate full of sandwiches and bring another packet of biscuits. Someone ate the last lot.'

'I believe that was you.' Valentine grinned.

After a quick lunch the team returned to their tasks. Meadows blocked out the noise as they made constant telephone calls. He stood at the incident board updating the notes and trying to make the connections.

It all centres on Bethesda House. But what is Tara's connection to Bethesda? The child she placed in care? Or more likely the child was taken away from her. Joan said she lost the child. Tara must have tracked him down. It makes sense – why else leave the money to Bethesda? But why was she killed? Did she find out about the abuse, raise questions, or was she involved with Alan as a way to get close to her son? Maybe she knew Alan's killer, or was a witness. No, it's more than that. There has to be a second child: one in Bethesda, the other one protecting them and seeking revenge.

Meadows ran his hands through his hair.

Finding Tara's son is the key and maybe that will lead us to the killer.

He left the team to continue with their enquiries and headed for the doctors' surgery in Ynys Melyn with Edris.

* * *

There were a few people milling around in the community centre where the doctor's surgery was housed, cleaning up after the local children's playgroup. Meadows' eyes were drawn to the large posters advertising vaccinations and help for the elderly in the winter as he walked through the building.

'You can smell the germs in the air,' Edris said as they headed for the reception area. 'They all sit here itching and coughing. You soon get sick sitting in here.'

'It's a doctors' surgery, what do you expect?'

'They should stay home until they get better and not infect the rest of the population.' Edris laughed.

'You're such a caring soul,' Meadows said. 'Puts the rest of us to shame.'

'Dr Reynolds is expecting you,' the stern-faced receptionist said as they approached the desk. 'You can go straight in, first door on the left.'

Dr Reynolds, a stocky man with brown curly hair, stood up from behind the desk and held out his hand in greeting. Meadows shook it and took a seat.

'Thank you for seeing us.'

'Shocking news.' Dr Reynolds shook his head sadly. 'It's not the sort of thing one would expect in a village like this. I've taken a quick look through Tara's records. As you'll already be aware, she was a heavy drinker. She was admitted to a rehabilitation centre in 1997 for drug and alcohol abuse. Since then as far as I can tell she has been clean of drugs. Other than the occasional prescription for antibiotics and a referral to the sexual health clinic there isn't anything that stands out.'

'We're particularly interested in Tara's pregnancies,' Meadows said. 'We believe she had a child in 1988 or 1989 and another sometime later.'

Dr Reynolds swivelled the computer screen and scrolled through the information. 'Yes, November 10th 1988. Tara gave birth to a boy in Cardiff University Hospital.'

'By caesarean section?'

'No, normal delivery.'

'Tara has a scar from a caesarean, so she must have had a child at a later date,' Meadows said.

The doctor continued to scrutinise the notes, his face creased in concentration.

'There doesn't appear to be any mention of a second birth.' He checked back through the notes. 'Ah, there is a note of an initial consultation following a positive pregnancy test. No notes of a follow-up appointment.' The doctor turned away from the screen.

'Is it possible that she had the baby with no record?' Edris asked.

'It's possible. Tara moved around using several practices before she settled here about ten years ago. All the medical records were transferred to computer and it has been known for some information to go missing. I'm not saying that is the case here.'

'What about if she didn't receive any medical attention?' Meadows said. 'Would someone have followed it up?'

'No, one would expect the mother to keep up regular checks. It's a risk to both mother and child not to monitor the pregnancy but given Tara's past history with alcohol it's conceivable that she waited until the birth to seek medical attention.'

'Perhaps she was afraid social services would intervene,' Meadows said.

'I guess that may be the case; as it is I can't help you, so if there is nothing else.' Dr Reynolds stood, indicating that the meeting was over.

'Yes, thank you for your time.'

* * *

'Well at least you got a date of birth,' Edris commented as they left the building.

'We'll check it against the residents' files as soon as we get back. We should be able to narrow it down now.'

'Yeah, I guess, but there's no evidence that there is a second child other than the caesarean scar, and if she didn't get any medical attention it may have been too late and the child could have died,' Edris said. 'Then we're back to Blackwell's theory that it's all about money and that Jane and Miles have an accomplice who killed Tara.'

Meadows shook his head as he pulled out onto the main road.

'No, I don't think so. We keep looking and with a bit of luck Martin Hughes will come up with some information.'

As they walked across the police station car park Meadows heard someone shout his name. He turned and saw Martin hurrying towards them with a file clutched in his hand.

'I was hoping to catch you, I have some information that may help you,' he said.

'Great! So far we haven't had much luck,' Edris replied.

Meadows led the way into an interview room and dragged three chairs around the table.

'Sorry it's taken me so long to get back to you. Some of the information was difficult to get hold of, particularly with regards to Liam, his case was initially dealt with in another county.' He opened the file. 'I looked into Kevin's background. His mother, Janet Ellis, left the family when he was seven years old. She divorced her husband shortly after and moved to Devon. She remarried and had a further two children. I spoke with her this morning, so I think you can rule her out.'

'So that leaves Liam.' Meadows battled with his patience, he wanted to take hold of the file and devour the information.

'Yes, Liam is the son of Tara Lane.'

'You were right,' Edris said. 'Tara does have a son in Bethesda. When was Liam born?'

Martin consulted the notes. 'February 3rd 1992.'

'Then we are looking for his brother,' Meadows said.

'Brother?' Martin looked confused. 'No, Liam has a sister. I had the files sent over. Tara gave birth to twins, a boy and a girl. Delivered two months early.'

'By caesarean section?' Meadows asked.

'Yes. As you already know, Tara was a heavy drinker and the twins were born with foetal alcohol syndrome. They spent the first few months of their lives in hospital.

Liam had complex medical needs, impaired immune system, epilepsy and an atrial septal defect.'

'A what?' Edris asked.

'A hole in the heart,' Martin explained. 'As you know, he later developed learning difficulties.'

'And the girl?' Meadows asked.

'Much the same. Complex medical needs. She was born with only one functioning kidney.'

'So are you saying the girl is also in care?'

'No. Social services filed a court order to have the twins removed from their mother's care. The girl was adopted by a Mr and Mrs Johnson, they called her Annabel.'

'Anna.' Meadows looked at Edris.

'So she does exist.' Edris leaned over to take a closer look at the file.

'What about the older brother, was he taken into care?'

'There is no mention of an older brother in any of the files. From what I have read Tara didn't have any other children.'

'Maybe he died,' Edris said.

'I'll look into it,' Martin offered.

'Do you have a name for the twins' father?'

'Yes, Dean Casey. He had no involvement with the twins, he would've been informed of the care order and the adoption if they had been able to track him down.'

'Do you have an address for the Johnsons?'

'Yes.' Martin moved the file in front of Meadows.

Meadows scanned the contents of the file before copying down the address. 'Thank you. You've been a great help.' He shook Martin's hand before leaving the interview room and hurrying up to the office.

'There is an Anna,' Meadows announced. 'She is Liam's twin sister.'

'So she does exist.' Paskin looked at Blackwell.

'Where is she?' Blackwell grunted.

'That's what we have to find out, I'm heading off to Newport with Edris to see Anna's adoptive parents. Hopefully they will tell us where we can find her.'

'So you think that she's the one responsible for the murders?' Valentine asked.

'I think she has something to do with it.'

'But who's helping her?' Paskin asked. 'You said there was more than one person involved in Alan's murder.'

'I would guess her older brother.'

'There's another one?' Blackwell looked up from his desk.

'Yes, but social services have no record of an older child. We need to track down the father, Dean Casey, and find Tara's children before someone else dies.'

'You think they have another victim lined up?' Blackwell asked.

'I think this is far from over,' Meadows said before leaving the office.

Chapter Thirty-one

'I feel like I've been on that motorway all day,' Edris said as he climbed out of the car and stretched.

'Well, let's hope they don't find Dean Casey in London.' Meadows grinned as he zipped up his coat. He could feel the evening chill penetrating his clothes and biting at his skin. 'Looks like the Johnsons are in.'

He looked towards the house which was set back off the road. Light leaked through the blinds casting a soft glow in the darkness.

'Nice place,' Edris commented. 'Two new cars, nice neighbourhood, bit of a contrast to Tara's place.'

'Yes, I guess, but what about the people inside the house?' Meadows looked at the neat flowerbeds and kidney-shaped lawn and imagined a mature garden to the rear, with decking and a swinging seat where the Johnsons sipped wine on a summer evening. 'Daniel Johnson is a bank manager and his wife Cordelia a school secretary. Annabel is their only child. We can't assume she had a happy childhood.'

'I doubt she wanted for anything. The alternative would have been an alcoholic mother.'

'But was she loved? If Tara had kept her children would she have cleaned up her act? Is Annabel angry enough to be involved in the murder of her mother? If so, why? Because Tara left her son in care to become a victim of abuse or is it more than that?'

'That's a lot of questions.' Edris laughed.

'Come on, let's see if the Johnsons have some of the answers.'

The front door was answered by a slender man dressed in a charcoal suit, crisp white shirt and paisley tie.

'Daniel Johnson?' Meadows asked.

'Yes?' He looked suspiciously at the visitors.

Meadows quickly introduced himself and Edris as he showed his identification. 'There's nothing to worry about,' he added, noting the concern that flited across Daniel's face.

'Who is it?' A woman appeared next to Daniel, chestnut hair cut into a sleek bob, her face carefully made up. She wore a pale pink jumper and black skirt.

'It's the police. Nothing to concern yourself about.' He shooed her off and turned back to Meadows, his expression stern. 'I'm afraid it's an inconvenient time for you to call, we are just about to eat.'

I bet he's used to getting his own way.

Meadows forced a smile. 'I'm sorry to trouble you but it is important we speak with you and your wife.'

'Can't it wait?'

'I'm afraid not.'

'I suppose you'd better come in.' Daniel led them to a formal sitting room where Cordelia hovered by the door.

Meadows' eyes roamed around the room. It was immaculate, with a deep pile cream carpet and brown leather suite. Modern art decorated the walls. There were no family photographs or ornaments; it looked like the room was never used.

'Take a seat,' Daniel said before sitting down in the armchair and leaning back, crossing his legs and folding his hands on his stomach. Cordelia perched on the other armchair, legs crossed at the ankles and perfectly manicured hands resting on her knee.

Meadows and Edris took the sofa which was spacious enough to fit four people.

'What can we do for you?' Daniel asked.

'You may have heard on the news about the recent murder of Alan Whitby in Ynys Melyn,' Meadows began.

'I read something about it in the paper. It was in the residential home, was it not?'

'Yes.'

Be careful, we need to find Anna and if they believe she is involved they will protect her, if only to avoid scandal.

'We're interviewing everyone that has a connection with Bethesda House.'

'Well I don't see what that has to with us,' Cordelia said.

'We believe your daughter, Annabel, may be connected.'

Daniel frowned. 'I don't think Anna would know anyone in that area, let alone a residential house.'

'Your daughter was adopted,' Edris said.

'Yes?' Daniel replied. He glared at Edris as if he had made a criticism.

'Were you aware that Annabel has a brother?' Meadows asked.

'Yes.' Cordelia's voice was barely a whisper. 'It wasn't an easy decision to make.'

'You mean to split the twins and just take one?' Edris said.

'Don't make judgements when you don't know the circumstances,' Daniel snapped.

'The twins were in poor health.' Meadows looked at Cordelia. 'I imagine they would've required a lot of care and attention.'

'Yes, we felt that it would be better for Anna and the boy to go to separate loving families where they would receive undivided attention.' Cordelia looked down and smoothed the edge of her skirt.

Meadows sat forward. 'What about the older brother?'

'What older brother?' Cordelia looked genuinely confused.

'There were only the twins as far as we knew. We weren't informed of any other children,' Daniel said.

'Anna's twin brother, Liam, was not adopted. He has spent his life in care and is currently a resident of Bethesda House.' Meadows watched Cordelia closely for a reaction and saw pity in her eyes.

'I'm sorry to hear that,' Cordelia said. 'We weren't given any information on Anna's brother after the adoption.'

'Does Anna know that she's adopted?' Edris asked.

'Yes.' Daniel stiffened.

'And that she has a twin brother?' Meadows asked.

'No, we didn't tell her.'

Meadows noticed a look pass between husband and wife and wondered what they were omitting. 'Did she try and find her biological parents?'

'No, I don't think so.' Daniel moved back in his seat.

'Perhaps it would be better if we talked to Anna,' Edris suggested. 'Could you give us her home address?'

Cordelia fiddled with her necklace. 'We don't have an address for Anna.'

'Telephone number?' Edris poised his pen over his notebook.

'No, she changed her mobile number.'

'What about a work address? Does Anna have a job?' Edris looked at Daniel.

'She was working for Barnes and Evans accountants in Cardiff. She got the job when she left university but from what I understand she left a few years ago. I can't understand why. It was a good job with future prospects, she would have done well there.'

'When was the last time you saw Anna?' Meadows asked.

'She came to visit last night.' Concern flitted across Cordelia's face. 'Is Anna in some kind of trouble?'

Meadows looked from Cordelia to Daniel, wondering how much to tell them.

'Anna's biological mother, Tara Lane, was found dead in her home yesterday morning. We are treating it as murder. Please, Mr and Mrs Johnson, if you have any information that could help with our inquiries please tell us. It's very important that we talk to Anna. Do you know where she is or if she's had any contact with her biological parents or brother?'

'I need a drink.' Daniel rose from the chair and crossed the room to the drinks cabinet where he took a glass and poured a large whisky.

'Our relationship with Anna has been a bit strained over the last couple of years,' Cordelia said timidly.

'Strained? It's been non-existent, then she turns up yesterday full of apologies and asking our forgiveness,' Daniel fumed. 'We couldn't have treated her any better than we would've our own flesh and blood.'

'Please, Daniel.' Cordelia put her hand to her temple. 'You saw what she was like last night.'

The anger slipped from Daniel's face and Meadows saw a glimpse of sadness in his eyes as he moved back to the chair.

'When we brought Anna home from the hospital our lives changed. We became a family. It was something we'd only dreamt about.' Cordelia looked at Daniel and gave him a sad smile. 'After a while we put the adoption behind us and she became our child, we never thought of her any other way. As the years went by the adoption became a distant memory, as if it never happened.'

'You never told her about the adoption?' Meadows asked.

'It was never the right time.' Daniel took a gulp of his whisky. 'We initially discussed the issue and decided to wait until she was old enough to understand, but that time never came. Her grandfather died, which she took badly, then she was sitting her exams and off to university. It didn't seem fair to unsettle her when she was doing so well. Then she left university, got a job, a boyfriend and moved out. She seemed really happy and had a bright future ahead. Then she became ill.' Daniel drank down the remnants of the whisky and stood to refill his glass.

Meadows imagined their perfect daughter going off the rails, quitting her job, maybe turning to drink and drugs like her birth mother.

'Did Anna have a breakdown?'

'No.' Cordelia looked shocked at the suggestion. 'Anna was born with only one functioning kidney, she was a very poorly child. In time she got better and had no health problems for the rest of her childhood. She was just like any other teenager, going to university, then settling down into a job. She started to complain about feeling tired and lost a lot of weight. We took her to a specialist who diagnosed the early stages of renal failure. She had treatment and seemed to be managing, then the condition worsened.' Tears glistened in Cordelia's eyes and she looked away.

Daniel moved behind his wife and laid a hand on her shoulder. 'The doctors told us that Anna would continue to deteriorate and would eventually end up on dialysis. The best hope for Anna was a kidney transplant. Both Cordelia and I were tested, but obviously we weren't a match.'

'So you had to tell her about the adoption,' Meadows said.

'Yes.' Cordelia seemed to have composed herself and sat stiffly in the chair. 'Naturally she was upset at first but we promised to do everything we could to help her find her biological parents. She wanted to do it alone so we respected her wishes. She became curious and, I suppose, a little excited. She would come over in the evenings bursting with excitement as she told us of her progress.' Cordelia let out a slow breath. 'Then one day she turned up yelling how we had ruined her life, she was furious, crying and screaming. She took off and we never saw her again until last night. We tried to track her down but she'd left her flat and job, there was no trace of her.'

'Do you know what upset her so much? Did she mention that she had found her biological parents or her brother?'

'No, like I said, she was screaming and crying. It was like her world had crashed down and it was our fault.'

'And last night you said she had come to make amends.'

'Yes, it seemed like that. She said she knew we didn't intentionally keep the truth from her and that we were only protecting her, then she said she wanted to thank us for all that we had done for her. It was as if she...' Cordelia voice cracked.

'As if she what?' Meadows leaned forward.

'As if she was coming to say goodbye for good.' Cordelia wrapped her arms around her body.

'She didn't say that,' Daniel said.

'No, but that's the feeling I got. She looked so frail and at times she struggled to catch her breath.'

An image of Leah flashed across Meadows' mind.

Frail and breathless. All the medication in the bathroom cabinet, the grey roots on her scalp that she tries to hide. No, not grey – white, white-blond like Liam.

'Do you have a recent photograph of Anna?'

'I'll get one for you,' said Cordelia.

'Do you think Anna is in danger?' Daniel asked as soon as his wife left the room. 'If some maniac has killed her biological mother and a man in her brother's home then she could be a target.'

Or the killer.

'We have no reason to think that Anna is in immediate danger but it is vital we talk to her, so if there is anything else you can think of that might help us find her.'

Meadows turned around as Cordelia came back into the room.

'This was taken few years ago, it's the most recent we have.'

Cordelia handed Meadows the photograph. The smiling girl had a fuller face, colour in her cheeks and long white-blond hair, but was still recognisable.

'Leah.' Meadows handed the photo to Edris.

'Leah? That was the name she was given when she was born. Does she hate us that much she changed her name?' Cordelia turned to Daniel with pain etched on her face.

'She calls herself Leah Parry,' Meadows said.

'Do you know where she is?' Daniel asked.

'Yes, you mentioned earlier that Anna had a boyfriend. Can you tell us his name?'

'Cillian Treharne, but I doubt she's still with him. It wasn't really a suitable match.'

'Thank you for your help.' Meadows turned to leave.

'Can you tell us where Anna is?' Cordelia asked.

'I'm afraid not.'

'Then tell her we are here for her, no matter what.'

'I'll make sure she gets the message.'

* * *

Meadows took the slip road onto the motorway. The traffic was light and enabled him to cruise at a decent speed.

'Do you really think that Leah is capable of killing Alan and Tara? From what the Johnsons say it sounds like she's really sick,' Edris said.

'Yes but she isn't acting alone, she's definitely involved.'

'Cillian?'

'Possibly, but we still have to find her older brother. Liam said that he had to keep Leah safe. What if he means safe from the older brother? He could be our killer, and Leah knows about it. Maybe she let him into the building the night Alan was killed. She could've just arranged to meet him, perhaps she wanted to keep it a secret from Cillian and the only chance she had was the night duty. Then Alan turns up and things get out of hand.'

'What about Tara Lane? If Leah thought her older brother had killed Tara, surely she would've told us. She would be worried for her own safety.'

'She wouldn't come forward if she had witnessed Alan's murder and help dispose of the body. By pointing the finger at her brother, she would be implicating herself.'

'If there is a brother?'

'I'm certain there is.'

'You've been right about everything else.' Edris grinned.

'It doesn't mean I have all the answers. Maybe Leah is the main instigator. If she's that ill she may feel that she has nothing to lose.'

'Yeah, but killing your own mother…' Edris shook his head. 'That's a bit extreme.'

'Who knows what goes through people's minds when they are in that situation. If Tara hadn't continued to drink through her pregnancy then both Liam and Leah would have been spared a life of sickness.'

'And she changed her name. Why do that unless you have something to hide? All she has to do now is make Leah Parry disappear and go back to being Anna. I'm surprised she got away with it. Don't you need a CRB check to work in a care home? They would've checked into her background – and how does she get paid without a bank account?'

Edris stretched his arms behind his head.

'She could have changed it by deed poll, it's not that difficult.' Meadows moved to the outer lane to overtake a slow-moving lorry.

'Maybe Alan found out about her change of name and was blackmailing her. We know he was blackmailing Jane and Miles, maybe he made a habit of it. Leah wouldn't want anyone to know if she planned on killing her mother and wanted to stay close to her brother.'

'Good point,' Meadows said.

'But why wait until now? It's been over two years since she questioned Alex and Rhys about the abuse and longer since she found out about the adoption.'

'Something must have triggered her rage. I just don't see her as a cold-blooded killer. She would've been planning this for a long time and Alan's murder was planned, well some of it was, like drugging Gemma. Or maybe she just wanted Gemma asleep so she could spend time with her brother.' Meadows sighed.

'So, what now, do we bring her in?'

Meadows' phone trilled, interrupting the conversation. He hit the answer button and Paskin's voice came over the hands-free.

'I've found Dean Casey. He lives in Neath.' Paskin reeled off the address.

'Good work! We'll be passing there shortly so we may as well pay him a visit. Leah Parry is Liam's sister so we need to bring her in for questioning.'

'Do you want me to go to Bethesda and pick her up? She's on duty tonight.'

'No, let's see what information we can get from Dean Casey, Hanes should be up there by now.'

'Yes he is, Blackwell just came back from there. He went up earlier to talk to Liam and the staff. Apparently, Liam flew into a rage and hit him.' Paskin couldn't keep the amusement from her voice. 'He went back up to check that Liam had settled down.'

'OK, can you give Hanes a call, tell him not to let Leah leave the premises and to be on the lookout for Cillian. Arrest him if he shows up. I'll let you know what we find out from Dean Casey.'

Meadows increased his speed, he had a sudden sense of urgency which pumped adrenalin through his body, tensing his muscles and sharpening his mind.

Maybe I should have asked Blackwell to pick up Leah after all.

He glanced at the clock on the dashboard and turned to Edris.

'It's 10 p.m. The residents should be asleep. Hanes is there. I can't see Leah hurting Liam and Hanes will be on the lookout for Cillian. If we pick up Leah now it could alert her older brother, we don't know where he is or if he is watching the house. The last thing we want is to push him to do something else.'

'Or Cillian. We still have no evidence that the brother is still alive let alone in the area. Even if he is, then who else could they seek revenge on?'

'Who knows, we don't know what happened to him. He may not have been as fortunate as Leah.'

Meadows pulled up outside Dean Casey's house, a mid-terrace on the main road.

Edris peered out of the window. 'Doesn't look like anyone is home.'

'Maybe he's in bed. Let's hope he is and he can shed some light on the whereabouts of his son.' Meadows climbed out of the car and hit the knocker against the door several times. The noise echoed in the silence.

A few moments later a light illuminated the door pane followed by the sound of a key in the lock. Dean Casey peered around the door. His eyes were bloodshot and what remained of his white-blond hair stuck up on his head.

'Sorry to disturb you at this late hour.' Meadows showed his identification. 'We need to ask you a few questions.'

'I was asleep, I'm on early shift, starts at four, what's this about?'

'Tara Lane.'

'Tara? Now there's a name I haven't heard in a while. Lane? So she got married again.' Dean smiled.

'Perhaps it would be better if we went inside,' Meadows suggested.

'Yeah, no problem.' Dean tied the cord on his dressing gown and, yawning, led them into the kitchen where he flipped the switch on the kettle.

'I'm sorry to have to tell you that Tara was found dead in her home yesterday morning,' Meadows said.

Dean's hand hovered over a mug that hung on a hook. 'Dead? Tara? Bloody hell.' He ran his hand over his chin. 'I suppose I shouldn't be surprised. I thought the drink would get her in the end. Such a waste.' He pulled down the mug and threw in a tea bag.

'It wasn't the drink,' Edris said. 'Tara was murdered.'

Dean paled. 'Murdered?'

'Yes,' Meadows confirmed. 'You and Tara were married?'

'Yes, a long time ago.' Dean poured boiling water into the mug and stirred, he appeared to be struggling to absorb the information.

'When was the last time you saw Tara?'

'Um, I guess about 1992. I walked out on her and never went back. I'm not a suspect, am I?' Dean looked alarmed.

'No, but we are trying to trace Tara's children and were hoping you could help. I understand from Tara's mother that she was very young having her first child.'

'Yeah, she was fifteen when she got pregnant. I stayed with her but we were both just kids. She drank through most of the pregnancy but when the baby was born she seemed to settle down. Her mother helped out, my parents wanted nothing to do with us, thought Tara was a slag, never believed the baby was mine. Anyway, I left school and got a job and we moved in together. The place was a bit of a shithole but it was a start. I wanted to marry her but she kept saying no. It took about a year to persuade her but eventually she married me, I really thought we could make it work but Tara didn't like being tied down. She saw all her friends going out partying and she felt she was missing out on life.'

Dean sighed and took a sip of tea.

'What went wrong?' Meadows asked.

'She got pregnant again, this time she went completely off the rails. Drinking and taking drugs. I worked in the day and looked after the kid in the evening. She would roll home stoned, raid the cupboard and fall into bed. She wouldn't go to the doctors for a check-up. It was like if she pretended that she wasn't pregnant it would go away. Joan – her mother – tried speaking to her but she wouldn't listen.

'We got into a fight one night, she was high and I just couldn't take it anymore. I told her if she didn't pull herself together, I would take the kid and leave. The next morning she got up and shoved all of Lee's things into a black plastic bag. She told me I was boring and she wasn't ready to be a wife. I asked her about the baby, how she was going to manage with a new-born. She said that it was nothing to do with me, that I wasn't the father. So I left. That was the last time I saw her.'

'What happened to your son?' Meadows asked.

'I brought him up on my own. It was just Lee and me until he moved out, went to university, I'm so proud of him.' Dean smiled.

'So your son's name is Lee Casey?' Edris asked. 'No, only I call him Lee. His name is Cillian.'

'Cillian Treharne?' Meadows heard the surprise in his own voice.

'Yes, that was Tara's maiden name. We weren't married when he was born.'

'Thank you.' Meadows made for the door.

'Wait,' Dean called out. 'Is Cillian OK?'

'That's what we need to find out.'

Meadows hurried to the car and dialled Blackwell's number as he started the car.

'Pick up Cillian, he's Leah's brother,' Meadows instructed.

'Bloody hell,' Blackwell's voice boomed over the speaker. 'So there is another child and he's been right under our nose all along.'

'I'm on my way to Bethesda House to pick up Leah. I have a feeling that Dean Casey will be on the phone to his son as we speak. I'll meet you back at the station.'

'Have you got Harry's number?' Meadows glanced at Edris as he pulled onto the road.

'Yeah.' Edris looked sheepish.

'Call her and ask her to meet us at Bethesda, someone needs to be there to watch over the residents.'

Meadows kept his eyes fixed on the road as thoughts bombarded his mind.

What will Cillian do now he knows we're on to him? He'll call Leah – or will he go to Bethesda and try to run with Leah and Liam. They have nowhere to go. Maybe he will sit it out, just make some excuse why they didn't confess to their family connection. There's no solid evidence to connect them to Alan and Tara's murders but enough circumstantial…

Edris' voice broke his thoughts. 'She's on her way. I think I woke her up, she sounded sleepy.'

'With a bit of luck we'll get there before they decide to do something stupid. Leah will have already been warned. I don't think she will run and leave the residents without proper supervision. I think she cares too much for them.'

'Cillian may have other ideas.'

'That's what I'm afraid of. Blackwell should be there soon. Let's hope he gets there on time.'

'It's gross, don't you think, brother and sister in a relationship? Not to mention illegal.' Edris wrinkled his nose in disgust. 'We can get them for that at least.'

'They have separate bedrooms so there's no evidence that they have a physical relationship.'

'Yeah, but he was her boyfriend before she knew of the adoption.'

'So she wouldn't have known he was her brother. I can't see that charge standing up in court. Poor girl, it's no wonder she was so angry with her adopted parents for not telling her the truth earlier. It could've saved a lot of heartache.'

'Angry enough to kill her birth mother?' Edris asked.

'I don't know if she would have the strength to do it alone. All three of them are damaged in their own way.'

Meadows' phone halted the conversation. He sensed that it wouldn't be good news as he reached out and hit answer.

'No sign of Cillian,' Blackwell's voice boomed over the hands-free. 'House is in darkness and the car's gone.'

'Shit! Meet us at Bethesda House, I have a bad feeling he's gone there.' Meadows ended the call and dialled Hanes' number. The phone continued to ring until it switched to voicemail.

'Why isn't he picking up?' Concern laced Edris' voice.

'This isn't good.' Meadows switched on the siren and floored the accelerator.

Chapter Thirty-two

Cillian is very angry. I think the red is in his head. He keeps moving and talking, too fast, too many words, it hurts my head. He made me get out of bed, he said we have to go. It's dark outside, we don't go out in the dark, not allowed.

'Come on, Liam, Please. We have to go now. Remember we talked about going away, you, me and Cillian. We'll go somewhere nice and we'll be together.'

Leah is crying again. I don't think we're going to a happy place. Everyone is happy when they go somewhere nice.

'Why are you crying?'

'I'm just a little sad we have to leave, but we'll have fun, we can do lots of things together.'

'OK. I need to get Hard Hat and we have to take his bed.'

'No, Hard Hat can't come with us, we don't have room.'

I'm not going without Hard Hat, he's my friend. Who's going to look after him? He only talks to me. If I sit on the bed they can't make me go, I'll stay here until we take him.

'Liam! What are you doing? We have to go, move now!'

Uh oh, now Cillian's very mad. Ouch, that hurts.

'Let go, Cillian, I don't like you.'

'Do you want to stay here? You will never see Leah again.'

No, I don't want Leah to go away. It hurts my tummy. He's pulling my arm, hurting me. He's making the red come, hit, bite, make Cillian go away.

'I hate you, wanker! Bastard!'

'Leah, do something,' Cillian shouts.

They are pulling me. I think my arms are going to come off. If I keep my feet stuck to the floor they can't move me. The floor is sliding.

'No, get off, bitch. I hate you!'

'Shut the fuck up!' Cillian shouts.

Ouch, my head.

'Don't hit him!' Leah screams.

Leah is touching my head, I try to move away, I don't want her to touch, it hurts.

'What the hell's going on? Cillian, why are you here?'

Uh oh, Gemma looks mad. Gemma is never mad. I'm not supposed to be out of bed, I'm in trouble now.

'Stay out of this, Gemma, just go back to the sleep-in room. You didn't see or hear anything, understand?' Cillian steps towards Gemma.

Cillian doesn't want Gemma to tell me off. He's pushing her. No, too much shouting. He's hurting Gemma. Cillian is going to be in trouble. If I go back to bed maybe they will stop.

'No, Liam, come on we have to go.'

'I don't want to. Cillian is mean. He hurt my head.'

'He didn't mean to do that. Please, Liam, I don't want to leave without you.'

Leah looks sad again.

'Gemma will be angry.'

'No she won't, it will be OK.'

Leah smiles and takes my hand. I look back at my room before we go out the door. Too much noise, I put my hands over my ears but I can still hear them. Cillian is trying to push Gemma into the food store. He's going to make her cold like Alan. I don't want him to hurt Gemma, Gemma is my friend. Don't want to look.

'Let go of Gemma!'

Kevin, Kevin will make Cillian stop. He is bigger than all of us, tee hee, he will squash Cillian.

'No! Don't, stop, stop it, you are hurting him, don't hurt Kevin!'

Cillian has picked up the chair, oh don't like the noise. The chair breaks on Kevin, now Cillian is hitting Kevin's head with the chair leg. I don't want to see, my eyes are closed, I'm squeezing them and they hurt. I can still hear.

'Leah, make it stop!'

'Liam, come on.'

Leah is pulling my arm. I open my eyes. Kevin is on the floor, blood coming out of his head. Cillian has made him dead. I don't want Kevin dead. I want to touch him.

'Kevin, wake up, don't be dead.'

'Get up, Liam, Leah, help me we have to move.'

Why did you have to hurt him?

Leah is crying, Gemma banging the door, there's another noise. Yuk, blood on my hands, blood on my shoes.

'Get it off!'

'It's too late, Cillian, the police are coming,' Leah says.

Cillian is coming for me, I need to pee, and I'm scared.

Chapter Thirty-three

Meadows tore into Bethesda car park with the gravel flying as he hit the brakes and pulled off his seat belt. He could see the dark outline of Hanes slumped against the steering wheel of the patrol car. He moved quickly, yanked open the door and felt for a pulse.

'He's breathing,' Meadows called over his shoulder. 'Hanes?' He gently pulled the young officer back and rested his head against the seat.

Hanes gave no response. Meadows checked for injury, there were no visible signs. 'Take care of him,' he said to Edris before sprinting towards the house, his path illuminated by the headlights of Blackwell's car speeding into the car park.

Meadows could hear a high-pitched wailing as he opened the door. Eddy stood at the bottom of the stairs, hands over his ears and rocking violently.

'Eddy, are you hurt?'

Meadows dared not touch him. Eddy continue to wail, seemingly oblivious to Meadows' presence.

'Harry will be here soon. It will be OK.' Adrenalin spiked his skin and quickened his breath as he left Eddy and made for the sitting room. 'Leah! Gemma!' he called above the noise as he ran into the sitting room, his eyes darted around. Nothing. He checked the kitchen then went back into the entrance hall. It was then that he noticed the blood smeared on the floor.

Oh no, please don't let me be too late.

His heart beat wildly as he pushed open the door heading for the sleep-in room. 'No!' Raw pain gnawed at the hollow of his stomach as his eyes fell upon Kevin laying in a pool of blood. A broken chair was in pieces on the floor, one wooden leg covered in blood discarded at Kevin's feet.

Meadows knelt down and felt for a pulse. *He's alive.*

'Kevin! Kevin, can you hear me?'

Kevin tried to move his head as his eyes fluttered opened. 'Winter Man.' He smiled.

Meadows felt his stomach churn as blood trickled from Kevin's mouth. He took a hankie from his pocket and gently wiped Kevin's lips.

'You hang in there. I'm going to get some help.'

'Gemma,' Kevin croaked, his body shook and a low gurgling sound came from his throat.

Meadows became aware of the shouts and thumps coming from the cellar. He turned Kevin gently on his side, trying to ease his breathing. 'Gemma will be fine, you just rest.'

He pulled off his coat and laid it over Kevin.

'Bloody hell!' Edris stood staring down at Kevin.

Meadows looked up and saw Paskin and Blackwell rushing towards him. 'Get an ambulance and find the key for the cellar.'

Blackwell moved swiftly and rammed his body against the cellar door as Edris called an ambulance.

'Valentine is with Hanes,' Paskin said.

'Cillian.' Kevin's voice was barely a whisper.

Meadows leaned in close. 'I know, try not to talk now.' He stroked Kevin's head.

'Liam doesn't want to go.'

'Go where?'

'The place where no one's been.' Kevin's eyes rolled back in his head.

'What does he mean?' Paskin asked.

'I don't know.' Meadows leaned in close to check Kevin's breathing.

'Ambulance is on the way,' Edris said as the sound of splintering wood echoed in the corridor.

Gemma flew out of the cellar and threw herself down next to Kevin.

'He was trying to protect me,' she sobbed.

Meadows touched Gemma on the shoulder. 'He's still with us. Help is on the way.'

Fury bubbled in his veins. He stood and turned to the team. 'Find them.'

'They probably left before we arrived,' Blackwell said.

'Both cars are outside, they have to be in the house. You and Paskin take upstairs, Edris and I will cover down here.'

Meadows searched the ground floor checking all the rooms before meeting the others back in the entrance hall, where Harry had managed to calm Eddy and was trying to persuade him to go back upstairs.

'They're not here,' Blackwell said, panting.

'What was Kevin trying to say?' Paskin asked.

'The place that no one's been.' Meadows looked around. 'I've heard that before, Kevin showed me around the house the first time we came here.' He ran his hand through his hair as he tried to recall Kevin's tour. 'The bell tower!' He ran to the door and yanked the handle. 'It's locked. Harry, where are the keys?'

'There's only one, it's in the office.'

'They've probably locked it from the inside, if that's where they are,' Edris said.

'Give me a hand.'

Meadows threw his weight against the door. Blackwell joined in but the door wouldn't budge.

Meadows kicked the door in frustration. 'See if you can find something to break it down, I'll see if I can spot them from outside.'

He ran to the side of the building with Edris close behind but the large oak tree obscured his view. He moved further along willing his eyes to adjust to the darkness.

'There.' He pointed up to the roof where Cillian, Leah and Liam stood on the edge, Liam was rocking back and forth.

'They're going to fall,' Edris said.

'Cillian, get away from the edge!' Meadows shouted.

Cillian didn't respond. He grabbed Leah's wrist and peered over the edge.

Meadows stepped back to get a better view. 'Leah, come back inside. Liam is afraid, you don't want him to fall, do you?'

'It's too late,' Cillian shouted. 'This way we stay together.'

'They're going to jump.' Meadows turned to Edris. 'We have to find a way to get up there.'

'How? That door is solid and I doubt they have any ladders hanging around.' Edris looked around helplessly.

'It's not too late, Cillian.'

Keep him talking.

Meadows could feel the cold air biting his skin and imagined the three of them must be freezing up on the rooftop.

'I know you didn't mean to kill Alan.'

'You don't know fuck all,' Cillian shouted as he leaned forward.

Leah screamed but Cillian yanked her arm. Liam moved closer and took hold of Leah's other hand.

'I know about Tara, the drinking and drugs. I know the pain she caused all of you. This is not the only way. Leah needs medical attention and Liam is petrified. This is not what he wants. He doesn't understand. I know you want to protect them, now is your chance, come down.'

'This is the only way for us all to be together,' Cillian shouted as he teetered on the edge.

'No!'

Meadows watched in horror as Cillian stepped over the edge. Leah screamed as she was pulled over but the inevitable thud didn't come. To Meadows astonishment Cillian dangled in the air, his hand gripping Leah's wrist. Leah's other arm was stretched above her head and held by Liam, who was leaning back holding their weight with superhuman strength.

'He can't hold them much longer!' Meadows leapt at the oak tree and hauled himself up the trunk. He felt the bark splintering beneath his nails, pain stabbed at his cold hands but he kept climbing until he reached the higher branches. He could hear Edris shouting below among the sirens. The sky was lit up with flashing blue as an ambulance tore into the drive. He tried to block out the pain as the bitter cold air bit into his skin, numbing his fingers.

He saw an outstretched branch that ran parallel with the roof, he gripped it and lowered his legs, not sure if it would hold his weight. It took all his strength to move along the branch, one hand over the other, and his arm muscles screaming in protest. The branch bowed as he took one last swing and catapulted his body onto the roof ledge.

'Hold on, Liam.' He could see Liam's face contorted with the effort of holding onto Leah.

Meadows reached over the edge and grabbed Leah's arm.

'Let me go,' Leah pleaded.

'No, you don't want to do this. Liam doesn't want you to die.' Meadows could see Cillian was struggling to hold on.

The only way to save Leah is if he lets go.

Below, Edris, Paskin and Valentine looked on helplessly.

'Get a ladder or something to break the fall!' He shouted but knew there wasn't enough time. 'Cillian, you're going to have to try and pull yourself up.'

'I'm coming!' Blackwell appeared on the roof and started to make his way towards them.

'I love you,' Cillian said.

'No, don't!' Meadows shouted.

Leah's screams rent the air as Cillian let go of her wrist and fell with a sickening thud.

'I've got you, buddy.' Meadows turned his head to see Blackwell wrap his arms around Liam and pull him away from the edge.

'Let me go,' Leah begged.

'No, you don't want to die and Liam needs you.'

Meadows pulled with all his strength and dragged Leah over the ledge to safety.

'Leah!' Liam wrapped his arms around his sister.

'Let's get them inside.' Meadows could see Leah trembling violently. He took hold of her arm and guided her off the roof with Blackwell and Liam following behind.

They were nearing the bottom of the stairs, where the bell tower door lay torn off its hinges, when Leah broke loose and ran for the front door. Meadows gave chase and caught hold of her by the oak tree.

'Let me go to him,' Leah sobbed.

Meadows held her tightly in his arms as snow speckled the dark sky and landed on Cillian's broken body.

Edris walked towards them shaking his head.

'There's nothing you can do for him now, come back inside.'

Meadows turned to walk Leah back to the house and saw the paramedics bringing out Kevin.

'Look after her.' He passed Leah to Edris and sprinted towards the stretcher.

'How is he?'

'He's lost a lot of blood.' The paramedic looked solemn.

Meadows took hold of Kevin's hand. 'You hang in there, Kevin. You have a snowman to build.'

Kevin opened his eyes. 'Winter Man.' His voice was weak as he stared up at the sky. 'You made it snow.'

'No, you did. It's snowing just for you.' The words caught in Meadows' throat as Kevin's eyes closed and his body started to convulse.

Chapter Thirty-four

'How is she today?' Meadows asked the doctor who had just come out of Leah's room.

'No improvement, she's still refusing treatment. I give her a week at the best.' The doctor shook his head sadly. 'There's not much we can do without her co-operation. I'll ask the duty psychiatrist to assess her but if I'm honest I would say she's of sound mind. Grieving and understandably a little depressed but not enough to warrant a section order.'

'It's important I talk to her, maybe then she'll change her mind.'

'OK, but not for long, she is very weak.'

Meadows pushed open the door. Leah looked like a doll laying in the hospital bed, her skin was as white as the sheet that covered her. She had an oxygen mask on her face and wires led from her chest to the monitor next to the bed.

'Hello, Leah, can we talk?' Meadows approached the bed.

Leah pulled the mask away. 'Have you come to arrest me?'

'No.' Meadows took a seat. 'But I do need to ask you some questions.'

She nodded and struggled to sit up. Meadows adjusted the bed and propped a pillow behind her back then poured a glass of water.

'I need you to tell me what happened.'

'You know by now that Cillian is my brother.'

'Yes.'

'We met when I was still at university. I was out partying with my friends, we were celebrating the end of exams. We hit it off straight away and then spent every spare moment together. We moved into the flat, both of us were working and life was great... it seems like such a long time ago.' Leah pushed her hair back from her face.

'Then I got ill, I started on medication but knew it wouldn't be long before I needed dialysis and eventually a kidney transplant. My PRA levels were high which made it more difficult to get a match, something like a five percent chance. So Mum and Dad had to tell me about the adoption. I had no idea, no suspicions. I was upset at first but Cillian said he would help me track down my real family, he said it would be exciting.'

Her breathing became laboured.

'Take your time.' Meadows handed her the oxygen mask and waited until her breathing became easier. 'It must have been a shock for you to find out you were brother and sister.'

Leah pulled the mask away. 'You've no idea. Our world came crashing down, we were in love but at the same time disgusted. I felt dirty and ashamed. We couldn't be together anymore but we weren't ready to let go, so we decided to stay together as a couple without the physical relationship. We should've split up. I blamed my parents, hated them for keeping me in the dark.'

Meadows could see that she was tiring but wanted her to move on with the story.

'You found Liam.'

'Yeah.' Leah smiled. 'But I didn't know how to introduce myself or if he would understand. I started reading up on his condition and the history of Bethesda House. It was then that I came across the abuse case. I needed to make sure that Liam was cared for. I couldn't do that with weekly visits so we decided it was best that we went to work there. I changed my name back to what it should have been but chose Parry so no one would make the connection. Getting into Bethesda was easy. We got some false references, passed the CRB checks and we were in.'

Leah put a hand to her chest.

'Are you OK to continue?'

Leah nodded. 'I loved working with Liam but it was hard not telling him he is my brother. I started to notice the lack of empathy Alan had with the residents. By this time I had befriended Gemma and she told me about Alan's involvement in the abuse. I talked to Alex Henson and Rhys Owens who confirmed the story.'

'But you didn't do anything about it at the time?'

'What could I do? As long as I stayed at Bethesda I could keep an eye on Liam. I started on dialysis, it wasn't too bad at first, and I could do it at home and run it overnight. It was difficult when I had to take the turn on the night shift. Cillian wanted to give me one of his kidneys but it wasn't a good match and he had his own health problems, he just hid them well. I guess we were all broken in our own way. Broken dolls our mother threw away.'

Leah turned her head and wiped a tear from her eye.

'I don't think Tara had a choice – social services intervened.'

'She had a choice.' Leah turned back to face Meadows with blazing eyes. 'She had a choice not to drink, not to take drugs and to think of her children, but no, she was too selfish.'

The heart monitor increased tempo as Leah once more struggled for breath.

'Try not to upset yourself.' Meadows handed her the glass of water. 'What happened with Alan?'

'I noticed his attitude towards the residents was becoming cruel, particularly towards Liam and Kevin. He was clever though, he did it in such a way it would be difficult to make a complaint.'

'So you decided to get rid of him?'

'Not in the way you think. We planned to frame him in a compromising position. I spent months flirting with him but only when we were alone. I arranged to meet him that Monday night, I told him I'd leave the cellar door open and make sure we were alone. I slipped some diazepam into Gemma's hot chocolate – it didn't take long for her to fall asleep. I was supposed to do the same with Alan, then Cillian would come and we would put him in bed with Nicole. When the staff came in the morning he would be caught and it would be instant dismissal.'

Meadows felt a flicker of anger. 'What about Nicole? Did you not think of the distress it would cause her?'

'Nicole was never going to be in danger and she wouldn't have thought anything of it, her mind is innocent. It was for the benefit of all the residents and the only way we could think of getting Alan sacked.'

'What went wrong?'

'Alan turned up early, he had already been drinking and brought a bottle of wine. I had already opened a bottle and had planned to put the crushed diazepam into the glass. He came into the sleep-in room, he was in a strange mood, agitated. His hands were everywhere.'

Leah screwed up her face in disgust.

'I tried to distract him but he was eager to... I deliberately dropped my glass so it smashed on the floor. Alan went to the kitchen to get another one which gave me time to put the drugs into his glass. Then I heard Alan shouting, he had caught Kevin in the kitchen eating ice cream. He was so vile, calling Kevin all sorts of names, it made me more determined to carry out the plan, no matter what it took. Liam came out of his room to see what all the noise was about. Alan said he would leave and that he obviously wasn't going to get what I promised. I told him I would settle them down. I persuaded Liam and Kevin to go back to bed and Alan suggested we go down the cellar where we wouldn't be disturbed. He drank down the wine with the diazepam but it didn't seem to have much effect. He grabbed me, tearing at my clothes…'

Leah rubbed her hands over her face. 'It makes my skin crawl just thinking about it. He started to pull down his trousers, I…'

'It's OK, I get the picture.'

'He called me a prick teaser, then pinned me against the wall, I scratched at his face, but he took no notice. Liam must have heard because he came down the cellar steps. Alan had his back turned so didn't see him. It just happened so quickly, Liam grabbed the iron from the shelf and started hitting Alan. Cillian came then but it was too late. Alan was on the floor, there was blood everywhere. Liam didn't mean to kill him. He was trying to protect me.'

'Why didn't you call the police?'

'We were afraid. Liam would've been taken away and how would we explain Alan and Cillian being there? I took Liam to his room, showered him and put him in fresh pyjamas. I gave him a sedative and he fell asleep.'

'Cillian had already cleaned up most of the blood by the time I went back to the cellar. He came up with the idea of the freezer, he'd been watching all those crime scene documentaries and thought it best that Liam found the body so any hair or DNA could be explained. We put Liam's pyjamas in Alan's car with the food from the freezer then used the hoist to put Alan in.'

'But he wasn't dead.'

'I swear he wasn't breathing. We wouldn't have put him in there to die if we had known.'

'The diazepam mixed with alcohol likely made his breathing very shallow. Didn't you check for a pulse?'

'No.' Leah bit her bottom lip. 'We panicked. We weren't thinking straight.'

'What about Tara?'

'I don't know what happened. We were so scared that we were going to be found out, every day I woke up feeling sick and afraid. I didn't realise at first that my health was deteriorating. That weekend I had been into hospital, the anaemia and high blood pressure was causing a strain on my heart. So now not only had my one kidney failed, my heart was giving up. I told Cillian I wanted to stop the dialysis, there seemed little point. I told him to let me go and I would leave a letter confessing to the murder of Alan, that way Liam would be safe. I guess it must have pushed him over the edge. I really don't know if he went with the intention of killing her or just to make her feel some of our pain. I didn't know she was dead until you came to Bethesda asking questions.'

'He did intend to kill you and Liam.'

'No, he just wanted us to be together.'

'Why won't you try to help yourself? A court would be sympathetic and with your medical condition I doubt you would get a custodial sentence.'

'There's nothing left to live for.' Leah's voice trembled.

'There's Liam. You're all he's got.' Meadows gave her hand a gentle squeeze. 'Come on, you have to try. Liam used all his strength to save you, he doesn't want you to die.'

A tear rolled down Leah's cheek and she turned her head away.

The door opened and Edris peeked inside. Meadows nodded.

'You have a visitor, Leah.' He stood and walked to the door.

Liam rushed into the room.

'Leah!' He threw himself on the bed.

Dean Casey stood in the doorway. 'Thank you,' he said to Meadows.

'I'll leave you three alone.' Meadows looked back and saw Leah stroking Liam's head. He smiled and left the room.

'You're taking a bit of a risk sending Liam in,' Edris said.

'I have to give her a reason to live. I just hope it works.'

Chapter Thirty-five

Meadows and Edris stood outside Bethesda House, watching the residents climb into the minibus which would take them to catch a plane to Lapland. Harry stooped beside them and set down her case.

'Are you looking forward to the trip?' Meadows asked.

'Yeah, I don't know who's more excited, me or the residents. It's just a shame that some of us won't be going. It's still hard to believe. Leah and Cillian…'

'Try not to think about it.' Edris touched her arm.

'I heard Jane and Miles were released on bail.'

'One of the conditions is that they don't come near here,' Meadows said. 'The case will go to trial and I would imagine they will both get custodial sentences.'

'Good, well I better go.'

Edris leaned in and kissed her on the cheek before she climbed on the bus.

'Dare I ask what all that was about?' Meadows grinned.

Edris looked coy. 'I'm sort of seeing her.'

'What about Valentine?'

'Well, that didn't work out.'

'Didn't work out? When have you had the time to… oh, never mind. I hope you haven't left her broken-hearted.'

'No, actually she used me, took advantage of my body then told me she didn't want a relationship.'

'Good for her.' Meadows laughed.

'Winter Man!' Kevin came lumbering out of the front door dragging his pink and white spotted suitcase.

Meadows felt his heart swell and couldn't help the grin that spread across his face as he walked towards Kevin. He could see that the doctors had shaved his head and a row of stitches were visible beneath the stubble. His eye was swollen and his cheek a purple-yellowish hue.

'I'm so glad to see you back on your feet.' Meadows embraced the big man. 'I have something for you.' He took a scarf from his pocket and handed it to Kevin. 'It's for your snowman. My mum knitted it for you.'

'You have a mum?' Kevin's eyes were wide.

Meadows laughed. 'Yes.'

'Come on, Kev, you better get on the bus, you don't want the plane to leave without you.' Gemma smiled. 'He was determined to come on the trip, the doctor thought it would do him good.'

'I doubt they would've been able to stop him. You have a great time, Kevin, take a picture of your snowman and I'll come and see you when you get back.'

'Bye bye, Winter Man.' Kevin grinned and climbed on the bus.

'You know you frightened the life out of me climbing that tree,' Edris said as the bus pulled out of the car park.

'You needn't have worried. Circus performers used to come to the commune when I was a kid. I was pretty good at trapeze and tightrope.'

'You're full of surprises.' Edris laughed. 'Shame you don't have the same skills with women.'

Meadows grinned. 'I think I'll leave that up to you!'

'Christmas dance is coming up. Why don't you ask Daisy?'

'Maybe I will.' Meadows smiled as he watched the bus fade into the distance.

List of Characters

Bryn Mawr police station:

Detective Inspector Winter Meadows
DC Tristan Edris
Sergeant Dyfan Folland – Custody/Desk Sergeant
DS Rowena Paskin
DS Stefan Blackwell
PC Reena Valentine – uniform officer
PC Matthew Hanes – uniform officer
Chief Inspector Nathaniel Lester

Bethesda House:

Alan Whitby – assistant manager
Jane Pritchard – manager
Leah Parry – support worker
Cillian Treharne – support worker
Gemma Scott – support worker
Miles Flint – support worker
Harriet Maddox – support worker
Danielle Isaacs – support worker
Liam Casey – resident

Kevin Ellis – resident
Edward Pritchard (Eddy) – resident
Steven Howell – resident
Vanessa Owen – resident
Nicole Lewis – resident
Jason – replacement manager

Others:

Daisy Moore – pathologist
Melanie Whitby – Alan's wife
Tara Casey – murder victim
Martin Hughes – resident social worker
Fern Meadows – Winter's mother

If you enjoyed this book, please let others know by leaving a quick review on Amazon. Also, if you spot anything untoward in the paperback, get in touch. We strive for the best quality and appreciate reader feedback.

editor@thebookfolks.com

www.thebookfolks.com

Also available:

Following a fall and a bang to the head, a woman's memories come flooding back about an incident that occurred twenty years ago in which her friend was murdered. As she pieces together the events and tells the police, she begins to fear repercussions. DI Winter Meadows must work out the identity of the killer before they strike again.

When a toddler goes missing from the family home, the police and community come out in force to find her. However, with few traces found after an extensive search, DI Winter Meadows fears the child has been abducted. But someone knows something, and when a man is found dead, the race is on to solve the puzzle.

When local teenage troublemaker and ne'er-do-well Stacey Evans is found dead, locals in a small Welsh village couldn't give a monkey's. That gives nice guy cop DI Winter Meadows a headache. Can he win over their trust and catch a killer in their midst?

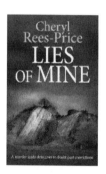

A body is found in an old mine in a secluded spot in the Welsh hills. There are no signs of struggle so DI Winter Meadows suspects that the victim, youth worker David Harris, knew his killer. But when the detective discovers it is not the first murder in the area, he must dig deep to join up the dots.

All available FREE with Kindle Unlimited and in paperback.

Printed in Great Britain
by Amazon

72100561R00168